Agnes Sligh Turnbull

THE RICHLANDS

COLLINS

St James's Place, London

1975

William Collins Sons & Co Ltd
London · Glasgow · Sydney · Auckland
Toronto · Johannesburg

First published 1974
©Agnes Sligh Turnbull 1974

ISBN 0 00 221690 6

Made and printed in Great Britain by
William Collins Sons & Co Ltd Glasgow

THE RICHLANDS

In *The Richlands* Mrs Turnbull has written not only a strong novel, but a warm and very moving one. The setting is rural Western Pennsylvania in the nineteenth century and the central character is Jim Ryall, who rejects a college education in order to manage the great family farm he loves so much.

As the story proceeds the reader is given not only details of a vanished time and way of life, but the deep emotional crises through which Jim passes as he and his two younger brothers, with Duncan, their devoted Scottish servant, live on in the large stone house.

Two women enter Jim's life: his pretty bride, Peggy, with whom one of his brothers falls in love, and the gentle Phoebe who later cares for his children as she quietly studies him. For Jim's normal ambition for the great farm grows into an overwhelming and consuming one which alienates his brothers.

The novel's minor characters are clearly drawn: the Scotchman, whose cheerfulness and humour help the family over difficulties but upon whom lies a shadow from his past that gives mystery and suspense to the story; also the beloved old Aunt Polly who comes in cap and apron for the main events of cidermaking, husking, butchering and *birthing*.

But through all the vicissitudes, the work of the farm must go on. As the harvest follows the planting, so does life come to its season of fruitfulness at The Richlands. Through love and suffering, Jim learns to curb his ambition and finds a happiness greater than he had dreamed of knowing.

by Agnes Sligh Turnbull

NOVELS

The Rolling Years
Remember the End
The Day Must Dawn
The Bishop's Mantle
The Gown of Glory
The Golden Journey
The Nightingale
The King's Orchard
Little Christmas
The Wedding Bargain
Many a Green Isle
Whistle and I'll Come to you
The Flowering

NON-FICTION

Out of My Heart
Dear Me: Leaves from a Diary

FOR CHILDREN

Jed, the Shepherd's Dog
Elijah the Fish-Bite
George
The White Lark

VOLUMES OF SHORT STORIES

Far Above Rubies
The Four Marys
This Spring of Love
Old Home Town

THE RICHLANDS

Chapter 1

It was not quite sunset, yet the day was fading. A long
shadow had fallen across the eastern end of the big stone
house; the leaves of the maple on the path to the barn on
one side and those on the way to the springhouse on the
other all had a bright, quickening light on them, while
over all the sky there spread a faint gleaming color which
told that the sun would soon show his full glory.

The young man on the chestnut horse looked around
him as though his eyes could never take in enough of the
scene. He sat easily without a saddle, the reins loose in
his hands, now and then caressing the horse's neck or leaning over to stroke her nose, while the animal responded
with quiet movements of affection.

They had been standing so for several minutes as the
young man looked over the wide, wide fields around him,
his eyes dwelling upon the new green wheat, the rich
brown furrows, the newly growing rows of corn, the wood-
land on the hill, the maple sugar grove, the walnut clump,
field upon field stretching in incredible fertile distance,
east and west. "The Richlands" it had been named on
the old maps and deeds and so it had remained in common

speech. For several generations now it had remained in one family, so the name of the family and that of the land were usually spoken together: The Ryalls of The Richlands. It was the young Jim Ryall who sat now on his horse surveying the expanse of cultivated field before him. He had come out to make a decision that could no longer be postponed. His father was pressing him daily for his answer, and he himself knew that his own peace of mind, and perhaps the love of his heart, demanded it.

Jim knew that the strain of all this which now stabbed him had begun in his father's own youth, for Judson Ryall's whole mind had been set upon an education. Then just when the way toward it seemed open, *his* father had died and the management of The Richlands had fallen upon him. Bit by bit, Jim had gotten the story. Judson's heart had been sore for he had loved his parent; but besides that, his golden dream of academy and then college and a profession looming in the distance were all dispelled. He was conscientious. He knew no hireling could take his place. Jim smiled to himself now as he remembered the old family saying: "There's no muck like the farmer's boot."

So Judson Ryall had patiently buried his dream, and as the years passed made The Richlands indeed the best farm of the countryside. But while he worked with skill and diligence, it was plain that he never really loved the soil. He was too good a man to keep an enemy in his bosom, but as he ploughed and harrowed and reaped, Jim realized sometimes that his father felt the great fields had stolen from him the desire of his heart.

When Jim was about twelve, the country schoolteacher

had come to spend the night, as was the neighborhood custom. After dinner, Jim, all ears, had sat listening at the top of the backstairs.

"You have an unusual boy here, Mr. Ryall, and a brilliant one. He does better in his books than all the rest of them put together. He must go on to the Academy."

"You say so?" Jim, straining to hear, had been amazed at the quaver in his father's voice.

"I do. It would be a waste of talent not to send him. And I'm sure you can afford it — with Richlands," he added.

"And beyond that you are thinking of Jefferson College, maybe, and — a profession?"

"But of course. I'm only a country schoolteacher with too few brains, I fear, but I can recognize them in anyone else. This boy has brightened many a monotonous day for me."

Jim had crept to bed but he had still listened to the sounds from below. He had heard his mother's voice, now sadly silenced, directing their guest to the little bedroom off the kitchen because it was the warmest. Then came the banking of the great fireplace and the steps of his parents as they climbed the stairs. Their room was next his own. He had sat up, alert. He remembered their words over the years, in substance if not to the letter.

"The *boy*!" his father had spoken in a low, tense voice. "What think you now of the *boy*!"

"We have three boys," his mother had answered calmly, "and to me none is worthier than another."

"But the schoolmaster! He said Jim had brains, had the gift, could go on to college, even get into a profession!"

"He's got one already. The Richlands. It's enough to

4

keep all the boys busy. And there's another thing, Judson. A profession can fall to pieces under you; we've seen it happen. The land never fails you if you treat it right."

His father had made an irritated sound. "Ach! There's no use talking to you."

"Turn over and go to sleep," he remembered his mother had said. "Let things fall out as they will."

The gist of this conversation was in Jim's mind now as he sat on Beauty, surveying the fields lighted suddenly by the blaze of the sunset. He laid his face for a moment on the horse's neck, and then slowly drew the reins and rode back to the barn. There he took in great breaths of the hay and straw and the good smell of healthy, well-kept horses mingled with a faint, aromatic strain of greased harness which a city man could not have identified. Jim checked the bedding and the mangers and then gave each horse a very small extra portion of "shorts" from the bin — for a treat, he thought to himself, even if they don't know.

He stroked Beauty's nose and went out, her affectionate whinny following him. In spite of the weight on his heart, Jim smiled as he thought of the cow stable adjoining the horses' domain. He never relished the redolent odors there though he could milk as fast as anyone. His younger brothers, Dave and Tom, moved down the opposite path now to the springhouse, carrying their buckets brimming with milk, most of which they would empty into the big crock that stood in the little running stream, there to await churning time. In a smaller pail, one of the boys would bring back enough for the household use. The routine was exact; with animals involved, it had to be.

Jim was near the back porch now and could see his father washing his hands in the tin basin that stood on the bench. He dried them on the rough towel but did not look up until Jim was close to him.

"Well, I guess I know your decision," he began in a voice harsh with feeling. "I saw you sitting out there a long time on Beauty, looking over the land. Tell me in your own words."

Jim swallowed painfully. "It hurts me to disappoint you, Father, but I can't leave Richlands. If I went on to college and maybe studied law the way I know you'd like, I'd be shut up in close, musty rooms for the best part of years to come, while here there would be the ploughing and planting and harvesting and all the rest. I can't leave this, Father. I guess I was born for it. Say you forgive me."

"Well, of course," Judson brought out slowly. "It's not a matter of forgiveness. I'll not deny I'm disappointed. I suppose it's part vanity; I always wanted to be a lawyer. You'll need a wife, Jim. Maybe you've picked one out already."

"Yes, I have. And I meant to tell you about her soon. It's Miss Peggy Prentice. You've maybe not seen her for they go to the church at the Four Corners. I was thinking of bringing her over for a Saturday night and Sabbath. Of course, with no woman here — oh, I miss Mother still. I'll never get over it, I guess."

"Nor I," Judson said heavily. "As to bringing your Miss Peggy over for a visit, I think it would be very nice and would brighten us up a bit. Duncan can turn out a good meal and," he added, smiling, "I would always be here to watch over you." Then he changed expression and looked gravely into his son's eyes. "I trust," he said, "that you are a man who can *wait*."

Jim's head went up. "I certainly am. How could you think otherwise? When you see Peggy, you'll understand how impossible anything else would be to me. We had thought of getting married next fall or in the early spring. Peggy wants to finish a couple of quilts and have a good few crocks of apple butter and pickles to leave behind her. Her mother's been gone longer than mine, so she's had to keep house for her father and uncle. They want her to get married, though. Her father says it's no life for a young girl there with two old men. He seems to approve of me, but he's a quiet sort."

"He is that," Judson agreed. "I've often met him at the blacksmith's over the hill here, and have tried to get him into conversation but it's always like trying to squeeze butter from a turnip. They're good folk, though, the Prentice men, and I'll be glad to see your Miss Peggy. By the way, you'd better tell your news to Duncan and the boys." He called through the kitchen and at once a man appeared in the doorway.

He was a bandy-legged little Scotchman who looked as though he should have bagpipes under his arm. His chest was broad, his arms as long as his legs were short. "I could tie me garters without stoopin'," he often said. "That is, if I wore garters." His face was Scotia in the flesh: eyes a clear blue, nose straight and prominent, cheeks mottled red from many a weather, chin strong as iron, with a dimple in it.

"An' what's goin' to come of them other two you've got, Master Ryall? Down there by the springhouse they are, kickin' an old bucket round an' us needin' a pail of milk now for the supper. I've often telt you—"

"Yes, yes," Judson said mildly. "The boys have worked hard all day and need a little fun. I called you, Duncan, to hear a bit of news. Go ahead, Jim."

Jim looked into the blue eyes staring at him. There was a close bond here and he didn't miss the tense look, almost of fear, in the older man's face.

"Ach, I could ferret it out without you tellin' me. You'll be off come fall to this college, like enough, and from then on we'll never see a glinter of you."

"You're all wrong, Duncan. I've decided to stay on at The Richlands and be a farmer. And get married within a year," he added, his face beaming, "to the prettiest girl in the world, most likely — Miss Peggy Prentice."

The Scotchman shook his head as though to rid himself of the mist in his eyes, then gave Jim's shoulder a resounding slap. "God a'mighty, lad!" he said, "God a'mighty! I've got to go an' be lookin' at me soup!"

As a rule, the meals at The Richlands were rather quiet, especially during the recent years, when Sarah, the mother, was gone, but tonight there was gay talk and much chaffing. Duncan, who had recovered his poise, led the teasing and the younger boys gleefully fell in with it. Dave, at eighteen, was as tall as Jim and only a year younger. Tom was fifteen, still growing and pure blond as his mother had been. His brothers, while not swarthy, had gray eyes instead of blue, and mildly fair complexions made a shade darker with the imprint of the seasons.

Just now, Dave was speaking with some irritation. "He's not old enough to get married, Father. He's only a year ahead of me. What would you think if *I* got a wife?"

"Well," Judson said quietly, for he had not joined in the gay talk, "it seems as though farmers marry young."

"Why so?"

"I'll tell you," Tom said bluntly. "It's because they want children to help with the work."

Duncan struck the table with the lalo of his hand. "Listen to the unnatural critter," he said, "forgettin' the big part of it all. Why it's *love*, lad, that makes a man want to marry if he's a man at all. Your father's got a copy of Bobby Burns's poems in his bookshelves. Read it an' you'll be findin' out. Oh, I'll say you one now. Mebbe not word for word but enough." He raised himself with his hands on the table and, in a voice they had never heard before, repeated the words as he looked off over their heads.

> "Oh, me love's like a red, red rose,
>   That's newly sprung in June;
>   Oh, me love's like a melody
>   That's sweetly played in tune;
>
> Sae fair art thou me bonnie lass,
>   Sae deep in love am I
> That I will love thee still, my dear,
>   Till a' the seas gang dry;
>
> Till a' the seas gang dry, me dear,
>   An' the rocks melt i' the sun;
> Oh, I will love thee still me dear
>   Till the sands o' time be run."

Judson wiped his eyes and Jim, his face scarlet, watched Duncan with fascination. It was Tom who broke the silence. "Why, Duncan, you're wonderful! Where did you ever learn that?"

"When I was a bairn, me mither used to sing it to me. Get on wi' your supper now an' quit your bletherin'."

"But we thank you, Duncan," Judson said. "I hope you'll recite us another poem sometime again. We didn't know you had this gift along with all your others. As to this pudding, now, I'll venture no woman could make a better."

"I thank you, Master. It's a pleasure to serve you. As to you, young rascals," he added, changing his tone and looking at the younger boys, "I want no more of this kickin' up your heels after milkin' till you've brought the house pail in. I swear it was only half-full this afternoon, an' us havin' puddin', too."

The boys grinned and promised. They teased Duncan and joked with him but still respected him and did as he told them.

Tom suddenly spoke now. "And what's Aunt Polly going to think of all of this news?"

There was a second of silence; then Judson broke it. "I think she may be the most pleased of anybody. You should be no later than tomorrow going to see her, Jim."

"I won't be," the young man said, smiling as though the thought was a pleasant one.

Before they all went to bed, the next day's plans had been made. Jim would start early in the morning, riding Beauty over the rolling hills until he reached Eldersridge Academy where he would tell his decision to the head-master, known to all as "Pater" Donaldson. After this interview he would ride back to Aunt Polly McDowell's to spend the night, then on to the Prentice home to spend the following one.

Duncan lighted the row of candles as usual, Judson leaning his hands on the table while he read for an hour or two before retiring to the "kitchen bedroom," as it was called, where he had slept with Sarah in the faint warmth diffused from the great fireplace. The boys, tired out from work in the fields, stomped up the wooden stairs to their room where they would be deep in slumber when their heads touched the pillows. Jim said good night slowly to Judson with as much tenderness as he dared, for he knew he had sorely disappointed his father that day. At last he took his candle, waved to Duncan who was banking the fire and in a short time was in his own bed, wakeful, his heart thudding from the excitement of his mind.

Finally, all sounds ceased in the house. He turned on his pillow and was almost asleep when he woke to the sound of the door hinge creaking. He roused with a start. Duncan stood there in the long-tailed nightshirt which Sarah had once made for him and of which he was inordinately proud. "It covers up me bandy legs," he had often told the boys.

Now he advanced with a conspiratorial air toward the bed.

"What on earth are you up to," Jim said, "waking me at this hour of the night?"

Duncan grinned broadly and lapsed, as he usually did when excited, into his native dialect. "Weel, lad, I'm comin' for to celebrate! You stayin' on wi' us at Richlands an' goin' to marry on a bonnie wee lass! If that's no cause for celebration, I'm no a Scotchman!"

He carefully drew from behind his back a bottle of whiskey and two tin cups and set them on the small table while Jim, looking askance, sat up and threw his legs over the side of the bed.

"Duncan," he said, "this is dreadful. You know how my father feels about drink. He won't have a drop in the house. How did you get this?"

Duncan winked. "I hae an errand betimes to New Salem an' there's a man there has a big closet in his hoose. I get what I go for and here I keep it, in me ain room cupboard, an' none's the wiser. Ach, lad, you should ha' seen me faither. Always had his whuskey but never 'under the influence' as the sayin' goes. He said a man that couldna' hold his liquor ought still to be on a nursin' bottle." Duncan chuckled. "That just minds me. I can still see him standin' up in our old kitchen drinkin' doon a great swig an' then lickin' his lips and sayin' to me when I was hardly more than a bairn, 'Eh, laddie, if me mither had give this at the breast I wadna' be weaned yet.' " His chuckle became a guffaw, to which Jim added a faint giggle as he watched the door anxiously.

"Now Duncan —" he began sternly. But Duncan was already pouring from the bottle into the tin cups, generously into the one and more sparingly into the other which he pushed toward Jim.

"Let's have nae mair bletherin'. You'll surely drink to your pretty lass. You've tasted this before, have you no?"

Jim colored. "Once. A fellah at the Academy had a bottle and he passed it all round for a joke. Don't you put a little water in it?" he asked.

"Water!" Duncan all but shouted. "Would you be spoilin' one of God's fine gifts? Drink it neat! It'll

make a man of you. Come on. To The Richlands an'
Miss Peggy Prentice!"

He drained his cup easily and Jim finally finished his
by taking small sips between coughs. Then Duncan
picked up the bottle and cups and eyed his young friend,
well pleased.

"Well, we celebrated! We drunk a toast! Good night,
lad."

"Thanks, Duncan. I know you meant it kindly, but I
still feel worried about my father. You know this is
getting to be a real Temperance Community."

Duncan snorted. "Ever been to a barn raisin', lad?
No, you're too young. Weel, I'll tell you something.
Them mighty beams ain't raised on *water*." And with
this parting shot he went out, leaving Jim to lie for a
minute reviewing the scene and then fall, almost instantly,
asleep.

The next morning was fresh and clear with all the bod-
ing of a fine day. It was early but Judson and Duncan
were already down. As Jim dressed, he remembered his
mother's usual remark about the two men: that they put
the cats to sleep at night and wakened the birds in the
morning.

"Well, you've got a fine day for your travels," his father
said as his son entered the kitchen. "You still think you'll
head for the Academy first?"

"I think so. I'd like to get the longest lap behind me
when Beauty and I are both fresh. Besides," he added, not
meeting his father's eyes, "I know Pater Donaldson will be
disappointed at my decision just as you were. I can't
bear to have that news hanging over me untold."

"Yes, yes. Maybe you're right. He had great plans for you. Well, eat a good breakfast and get on your way."

Duncan turned from the stove with a plate of pancakes. "Buckwheat," he said with a slow wink. "Only one thing better for the stomach. Eat it, lad. I've made plenty an' the maple syrup's nice an' hot. Where's them lazy louts upstairs? They ought to be down by this time, Master."

"Oh, it's early," Judson said. "They're pretty good about starting the day. When we get this one here off, I'll rouse the boys if they aren't awake by then."

But they were, ready to join Judson and Duncan on the back porch as they waved and shouted to Jim who, seated smartly on Beauty's new saddle, moved out toward the open road.

"Good-by! Good luck! Don't stay too long! Tell Peggy I sent my love!" This from Tom. "Tell her I wish I'd seen her first," from Dave.

"Don't be impudent!" Jim called back, grinning. "I'll likely be at Aunt Polly's tonight and back here the day after tomorrow."

As usual, Duncan had the last word. "When you're courtin', mind your p's and q's now," he yelled in a voice that could carry over the farm. Then the sounds grew dim and faded away as Jim struck Beauty's flank lightly with his hand and she cantered up to the top of the first small hill. Here Jim drew rein and looked back at the farm as though to fortify himself for the trip ahead. In the bright morning the stone buildings stood out clearly: house, barn, springhouse and wagon shed, the latter being the remains of the old fort that had protected the family from the Indians in his grandfather's time.

There was visible now also something that looked like

a delicate pink cloud resting below and beyond the barn. Jim smiled. That expanse was not a cloud; it was the apple orchard in bloom. As he had walked through it yesterday, he had been much more intoxicated by the perfume than by Duncan's whiskey.

"How could a man miss all that? I say, Beauty, how could he leave it to be shut up in close rooms for the rest of his life?"

He took another long, satisfied look and then, telling Beauty they must hurry, set off at a brisk trot, watching the passing woods and fields with keen eyes. His thoughts, however, were upon the Academy to which he was going. Though ignorant of others, he yet knew that this one, Eldersridge, was unique. A young man fresh from college and divinity school had once come to one of the Western Pennsylvania hills to preach in a small country church there. Soon a farmer came to arrange for Dr. Donaldson to tutor his son for college. Then a second lad came and a third. Within a year, the little parsonage was full to overflowing and more boys were clamoring for admission, so a group of farmers with their sturdy, teen-age sons came to the Ridge, and on its slope put up a building to serve as a dormitory and a few classrooms.

When this became too small, the students themselves built small shacks or cabins in each of which two boys kept "bach." Here they warmed themselves and did their simple cooking by small wood stoves and studied their Latin, Greek and math by candlelight.

Jim well remembered his first trip. His father had driven him over in the spring wagon in the back of which, in addition to cooking utensils, was a straw tick (his cabin mate would bring another), blankets and a homemade comforter, crocks of sausage and lard, a ham, a flitch of bacon, a sack of dried apples and one of corn meal, loaves of bread, a big box of sour-milk cookies and everything else his mother could think of for his comfort and pleasure. "And mind," he could still hear her say, "on a cold night, if you're tired, just stir up a big pot of mush. It's filling and tasty. You can easily get milk and butter from the nearest farm, I'm sure, And remember —"

She had told him so much that most of the cooking had fallen to him, his mate, Bill McBane, not being so well instructed. But the boys had been congenial and Jim was even now thinking that when he married he would like to have Bill "stand up" with him. Bill would be home, for he was needed on the farm and could not go on to college as he would have liked.

"But not me!" Jim spoke aloud. "Not me!" Then he chuckled as he drew Beauty to a stop to rest her. "When I get to Pater Donaldson's I'd better say, 'Not I!' "

The word "Pater" fell easily from his lips as it did from those of all the students. Not only were they rooted and grounded in Latin from their first day on, but their affection and respect for their great teacher seemed to demand a special title to set him off from the various assistants. Pater himself smiled and made no comment.

Jim and Beauty were climbing up the long slope of the Ridge now, and soon the Academy building with the white parsonage across from it and all the little cabins showing up against the new green came in sight. As they neared the center Jim could see Pater Donaldson out in his garden. He rode over to the hitching block, twisted the reins around the saddle pommel, then drew the tie-rope from one of the saddlebags and also an old cloth with which he carefully wiped Beauty's back for she was sweating after her long canter. "I'll gait her to a pace going back," he thought as he fastened the rope to the block's ring. "It will be easier for her in the heat." For after the cool of the early morning, the sun was shining vehemently and Jim felt his own shirt damp beneath his coat.

He opened the gate and entered the garden and Pater Donaldson looked up in surprise.

"Why, Jim, this is pleasant! No matter why you've come, you are most welcome. I believe, though, I know your reason. In a sense, I think I've been waiting for you."

Jim flushed with embarrassment. "I had to come, Pater, to tell you something right away, even though it may hurt you."

The older man looked at him keenly. "Come into the house and we can talk at leisure."

He led the way around to the front door and into the parlor with its ingrain carpet and armchairs. "Now, what's lying on your heart, my boy. You look worried. By the way, you'll be pleased to know that I've just written letters of recommendation for two of your class to Jefferson College." He leaned forward, his usually serious face lighted and his gray eyes twinkling. "And here is something that makes all the work worthwhile. The president of the College writes that, from now on, every boy coming from the Academy will be accepted without further examination. Now, that's my news. Go on with yours."

Jim felt himself shrinking in his chair. "That's wonderful, Pater, but I'm afraid I'm going to hurt you as I have my father. Ever since Commencement, I've thought and thought, considering every side to it, and I've decided not to go to college. I'm going to stay on the farm."

Dr. Donaldson looked at him in astonishment and pain. "You can't mean it!" he said. "With your ability, your *mind*. Why, Jim, I have pictured you on a judge's bench! Maybe I've been too lax in my praise and in explaining what I felt was your potential. I can't believe you've given this enough thought."

"I'm sure I have," Jim answered gravely. "The thing is, I love the soil. I love Richlands. It's born in me from my mother, I guess. Wherever I went, my heart would always be with the farm."

"But God has endowed you with a *brain*, Jim. Any strong young man can plough a furrow."

"Not a straight one," Jim said smiling. "But I can."

There was silence for a few moments and then the man smiled, too. "It's a shock, Jim, but I've got to accept it. I can trace now all that led up to this. The many times you asked for days' absences, it wasn't that your father needed you; it was that you needed the farm, wasn't it?"

"I'm afraid that was it. I do thank you for understanding, Pater, for it's awfully hard for me to disappoint you. I must be getting along now, for I want to reach Aunt Polly McDowell's before it's too late. I'll stay there the night, but I had to tell you first."

"And I appreciate that, Jim. Give my respects to Mrs. McDowell. A great old lady she is, and I have a feeling she will not be as shocked as I've been over your news. But won't you stay for some lunch?"

"Thank you, but I have some in my saddlebag and quite a way to go."

By the time they were both back to Beauty, the leave-taking was not too sad. "It could have been a good deal of sinful pride on my side," the old man said. "I must watch out for that. 'He that is down need fear no fall; He that is low, no pride.' Remember that when you are ploughing your straight furrow, Jim."

"Oh, I will," Jim said gravely, "but I've got ambitions, too. I want to make The Richlands a really great farm." Then he leaned over Beauty's head. "One thing I haven't told you. After I've been to Aunt Polly's, I'm going on to the Prentices'. You see, Peggy and I are going to be married."

"So! The secret's all out. But Jim, aren't you pretty young to be thinking of marriage?"

Jim laughed. "Well, they say my grandfather grew out of his wedding suit. And my father was pretty young himself. I guess it runs in the family."

"Well, well!" Pater Donaldson said, "Peggy's a 'bonnie wee lass,' as your man Duncan would say. Blessings on you both, my boy. When you're ready, if you want me to tie the knot I'll be proud to do it."

"We will, and thank you for everything." Jim called as he started away, giving a last glance at the cabin he had shared for four winters with Bill McBane. They had been congenial both in work and fun and Jim now missed the companionship. He thought again that he would certainly like to have Bill stand up with him when he got married, if that didn't hurt his brothers' feelings.

But he felt happy as he always did as he went toward Aunt Polly's. She was really his father's aunt, tall, spare, spry as a cricket, of what age no one was quite sure. When anyone brought the subject up, she merely said, "None of your business," and fell to discussing other things. Of late years, along with her black, cambric muslin dresses, she had worn a white cap and white apron which were the marks and symbols of feminine maturity. Aunt Polly, however, had always carried them lightly. Her hair was not yet white, her gray eyes twinkled with frequent mirth, her cheeks, though wrinkled, were rosy and her smile brought something almost like youth to her face. She not only did her housekeeping and cooking as she had always done, but usually had a quilt half-finished in the frame by the kitchen's sunny window.

Jim kept thinking of her as he rode along and of how much she had meant to him over the years, especially since he had lost his mother. Uncle Charley, her husband, was a slow, quiet man. Indeed, there were those critical ones who said he was a "cipher at the wrong side." This was not quite true. He had worked his small farm well enough to make a living and was now nearing Aunt Polly's own spare eighties, plump, easy-going, gentle and generally content with life.

Jim had always loved to go to Aunt Polly's. This time, bursting with news which he felt would be well received, he finally turned happily into the familiar lane and was soon knocking at the back door. It was opened by Aunt Polly herself, with a long curl of apple paring around her finger.

"Jim!" she cried out as she kissed him. "Who would have thought you could smell apple pie this far off? Come away in and sit you down and tell me what brought you."

She looked at him shrewdly. "You've brought news! I can see it by the twinkle in your eyes. Out with it now while I set this pie in the oven."

"Oh," Jim said as he drew great breaths of the homely kitchen's air. "I always like the smell of this room. Were you baking bread this morning?"

"Oh, just a few bit loaves. Do you want a heel spread with butter?"

"I can't wait."

Aunt Polly cut the crust from one end of a loaf, spread it liberally with the yellow butter she had churned, handed it to her young kinsman and then sat down in the big wooden rocker and looked at him expectantly.

"You're only a boy, liking the loaf heels and all that, but there's a man inside you, Jim. I can see it. Tell me what's brought you today."

"I've made up my mind, Aunt Polly. I'm going to stay on the farm."

She didn't speak at once and then she clapped her hands together. "If you could have heard my prayers this last twelve months you'd know how I feel. 'O Lord,' I always prayed, 'Thy will be done and all that but just grant Jim may stay on at Richlands.' You see? I give Him a little nudge every time, and don't tell me prayers are never answered!"

Jim almost dropped his buttered crust in the laughter that followed. Aunt Polly plied him with questions. How had his father taken it? Had he seen Pater Donaldson? And was it true that Peggy Prentice was his girl?

At all the inquiries, her eyes were bright and her face eagerly showed her fondness and her interest.

"How did you ever hear about Peggy and me?" Jim ended his replies. "I thought I had kept it so quiet."

"I'll tell you something." Aunt Polly leaned toward

him. "Of all the gossips, men are the worst. Your Uncle Charley, now, can take the horses to the blacksmith shop at the Cross Roads and come home as full of news as a comb's full of honey. I just sit here and all the happenings are brought right to my armchair. Well, as to Peggy, she's a sweet, delicate-made child. You're a big, strappin' creature, Jim. If you marry her, you'll have to treat her gently. I'll lay down the law to you, mind, before your nuptials."

"Good!" Jim answered. "You know I've always taken your advice."

"Well, what's that cantankerous little Scotchman of yours up to now?" Aunt Polly inquired when she had satisfied herself on all other points.

"Oh, he's a good soul. He can plough a field and then come in and make as good a supper as a woman could — except you," he added loyally.

"When he comes here on an errand, something happens to my tongue. I fall into broad Scotch which I thought I'd forgotten for fifty years. I don't say I'm fey, though my mother was said to be in her youth before she left Scotland to come here, but there's something queer comes over me when this Duncan's around. I keep thinking, where did he come from, droppin' in here on a winter's night with only a few clothes to his back? He had the manners of a well-trained servant but of one who had taken his leave in a hurry. But what's his story? That's what I'd like to know. And nary a haet can you get out of him."

"Oh, I don't think there's a mystery about him. I was pretty young when he came to our house. I remember

Uncle Charley drove him over and said to my father, 'Here's a man wants a job. We don't need him but I thought you might.' My father said he did, and in a few minutes Duncan had accepted us all and gone to work like a bee and has never stopped since.''

"Well, so be it," Aunt Polly said. "I'm glad it's worked out and no one any the worse.''

"Why, how could we be —''

"I must get to the supper," Aunt Polly interrupted firmly. "You must be hungry after that long ride. Your Uncle Charley's out in the orchard. He'll be glad to see you and to hear what Dr. Donaldson had to say.''

"I'll go right out and meet him," Jim said. As he went toward the door he stopped before the dresser and touched a blue teapot with a loving hand. "It was out of this that the bills used to come to help me buy some extras while I was at the Academy," he said. "You'll never know, Aunt Polly, how much those bills meant to me. One thing about farming," he added "is that you can be land poor. Even with The Richlands, I may often lack ready cash, like my father.''

"Not if you manage right. Let that little Scotchman take care of the chickens and the milk cows. Then you'll have butter and egg money when you need cash.''

"I'll remember. Oh, I do want to make a success of things when I really get to work. And lift some of the burden from my father, too. I think he looks a bit tired these days. Maybe he'll be glad yet that I'm staying on.''

"Well, well. Get along now to see your Uncle Charley. I'm glad I baked a gingerbread this morning. It ought to go right well with fresh applesauce. I have to keep up to the little Scotchman's cooking, you know.''

Jim ran to her, untied her apron strings with a boyish laugh and hurried out the back door, thinking how odd it was that he always had fun with Aunt Polly in spite of the fact that he had told her his inmost thoughts over the years.

It was a happy evening. There were no overtones of sadness or regret, so Jim basked in the loving favor that surrounded him, ate the supper with relish, played a game of checkers with Uncle Charley and watched with additional color in his cheeks as Aunt Polly showed him the quilt in the frame by the west window.

"It's the Wedding Ring," she explained to him. "And I'm going to save it for the young couple I like best! I guess from what you tell me it won't get faded before it's used."

There was more of the laughter which always broke out naturally among them, and then Jim slept at last in the low four-poster where he had spent so many nights from childhood on. When he lay relaxed, as he always did under this roof, he drew in the sweet night air with the scent of heliotrope and early roses within it and gave himself up to the joy of his coming meeting with Peggy the next day. "I wish," he thought, "that we could spend our wedding night here instead of at home."

He woke betimes, for Uncle Charley was an early riser, and was ready quickly for the hearty breakfast of pancakes and sausage, his favorite one, as Aunt Polly knew. When he was ready to set forth on Beauty, he shook hands with Uncle Charley and stooped for Aunt Polly's unfailing kiss.

"Oh, it's been good to be here," he said. "It always is."

The old woman looked deep into his eyes. "Give my best regards to your 'bonnie wee lassie,' as Duncan calls her. Say all the sweet things you know, Jim, but never a quick word. Every tender woman takes easy hurt. Mind now, Jim. God send you both happy!"

He kept looking back until the tall figure in the white bonnet and apron was lost to view. Then he rode on exultantly, thinking only of his love. Oh, she was pretty. From her shining brown hair with the soft wave in it, down to her little feet that tripped along while those of other girls went more slowly. Her eyes — what color were they? He never could tell about them except that they sparkled and gave him strange shivers as he looked into them.

"Now tell me," she had said once, standing close and shaking her head back and forth. "What color are my eyes? Quickly now."

"I — I can't tell. They never look the same twice."

"They're *azure*! I read it in a book. Now say it. *Azure, azure, azure!*" With each repetition she came closer, until he had caught her to him in their first long embrace.

"Don't do that again!" Jim said, when he could speak.

"Didn't you like it?"

"Too much."

She became at once grave. "You're right. I'm sorry. I understand. We'll forget all about it. But," she added, "my eyes are really blue, of course. Azure is just a fancy name for the color."

Now as he rode along he smiled at the qualities that made her half child and half woman. He had never been attracted deeply to any other girl. She was all he craved to complete his life and fulfill his love. And with the realization came a feeling of maturity which he had never felt at the Academy. It came with his newly made decision and also with the definite thought of marriage. Although he was passing then through a cool, wooded stretch of road, his face grew hot and a warmth filled his whole body. Of course he would wait as his father had said, but now he hoped he would not have to wait too long.

He reached the neat Prentice farm and rode along the locust-bordered land, smelling the perfume that Peggy had told him was her favorite in all the world. He could see the house, built of logs and cemented solidly between. It was as old as The Richlands buildings, though not as large by far, and had the same square lines which Jim admired without knowing why he did.

As he reached the end of the lane he saw a slight figure in long, checked apron and sunbonnet rise from weeding the peony bed to stare for a second as he threw the reins over Beauty's neck and jumped to the ground.

"Jim!" she called. "Jim, I never thought of you coming today, and me with an old dress on and my hair —"

She ran toward him and he caught her to him as she stumbled in her haste.

"Let me look at you." he said. "Oh, Peggy, you're so pretty. I don't care what kind of dress you have on. Take off your sunbonnet, though, so I can see your eyes better. And — don't tell me — they are azure blue! There, I got it all in. And they sparkle like stars and don't I get a kiss?"

"As if you needed to ask!"

They walked, finally, hand in hand around the house to the back porch, Beauty following, the loose bridle in Jim's hand. There they found Mr. Prentice, undemonstrative but plainly pleased to see his prospective son-in-law, and Uncle Bob who came from the open wagon shed at the sound of the voices. They all sat down on the porch steps in the late sunshine and, with Peggy's leading, the news was all told. Both men changed from their usual gravity to smiles as they heard of Jim's decision to remain at the farm. Peggy's satisfaction had already been voiced when the young people were alone. Then came the details of the talks with Pater Donaldson and Aunt Polly.

"And how's your father?" Mr. Prentice asked at last.

"Very well, I think, though he seems to tire easily. He's disappointed that he isn't going to make a lawyer of me as he had hoped. I'll try to fill him with good news when I get home. I think I should leave early in the morning, by the way," he added.

Peggy was a good cook and they all lingered over the supper table, her hand occasionally touching Jim's as she helped him to the food. Once when this happened their eyes met and held with such a look of love that Mr. Prentice rose from the table. "This has been a heavy day in the fields and Uncle Bob and I are both pretty tired. I think we'll go right upstairs and get a good start on the night's rest. We'll be seeing you, Jim, in the morning."

When they were alone, Jim and Peggy cleared up the dishes together and then, arms entwined, strolled back and forth between the blooming locust trees of the lane.

"Oh, it's so sweet," Peggy said, drawing in great breaths of the fragrance. "Some folks say locust trees attract lightning but we've never had one struck yet."

"I feel as if some kind of lightning had struck me," Jim said, half-laughing. "When do you think we can plan to get married, Peggy?"

"Oh, Jim, I wish it could be before *too* long. I shouldn't have been so set about finishing my quilts."

"Aunt Polly has one nearly done that she's going to give you. She says it's the Wedding Ring pattern."

"Oh, good! I love that, but I can't do those hard ones. Mine are just the old fashioned Nine Patch kind, but I've used pretty colors. About — the time, Jim," she said, blushing a little.

"I don't want to put it off longer than this fall. Oh, your father's good to agree to having you leave. They *will* be lonely, those men."

Peggy pressed his hand. "I'm glad you understand about that. I thought when we were — married, maybe sometimes you would allow me to drive over for a few days to do for them and clean the house and cheer them up a bit. Do you suppose I could?"

He held her close. "It won't be a question of *allowing* you, my dear. You must do what you wish. I will certainly not be your master." Then he laughed. "That's what Duncan always calls my father. Aunt Polly says he's been a well-trained servant someplace, but of course we don't know where. He likes you. He says you're 'bonnie.' And so do I! Oh, terribly bonnie!"

The kisses grew longer and the plans more ardently definite when they re-entered the house and waited for early candle-lighting time. Then, at last, Jim closed the door and drew in the latch string. There was one last embrace on the first step, then, with their candles, they climbed the creaking stairs to their own rooms.

If Jim had been happy on his outward journey, he was filled with joy as he turned Beauty's head toward home after his last farewells the following morning. Even his parting from Peggy had been "sweet sorrow" for they had

fixed a date for an early fall wedding. He had felt nothing
but deep pleasure in each house where he had been. Now
to tell it all to his father and to Duncan and the boys, too,
for they would all be waiting to hear!

When he came at last to the crest of the hill overlooking
Richlands, he reined Beauty and, with a great overflowing
of gladness, let his eyes take in again the scene he loved.
He knew at a glance just what relevance each field bore
to the whole year's fertility. He loved the big stone house
where he hoped one day his own children would be born.
Three generations, then, within it. He drew rein quickly, spoke to Beauty and in a few minutes was riding into
the yard. In his eagerness, he didn't take his horse to
the barn at once but tied her to the hitching post and went
on to the kitchen. No one seemed to be about, which
was strange, as they must have expected him about this
time.

"Father!" he called. "Duncan! Where is everybody?"

From the stairs, Duncan came into the kitchen. His
face twitched and his eyes were swollen. He went to Jim
and grasped both his arms.

"Laddie! Laddie!" he began. "I've sair news for you.
Your father took sick verra early this mornin' an' Tom rode
to New Salem for a doctor. He come along back with him
an' examined your father and says naething can be done.
It may be but a few hours. Can you go up now?"

Jim felt the room swimming around him, but he caught
a chair for a moment, straightened and said, "I'm ready."

Duncan led the way up the familiar stairs and into the
room where Judson lay, very still and white, upon the
pillow. Jim clenched his hands for steadiness and approached the bed as Duncan withdrew to the hall.

"Father! I'm here. I'm back."

Judson opened his eyes and slowly vision came. He tried to smile. "Jim," he said with difficulty, "I guess I'm content — now to — have — you   stay on — since I —" There were only a few soft breaths and then a great stillness.

Duncan, watching from the door, came forward quickly, drew the sheet higher and, taking Jim's arm, helped him down the stairs and back again to the kitchen.

"Sit you doon, laddie, an' I'll fetch you a cup of tea an' a bit of bread to stay you."

Jim sank into the chair he did not even recognize as his father's place at the table, and leaned his head on his hands while his legs trembled from the shock. His father! So strong, so sound! Like the big oak in the pasture field where the cattle always took shelter from the rain. He was the protector of the family. With him, his sons had always felt safe. And now —

Duncan came in with food and Jim drank the tea in a quick gulp and ate the buttered bread as though famished. It was strange he could do so, he thought, but at least he had strength now to speak.

"What was it, Duncan? What happened?"

"His heart, the doctor said, or sort of a stroke. I've noticed he'd been slowin' up a little but nothin' you could put your finger on, an' he never complained. I'll get you more tea."

When he had brought it and removed the plate, he stood before Jim, looking upon him with a great tenderness. "Is there anything more I could do for you, Master?"

Jim started as though he had been struck. "How dare you make such a joke at a time like this?"

"I'm no jokin," Duncan said slowly. "Already there's been a great change here, though mebbe you'll no be understandin' it yet. But whether you do or not, it's true. *You* are now the Master of Richlands.

Chapter II

A brightness had come to the old stone house. There was the sound of tripping feet hurrying here and there; there were frequent ripples of laughter and also of song. A blue-eyed girl sat now at the end of the table opposite Jim at mealtime and smiled upon the three young men and the one older one, all of whom, it seemed, had difficulty paying attention to their food. For after a month of heaviness and sorrow following Judson Ryall's death, Aunt Polly, staying with the family to lend her comfort and assistance, had talked decidedly to Jim one night.

"You said Peggy and you were planning to be married in the fall?"

"Yes, we were."

"And why wait? It's now you need a wife more mayhap than you ever will. This is a dark and heavy house now and I can't brighten it. I can't lift the sorrow when I'm feeling it hard myself; so, Jim, if Peggy is willing and her father, too, you ought to get married at once."

"But Aunt Polly, it might not look respectful to my father. Not that I wouldn't *like* to do it," he added.

"No, there would be no disrespect. Everyone who

knows the situation here will understand. You need a wife. You're already planning marriage, so let it be soon."

"I know Peggy had thought of a few guests and a little dinner or supper after the — the ceremony. I wouldn't like to start out disappointing her."

Aunt Polly smoothed her white apron and then slowly pulled her cap strings while she thought. "I have it," she announced triumphantly at last. "I'll stay on here for a bit longer, and when you and Peggy set the day let her come over here with her men folk that morning. And you'll want Dr. Donaldson, of course —?"

"I think he would come."

"And I'm sure of it. You and Peggy can each invite a couple of your young friends who are near enough. Then you can be married in the big parlor here and Duncan and I will have a late dinner for you, fit for any bride and groom. I'll bake my famous white layer cake and put a posy on the top of it. What think you of *this* plan?"

Jim drew a long breath. "It would be just about perfect if Peggy would like it."

"I'll warrant she will. The Prentice house is small and she'll have no real help. This way, she can forget everything but her dress and *you*. And of course, Jim, we'd have no loud singing or play-games or merry-making like at other weddings. We could be cheerful, though, and never cast a cloud over your happiness. Be sure to tell that to Peggy. I think this is just what your father would have wanted."

There had been a family consultation that night in which Duncan joined. As a result of it, Jim rode off to the Prentice farm the next day with his heart strangely full of both sorrow and excited happiness. Peggy had been more than satisfied as he gently unfolded Aunt Polly's plan.

"It will be such a relief to me," she said. "I had felt so burdened and alone with having no woman here to help me at my wedding. Now there will be Aunt Polly to see to me and answer my questions."

"Do you have questions?" Jim asked seriously.

"Oh, maybe a little one or two," she said, blushing.

"You can always ask me anything you wish," Jim said, his face very tender.

"I know. I love you."

It had been agreed that the marriage would take place a week later and that, soon after the wedding day, Jim would drive Peggy back to get her quilting frame and a few pieces of furniture from her own room which she wished to have, along with little oddments from her childhood. So it had all been settled.

Strangely, for this vain and transitory world, everything had worked out for the wedding exactly as planned. The boys, filled with delight that the pall hanging over the house had been lifted, brought in flowers for the mantel vases and boughs of hemlock for the fireplace. They fetched and carried according to directions as Aunt Polly laid the long, linen cloth and set the table on the wedding morning. Duncan, in tan trousers and a white ruffled shirt, muttered in broad Scotch as he watched over the skillets and pots.

"You're a good man, Duncan," Aunt Polly said once as he forced her into a chair to drink a cup of hot tea.

"Say I'm a 'guid mon,' an' I'll hear you the better," he returned.

Jim, watching, had felt his mouth twitching. Aunt Polly put a bit more sugar in her tea and sipped it gratefully, the color coming into her pale cheeks. All at once she set down the cup.

"Duncan, me 'guid mon,' I doot this tea's a bit laced, is it no?"

"Sup it up an' dinna' keep speirin' at me," was the grinning reply.

As she saw Jim watching them, Aunt Polly gave what in a younger woman would be called a giggle. "You see what your little Scotchman does to my tongue? I've never spoken broad Scotch since I was a child. Now I can slip into it as easy as my petticoat! Well, whatever that rascal did, it revived me. Now, I think we're all ready. Isn't that the Prentice carriage now?"

She ushered Peggy up to the room she would share with Jim and helped her out of her dusty frock and into the white ruffled muslin one she had made herself for the occasion. At last, after gentle confidences had been exchanged, Aunt Polly led down the bride who carried the flowers Jim had picked for her, looking herself like one of the roses in her bouquet.

They found the guests who had come from far away, along with Dr. Donaldson and Uncle Charley, already there; so after the greetings, the young couple took their place in front of the mantel with Bill McBane, his old cabin mate, beside Jim, and Jennie Homey, Peggy's best friend, beside her in a pink dress to match the roses. Dr. Donaldson, in his long-tailed coat, stood before them while the others, except Aunt Polly, stood stiffly around the wall. She sat in the big horsehair rocker and wiped away an occasional tear. Duncan took his place near the kitchen door so, as he said afterward, he could jouk out if necessary to watch the dinner.

There was first the long prayer, then the dissertation on the sacredness of the married estate. Then the Pater's voice broke a little as he looked into the young faces before him. "And remember, my children, be tenderly affectionate one to the other. As the Bible says, 'Never let the sun go down upon your wrath.' That means, if you have a little disagreement, make it up before you sleep. Always bear the burden of love which is no burden, and may God bless you."

With the Pater's eyes still misty, the vows were spoken and repeated and the ring that had been Sarah's was placed on Peggy's finger. Then came the final benediction while all who listened were most stirred by the strong words: "I now pronounce you man and wife."

Aunt Polly slipped out quickly while quiet laughter and much hand-shaking and some kissing went on in the parlor, but returned soon with her aristocratic air to say, "And now, ladies and gentlemen, will you kindly step out to dinner?"

There were outcries of surprise and pleasure as the guests saw the long table with its shining damask, old glassware and the "good" dishes with the ivy spray upon them that Sarah had always cherished. Aunt Polly had arranged the seating: the bride and groom together at the head with the bridesmaid and groomsman at either side. She would sit at the foot with Dr. Donaldson at her right and Mr. Prentice at her left.

"And Charley, you see to Uncle Bob Prentice, and the rest of you young folk just sit where you will."

There was a scraping of chairs and then all were seated

except Pater Donaldson who, at a sign from Aunt Polly, bowed his head and said grace. Then the talk became more general and small jokes went round and much laughter, always, however, within the bounds of a certain propriety as though the former Master of Richlands were there also to add his blessing.

The old-fashioned food was superlative, with some extras Duncan had added, such as small pancakes spread well with butter, sugar and cinnamon and rolled in tight little cylinders. He had made an incredible number of them but the young people, especially, could not get enough.

At last, though, it was time for Aunt Polly's layer cake and the sweet cider Jim had made himself from the early Maiden-Blush apples. Duncan set the cake before Peggy who, with a pretty show of shyness, received advice from all sides and soon had the luscious-looking slices on the tray Duncan held for her. Then, when all were served and the cider was being passed, Dr. Donaldson stood up, very straight, very dignified.

"A toast!" he said. "May God's blessing rest on the new home you've founded."

Aunt Polly rose quickly. "And may Jim and Peggy always love each other as much as they do today."

At the words, Dave spoke to his brother. "Oh, Jim, get Duncan to say the poem again that he said once before about my love is like a red rose. You remember?"

"Na! Na!" said Duncan, backing away.

"But Duncan," Jim urged, "you wouldn't refuse me anything on my wedding day, would you? Come on now, please!"

"Weel, weel, if you're so set on it." There was a tiny glint of pride in the steely eyes. So, standing behind Aunt Polly's chair, he recited the poem.

> "Oh, me love's like a red, red rose
>   That's newly sprung in June;
> Oh, me love's like a melody
>   That's sweetly played in tune —"

There was tremendous applause and a number of misty eyes. Dr. Donaldson was deeply impressed.

"Duncan, you have a real gift for speaking. I thank you for that pleasure."

"Another! Another!" chorused the young people.

But Duncan was backing away. "Na! Na!" he called over his shoulder. "One like that's enough." Then he stopped and turned with a mischievous grin on his face.

"I could give just a wee bit rhyme that's often said at Scotch weddin's," he ventured, looking at Jim, "if it ain't too bold."

"Nonsense!" Jim said, full of his great gladness. "On with it, Duncan."

He came closer and held his mug of cider toward Peggy and still in his tender voice repeated:

> "Sae fair an' sweet as our bonnie bride,
>   There could na' be another;
> An' ere the wheat be green again
>   May she be a happy mother."

There were blushes and laughter and many thanks to Duncan for his contribution.

"If I just live to see it," Aunt Polly whispered to Dr. Donaldson.

"Nonsense," said the good Pater, "you'll live to see a whole family round the hearth here."

When the cake and cider were all finished, there followed a general leave-taking, for there were many who had long distances to go. Dave and Tom brought around to the front the buggies, dogcarts, carriages and riding horses which had brought the guests. As Jim thanked Dr. Donaldson, he pressed a note into his hand. "And it's not a shinplaster," he laughed.

"My dear boy, I'll take a kiss from your bride and that's all." And he put the bill into Peggy's hand as he took his reward in stately fashion.

Finally, the last calls of good wishes faded, and no one was left behind besides the family except Aunt Polly and Uncle Charley. "We'll be off now," she said to the boys, "but we're taking the bride and groom with us just for the night — a little wedding trip! Duncan, you'll take care of everything and have a good supper for the newly-weds when they get back. You're a 'guid mon,' Duncan. And you boys have been strong and fine and I'm proud of you."

They stooped for her kiss and Duncan shook hands. "We'd ha' been hard put to it, without you, Ma'am."

"We'll go on now, then," she said, "and the others can follow. Good-by and thanks to you all."

It was a little later when Peggy, in a brown-checked gingham and a little bonnet to match, came down the stairs followed by Jim, each carrying a small hand satchel. They were shy as they made their good-bys, almost as though they were setting forth on a real journey. Dave and Tom were very quiet, sensing that their brother was leaving them now in a more subtle but definite way than when he had gone to the Academy.

It was Duncan who saw Jim and his bride out to the freshly painted buggy and handed him the reins. Beauty knew the touch and started at once.

"I'll see to things," Duncan called. "Blessings on ye!"

Up the little hill and down and then along the quiet valley and into the woods, and still neither spoke. At last Peggy drew a long sigh.

"This is really like a little wedding trip! I'm so glad we're going to Aunt Polly's. She told me she and Uncle Charley would be away to bed when we got there and we'd have everything to ourselves. I made this dress and the little bonnet myself, just hoping we would be going some- where, maybe even for a night. Do you like the bonnet? It's smaller than a sunbonnet, of course, but it has stays in to hold it out. I got the pattern from Jennie Homey after church one day." She paused to look anxiously at Jim.

"I love it!" he said. "But I'll soon be taking it off."

"Oh?"

"Don't you realize that I've never had a kiss from *my wife* since we were married? That one at the ceremony was just a peck, with everyone looking. So, here's a shady place."

He gently removed the little bonnet, becoming as it was, and with the reins slack, took his bride in his arms and kissed her long, possessively, rapturously. Beauty had been turning her head frequently to see the reason for the pause and now, at the touch on her reins, started off will- ingly. Peggy leaned back, relaxed against the buggy cushions. She folded the little bonnet and laid it in her lap with a side glance at Jim.

"I don't believe I'll put it on again," she said. "It is a bit warm."

Jim eyed her with delight. "You're a darling little hussy, but I didn't need a hint," he said. Then they laughed in sheer happiness.

It was late dusk when they arrived at Aunt Polly's. She had left two big candles burning on the kitchen table, and when Jim had cared for Beauty he and Peggy read together the note she had left for them propped against the cream pitcher.

You had early dinner, so you'll need a snack when you get here, I doubt. Jim, you know where everything is. There's fresh bread and butter and my new strawberry jam in the covered glass dish and plenty of gingerbread and milk. On my wedding day, my grandmother whispered to me, "Mind, there's more to marriage than four bare legs in a bed." Well, eat hearty and sleep well. I love you both.

Aunt Polly

At first they looked up from the paper, both coloring. Then they laughed. The communication was so like Aunt Polly; Jim folded it carefully and put it into his pocket to keep.

They ate ravenously of the food which somehow seemed exactly what they craved at the moment. When they had put things away, Jim held the two big candles for Peggy to see the Wedding Ring quilt with its soft pinks and blues, needing perhaps only another week's work before it would come to stay at the Richlands. Then, candles high, he led his bride up the stairs until they came to the room he had always claimed as his own. "I've dreamed of being here with you," he said, "and now it's really come true."

Peggy was misty-eyed as she went about looking at the
big four-poster, now all in white with its linen sheet folded
back over a pure, uncolored quilt, at the washstand with its
flowered bowl and pitcher. "And a little soap dish!" she
cried. "Why, the soap's *pink*! Is it boughten?"

"No. Aunt Polly, of course, makes her own, but she
has a little trick of putting into it, just before it's poured
out to harden, a little bit of any red fruit juice and it comes
out a pale pink. It's a secret, but she told me."

"Oh, I hope she will show me how."

When the candles were snuffed, they modestly undressed
and got into the big bed with its soft feather tick. Almost
at once there was a pitter-patter on the porch roof just outside their window. A sweet breeze came quietly with the
sound of the drops. Peggy spoke ecstatically. "Oh,
Jim, listen to the rain! And I *love* to go to sleep when it's
raining. Why, it just seems like the last lovely thing for
our wedding day, doesn't it?"

Jim drew her close and touched her hair with his lips.
"Perhaps not the *last* thing," he whispered.

And so it was that a brightness came to the old stone
house as the weeks passed. It was soon apparent that
Peggy, along with her laughter and song, had the talents
of an excellent housekeeper. She did her cooking with a
light ease, but good, substantial foods appeared on the
table. Duncan watched her proudly, as though he had
taught her all she knew. "Could you bake us a cake,
lass?" he inquired once.

"Oh, yes, I can. I never had as good a stove as this to
cook on before. And I can bake the bread in the bake
oven too. Why don't you let me?"

"Ach, it's heavy work, the firing an' pulling the loaves out an' all. You're too light-made for that, little Mistress. But a cake now —"

So Peggy made a pound cake with the cream and rich, yellow butter from the springhouse crocks, flavored it with arrowroot and sprinkled it with sugar. The men, eating it, declared with solemn conviction that it was the best cake they had ever tasted, even including Aunt Polly's wedding confection.

"Oh, I'll make it often for you," Peggy laughed, well pleased at its reception. "I know a few other things, too, that I'll try for you."

One was apple dumplings. When a basket of early Maiden-Blush apples were brought in one day, she had her dough ready. After paring and coring fifteen apples, she rolled each in a bit of buttered dough, crimped the edges close to make a ball, then dropped them all in gently simmering water. She served them at supper on a huge platter with the sugar bowl full and a great pitcher of rich milk. The apples were tender, the dough melted in the mouth, the old-fashioned soup plates held the creamy juice. The men ate until the last ball had disappeared; then, replete and speechless with satisfaction, they looked at Peggy as though she were a being from another world. Duncan, as usual, broke the silence.

"God a'mighty, little Mistress, what do ye call these here things we just et?"

"Apple dumplings! Did you like them?"

There was a roar of laughter and then the talk began. Duncan's questions were distinctly culinary.

"So, they're a bit like apple turnovers only not round, and boiled instead of baked, eh?"

"Now, look out, Duncan," Dave adjured. "Mind, we don't want you trying your hand at these. When we have dumplings, who makes them? All together now." — "Peggy," the brothers' voices shouted.

"Hear the ungrateful critters," Duncan grinned. "Slavin' me hands off cookin' for them when there was naebody else to do it." Then he stopped, smiling more widely. I'm just havin' a bit joke wi' them, little Mistress. You just make the dumplings for us as often as you can, an' blessings on ye! An' now you and the young Master go on into the sittin' room an' talk your own talk away from these noisy louts here, an' them an' me, we'll clean up the dishes."

When Jim and Peggy were by themselves, she looked up at him wistfully. "You never said a word about the dumplings."

He kissed her before answering. "I'll tell you why. I was afraid if I let myself go at all, I'd blubber right into the soup dish. You see, they were so delicious and I was so proud of you, I was afraid to speak. Are you satisfied? I could say it all over now if you wish."

She laughed. "No, no, everything is all right now. But you see, it's so very important to me that you think I'm a good cook. When do you think we could go over to my father's and pick up the things from there that I want? You know, the weeks slip away so fast. Can you believe it's nearly September?"

"I know. I've sort of put you off about that. It's been such a busy time with the haying and the harvesting. I'll tell you what we'll do. Friday of next week we'll start early for your father's. Then you can dust things up and do a little cooking and maybe sleep in your old room again. Would you like that?"

"Oh, yes!"

"I'll pack your things and we'll go to Aunt Polly's and spend the next night there. Then home by Sunday. Would it bother you to travel on the Sabbath?"

"Not a bit. Do you think it's wicked?"

"Well, no, I don't. I can't seem to be as strict about many things as my father was. But I was a little worried about you."

She giggled. "Now we don't have to worry about each other." Then, turning serious, "I'll tell you one thing I would like. When we get home Sabbath evening, I think we should have family prayers."

Jim was sober, too. "You are right. I should keep up that custom now that I'm the head of the house. Let's have them every Sabbath evening at bedtime. Now come on out and see the moon rise over the hay fields."

Duncan highly approved of the short trip as did the boys, though they shed many crocodile tears in the porch towel as they waved Peggy good-by. Jim had placed the buggy cushions instead of the regular ones on the seat of the light spring wagon. Peggy would have a more comfortable journey. He had also set a small wooden box in front of the dashboard upon which she could place her feet since they barely reached the floor of the wagon.

They set off at last up the first little hill and down the other, along the woods or the open roads. Peggy's head drooped sometimes against Jim's shoulder when the sun was hot, and then he let the horse go more slowly while he feasted his eyes worshipfully on the beauty of the young face that lay on his arm.

It was late afternoon when they reached the Prentice

farm. Peggy ran eagerly into the house and cried out in housewifely distress at the disarray. The men were still in the fields, so Peggy swept and dusted and put things to rights, then made the oven hot for biscuits and cut slices of flitch. This, with eggs and biscuit and jam, would make a good dinner for all of them. She was hungry herself after only the bread and butter they had eaten along the way.

When the men came in there was the good smell of bacon frying and biscuits browning. Mr. Prentice did a rare thing. He came over to Peggy and kissed her. He even told her how glad he was to see her and, for an undemonstrative man, this was going far. The uncle shook hands, a wide, wide smile of pleasure spreading over his face.

"I'm ashamed," Jim kept saying. "I was busy with the harvest, but that was no excuse. I'll do better from now on. I've been selfish."

But the meal was altogether a happy one. Peggy's big, fat biscuits were pronounced by her father to be the best she had ever made. "Just see what marriage will do for a girl," Jim said, grinning.

After all the review of the wedding and news of the progress of the work on both farms, Mr. Prentice said he had all the things Peggy wanted to take back arranged in the wagon shed so they would be together. "I suppose," he added a trifle wistfully, "you will want to make an early start tomorrow."

"We'll have to, if we stop at Aunt Polly's on the way," Jim said.

As a matter of fact, it was past supper time when the wagon at last turned in at the lane, but Aunt Polly saw them coming and had ham in the skillet when they were barely at the wagon shed. They settled comfortably to give the small bits of news they had, Jim making much of the pound cake and apple dumplings Peggy had made.

"He's just about bustin' with pride, this fellow! Look at him!" Aunt Polly said. "And no wonder, with a bride like the one he's got. Now get along out with Uncle Charley, Jim, while he beds the stock, and Peggy and I will have a little dish of chat all by ourselves."

When the men were gone, Aunt Polly took the girl in her arms, for she saw the tears gathering, and held her close while Peggy clung to her and asked her the questions she had, for there was no other woman to whom she could pour out her heart. After Aunt Polly had answered them all she saw how tired the girl looked, and when the men returned she made her demand.

"Now, Jim, you've both had two days' hard driving and you're ready to sleep. Go along right away to your old room and get a good rest, the two of you, and we'll talk more in the morning. Get on now, for Peggy's about done out up on that spring wagon. I never knew one yet that had decent springs," she added.

"I guess you're right, Aunt Polly. Do we need candles?"

"It's early dusk, but take one along. I doubt you know the way," she chuckled.

She kissed them both and they started up the backstairs with Peggy giving a last wave of her hand before she disappeared. Once again in the white marriage chamber, Peggy undressed quickly and sank with relief into the soft welcome of the big bed.

"Hurry, Jim," she said. "I've something to tell you."

"Are we to take the quilt now, after all?" he asked eagerly.

"No, not the quilt."

When he was beside her, she laid her face against his and caught his hand.

"You'd never guess! I've had a secret, but I wasn't sure until I talked to Aunt Polly tonight. Jim, we're going to have a baby."

The next morning, Aunt Polly walked beside the wagon all the length of the locust lane, as though loath to give the young people up.

"Now mind," she kept repeating, "don't worry about a thing. Anyone can tell you I'm as good as any doctor at a birth and I'll come over a couple of weeks early. Just don't lift heavy, and take things normal. Jim, you look out for her and put a flea in that little Scotchman's ear. I'll warrant after that he won't let her even lift a teaspoon. Good-by, now. Good-by and God bless you."

As the weeks went on, Jim and Peggy spent long evenings alone in the parlor talking about all the phases of the coming event. In spite of Aunt Polly's renowned skill, Jim felt Peggy should be in touch with the New Salem doctor.

"It will seem a long trip as time goes on," Peggy said.

"It's only three miles. And we've got to settle about what church we're going to attend, anyway. The baby will have to be baptized."

Peggy was thoughful. "That's true. The trouble is I won't know anyone in New Salem. We always went to the Four Corners because it was nearer to us and you all went to the Old Covenanter on the hill. We're all so scattered here. But your father was leaning a little to New Salem, wasn't he?"

Jim nodded. "He had already taken his letter and he lies there, so —"

"We'll go to New Salem," Peggy said positively. "After all, it will be exciting to see new people for I've lived such a quiet life."

"Remember, it's a very little village," Jim said laughing, "but I have heard there is a lady there who makes hats and bonnets in her parlor!"

"And the doctor?"

"He seems a bit gruff but he has the kindest eyes I ever saw, and when I spoke to some of the men in the General Store once, they couldn't say enough for him. 'A good man and a good doctor,' they all said. So I'd feel safer, Peggy, if you are in touch with him. We could maybe drive in one day when the September ploughing is over."

"Oh, I'd like that," she said.

Then something happened that drove the trip out of Jim's mind. During the mystery of coming motherhood, Peggy had changed. Her slender body had filled out ever so slightly, enough though to round her cheeks and her small breasts. Nothing else of the great fulfillment was yet noticeable under her Mother Hubbard aprons, but the fact was that with her pregnancy Peggy bloomed like a rose and her normal prettiness lay upon her as beauty. Her smile was more alluring, her eyes brighter, even her hair seemed to have a certain living quality it had not had before.

Jim could hardly keep his eyes off her at mealtimes as he watched her across the table, but he became increasingly aware that another was looking at her, too, with the same intentness. This was his brother Dave, and his eyes were also filled with desire. The shock of the discovery sent him hot and then cold. He was sure of but one thing. It had to be stopped. Those young eyes on fire must no longer look at Peggy. That was a soiling thing. And now, of all times, when she was carrying his own child.

He couldn't finish his dinner one evening because of the weight on his heart. Peggy was solicitous and Duncan irritated, for he had prepared it himself that night.

"So my cookin's no good enough for you now," he teased. "Glad enough you were to have it for many a year. Ah, well. I'll no be denying the young Mistress has a lighter touch wi' the vittles."

"Come, come," Jim said. "For heaven's sake, can't a man leave a bit of meat on his plate without stirring up such a hullabaloo? I maybe did a little too much ploughing. That's all."

"And it's nonsense to plough again in the fall." Tom spoke. "Spring's enough if you give the fields a good turnover. Father hardly ever did a second ploughing."

"It's just one more effort to make this the best farm in the county. That's what I'm aiming to do," Jim said.

Peggy broke in brightly to explain to Duncan just how she made her gingerbread and the meal was soon over, the boys jostling each other to retrieve another piece of cake from the pan. Jim touched Dave's arm.

"Meet me down in the lower field, will you? I'll be there." Dave looked up in surprise, then his expression changed to anger. "Is this a command, Master?" he sneered.

"Well, in a way," Jim said quietly.

He went out quickly with a wave of his hand to Peggy and made his way through the orchard and on to what was always called the lower field since if seemed to be in a bit of a valley. Here, when Dave came, they would be completely screened from the house. In a short time he did come, loping through the orchard and into the field where he faced Jim with a quizzical smile.

"Well," he began, "what's the big secret that we have to cross half the farm to talk about?"

Jim's face was white and troubled. "I don't know how to say this, Dave, but the fact is I don't like the way you look at my wife."

"So that's it, bridegroom. What's wrong with looking at her?"

"You know what I mean, Dave. You look at her as though you — you *wanted* her yourself."

"All right," Dave flared. "What if I do? Let's say it all out in the open. Here you bring right in amongst us a beautiful girl who would turn any man's head. And we have to look at her every day and be close to her and listen to her singing and laughing and know we can't touch her. We can only look and —"

"You mean Tom, too?"

Dave gave a hard laugh. "Oh, Tom!" he said. "I don't think he'd know what to do with a girl if he had one. Oh, he's just the brother, all right, but me —"

He took a step nearer and looked Jim in the eyes. "I'll tell you once and for all how it is with me and then you can shut up. When I hit the pillow at night and think of her in bed with you I feel torture. I've even *cried* with the pain of it. Me! I haven't cried since I was a kid.

Well, I have now, so that's how it is and there's nothing you can do about it."

"Oh, yes there is." Jim's face was scarlet and his voice furious.

"Like what?"

"Like this," Jim hissed as his right arm shot out and hit his brother on the chest. Dave fell back at once to the ground but was up in an instant and stood still. "You dirty skunk," he said. "You wanted the truth and I gave it you and you knock me down for it. Watch out now, you bridegroom, for I'll kill you if I can."

So they fought — vicious, cutting, bruising blows. They were both young and strong as steel, their muscles hardened by the heavy work of the farm. They had pummeled each other as boys, boxed and wrestled as they grew older, but none of this had prepared them for the desperate strength their bodies drew now, as though welded by fire. They each fell, lay to catch breath and then managed to get up and once again return fiercely to the encounter, each in a strange sense fighting for his love.

It was Jim at last who held up his hand weakly and crossed over unsteadily to Dave, his chest heaving with his labored breath.

"This is terrible, Dave. This is wicked. We've got to stop."

He threw an arm around Dave's shoulder and, supporting each other, they reached the orchard fence and leaned upon it. For a time, they did not speak. Then Dave said, brokenly, "You were right Jim. There is something can be done about it."

"What?"

"I can go away."

"No, Dave! Not that. Oh, God, I couldn't bear that. We've always been so close. Listen." His head rested on the fence rail and he could feel the tears on his bruised cheek. "Listen," he repeated. "There's something I want to tell you. Aunt Polly said to tell Duncan but to say nothing to you boys for a while as that might be easier, in a way, for Peggy. Dave, she's going to have a child."

There was no response.

"Did you hear me?" Jim asked.

"I heard you."

"But can't you see this might make a difference in your feelings? As the months go on — it's not due till March — Peggy may not be as lively or even as pretty as she is now. Aunt Polly warned me how it often affects women during the last waiting time. The whole situation now is different, and when you think it over you may see that. Won't you try?"

Dave gave a short, choking laugh not pleasant to hear. "No, I won't try, for there would be no use. You seem to forget I'm not a child. I'm a man just as you are and I love my brother's wife. I can't stay longer in the same house. It's as clear as that. I think I'll leave tonight. I couldn't take the made-up explanations and the good-bys in the morning. You and Duncan can make up a good story. I'll take my own horse," he added.

"But where will you go?"

"To Aunt Polly's. I'll tell her everything. She's a wise one. She'll understand. And there will be some farmer looking for extra help. At least the heavy summer work is done here. I wouldn't want to leave you in the lurch. 'The happy harvest days are gone,' " he quoted. "I read that once. Those days were the happiest of my life, only I didn't know then where I was heading."

They still leaned on the fence, still drawing long breaths, still speaking with difficulty though the lapses between the words were now growing shorter. When Jim spoke, his voice was full of misery. "This is a hard thing, Dave. I understand, but I'm sick at heart over it all. And to have you leave is like losing my right arm, for I've depended on you. And in the house you've been the one to keep the talk going. I'll miss you at every turn. I wish," he added, "that we'd never had that fight."

"Well," Dave said, "so do I. But maybe it had to be, before we could get all the venom out of us. We'll be plenty stiff in the morning, Jim."

"You're not able to go tonight."

"I'll manage. Let's get up to the house and get Duncan to fix us up a little. You go ahead and see if — if Peggy is out of the way."

"She's been going to bed early these nights. She gets tired."

The moon was up by now as the two went stiffly up the walk. "I never knew a fence could feel so soft to lean on," Jim said, and Dave agreed. At the house, all was quiet. Peggy had evidently gone to bed and Tom also, tired from his day of ploughing. Duncan looked at the two battered young men who entered the kitchen and for once said nothing at all. He worked fast, however. He brought a second basins, filled them both with warm water and witch hazel and then, with pieces of soft, old linen, began to wipe their faces gently and then let them bathe themselves as he brought warmer and still warmer water. While they were sponging their bruised bodies, Duncan slipped up to his room and brought down some of the contents of his bottle in a tin cup. Once back in the kitchen he heated milk, put into it a generous spoonful of honey and a very sparing amount from the cup.

"Now drink this and it'll warm up your insides," he said gruffly.

"Duncan, I'm going away. I'm leaving tonight as soon as I get myself pulled together. I have to go. You can draw your own conclusions," Dave said.

"I've been drawin' them this good while back," he said. "It's a sad business, havin' you leave, but mebbe for a while it's best. You'll go first to your Aunt Polly's, I doubt?"

"Yes, for a bit."

"Well, you've got moonlight to help you keep the road. I'll fix you a bite to eat along the way."

"Thanks, Duncan, for everything. That hot water and witch hazel certainly took the soreness out of me. And that drink! My, that went to the spot. What was in it, Duncan? Whiskey?"

"Mebbe one small drappie. Only used in emergencies," he added, "and I'll thank you that you have no more of *them*."

When Dave had quietly put his few clothes together for the saddlebag without disturbing the sleeping Tom, he came down, got his sandwiches and went to his horse tied at the gatepost, waiting. Duncan and Dave gave each other short good-bys, but Jim held his brother's hand when he was seated on his horse. His voice was husky.

"Dave," he said, "this is dreadful, your going away. It breaks me all up. I want one promise from you. If I ever get into trouble of any kind, bad trouble, would you come back and help me?"

"For God's sake, yes," Dave answered quickly. "Of course I would."

Jim drew a long breath. "That makes me feel better, somehow. It's no one's fault. I can see that. Least of all, Peggy's" he added under his breath. "Try to send us word where you are, Dave, and bless you."

Dave pressed his brother's hand but could not speak. He drew the horse's reins and the hooves clattered off into the pale moonlight.

Jim staggered back into the kitchen and sat down at the table, his head in his hands. Duncan came over and patted his shoulder.

"Aye, aye, laddie, it's a sair blow to us all. But I've been watchin'. It's mebbe better this way."

"What will I tell her?" Jim asked.

"Tell her you had a fight over the farm. She'll take that an' so will Tom. They know Dave's hot-headed. So get some rest now. Tomorrow's the Sabbath an' you can all sleep late. I'll no be disturbin' you. Dinna' fash your-sel' too much. Things have a way of levelin' off. Good night, Master."

When Jim woke in the morning, the sun was high and Peggy's place was empty. He had not heard her leave, but he could hear her voice and Tom's talking with Duncan below. "Good heavens," he muttered, "I surely took a sleep, but I guess I needed it."

When he entered the kitchen, there were cries both of

consternation and amusement. "Oh, Jim, you look dreadful!" from Peggy. "What hurt you?"

"You look as if you'd been in a fight," Tom laughed. "And there's no sign of Dave anywhere. It surely wasn't with him."

Jim looked at Duncan, who nodded. "The quicker you tell, the sooner they'll know," he said, "an' here's a plate of hot cakes for you."

"Well," Jim admitted, "you've guessed it, and I feel pretty bad inside about it. As well as outside," he added. "I suppose there has to be one person who decides what is to be done. Dave didn't like some things —"

"The fall ploughing," Tom put in. "He was grumpy about that."

"And he doesn't see the need of a bigger corncrib," Jim added quickly. "So one word sort of brought on another, and you know Dave's —"

"A pepper pot anytime. But where is he? He hasn't gone away?"

"For a time. It was moonlight, so he left last night for Aunt Polly's and will try to find work somewhere around for a while."

Tom whistled. "He must have got his dander up for sure. Well, I'll be your number one man now, Jim. I can accept your orders without fighting you, I'll promise you that." And suddenly a burden seemed lifted and they all laughed together, even while thoughts of Dave were still underneath with all of them.

"I'm sorry about church today, Peggy," Jim said ruefully. "We'll never make it anywhere now, and I'd promised to take you to New Salem. I hope you aren't too disappointed."

"And you with a face like that? I'm certainly not thinking of church. Oh, your *poor* face!"

"It's really a lot better. Duncan fixed us both up last night. But I'll tell you what. I've never taken you completely around the farm, for we've had such a busy summer. Why don't we go out now and 'ride the bounds' as my father used to call it. We'll take the spring buckboard and I can show you how big The Richlands really is. Would you like that?"

"Of course I would love it, if you're able."

Tom gave a great guffaw. "Oh, you can stop at the Bumpers' for a rest if you get tired. She hasn't been there yet, Jim. I don't believe she has even seen any of them, have you, Peggy?"

"Who are the Bumpers?" she asked.

"You can't explain them," said Jim. "You'd better just come on them suddenly if you can take the shock. Well, anywhat, let's start now on our little trip. It will do us both good."

"I'll hitch up for you," Tom said, going quickly out of the kitchen.

The day was mild and sunny with a dim fragrance of the autumn pervading everything. The large trees were still green, but subtle splashes of pink and scarlet showed here and there in the bushes which had sprung up along the fences. With the buggy whip as a pointer and a little normal pride in his voice, Jim showed his wife where one big field ended and, beyond a stout rail fence, another began.

"But does this never end?" Peggy asked in surprise.

"Oh, yes, eventually, but it's a pretty big tract, you can see. Now here's the sugar meadow. The leaves haven't turned yet, but when they do it's all a perfect glory, I think. And in the spring, when it's sugaring-off time, I think you'll like that. We always get gallons of syrup."

"What do you ever do with all the sugar? We only have three trees at home and what we always got seemed enough."

"Oh, we put it down in crocks and let it harden, and we always share with Aunt Polly for they haven't any —"

"Jim," she said suddenly.

"Yes, darling."

"I would like you to tell me the truth about something, if you will."

Jim swallowed nervously. "About what?"

"It's hard for me to ask this, but it seems I have to know. Did Dave's going away have anything to do with — with me?"

Jim flushed scarlet and for a long moment didn't answer as she looked up at him in alarm.

"Just tell me the truth."

"Yes," he said slowly, "it did."

She drew a long, sad sigh. "I was afraid of it."

"How did you know?"

"Well, his looks maybe, and once he held on to my hand when we were walking to the springhouse and when we got there he put it against his cheek. I just laughed, and from then on I tried to be more jolly and sang more and all that; but I think now that was not the best way. I should have been serious to show I knew and didn't like it. Oh, I feel so utterly miserable."

He put his arm about her as his voice became almost violent. "You must never blame yourself. You acted with him exactly the way you do with Tom."

"Oh, Tom!" she said softly. "He's such a comfort. He's such fun and would never — *never* think of anything like — like Dave. But I can't help feeling unhappy."

"You must put that thought away. You are my precious wife and just now you must not feel a care. Let's forget Dave for a while. He'll likely stay on at Aunt Polly's for a bit. Uncle Charley isn't so young anymore and could use some help. Besides, he's a very gentle man and Dave can boss him around all he has a mind to."

Jim found he could laugh, and Peggy joined him, if a bit shakily. "Now we'll be getting along," he said, "for just a little way farther we'll come upon the famous Bumper family and I'm badly mistaken if that doesn't drive everything else from your mind."

"Do they work on the farm?" Peggy asked a little later.

"Not if they can help it," Jim said. "That's why you've never seen them. Well, here we are."

The buckboard drew into a wide, beaten path and came to a stop as the occupants surveyed the scene. In front of a dilapidated shingle house, against a spreading elm tree, leaned a long, bedraggled-looking figure of a man: his hair apparently had not been combed lately, his face was dirty, his worn suspenders were fastened to his pants with twine and his large feet were bare. He left the tree and with surprising agility came over to the buckboard.

"Well, if it ain't young Master Jim," he said, in most ingratiating tones.

"Hello, Bumper."

"You know, I was just thinkin' of goin' over to see you to explain about this summer. I sure meant to be on hand for the harvestin' an' some of the fall ploughin' too, but —"

He suddenly assumed the position and a tone of extreme pain and continued, "I've had this turrible back all summer. It just hit me suddenlike —"

"About last spring ploughing time?" Jim asked with mock innocence.

"You're right," Bumper agreed. "That was the very time an' the blasted thing hain't ever left me yet. Mrs. Bumper can tell you I'm speakin' God's truth."

"Well, now, suppose we leave God out of this. I have something very important to say to you, though. Before winter comes, I want you to mend the side of this house where the shingles and clapboards are torn off. If you want to stay here, that *must* be done."

"Oh, sure, sure. Some of the children did that. This here your bride, Master Jim?"

"This is my wife, Mr. Bumper."

"Well, now, you sure picked yourself a beauty an' no mistake. You'd never think it, but when I married Mrs. Bumper she was as pretty as this one. Yes, sir! Of course now, childbearin' has worn her down some, but she's got a nice big family to pay her for her trouble."

"How many children have you? By last count," Jim added wickedly while Peggy smothered a giggle.

"Well, I'd say nine 'on the hoof' as it were, an' far as I know 'none in the oven,' as the old sayin' goes. Not bad for old folk like us, is it?"

"How are you going to feed them?"

Bumper shifted his quid to his other cheek. "Oh," he said jauntily, "we hain't never starved in the winter yet." Then raising his voice, he yelled, "Mrs. Bumper, come out. We got company."

At once there was a hurricane of children of mixed ages

streaming around the corner of the house, while Mrs. Bumper herself came through the door with one large child still breakfasting at the maternal font. She disengaged herself and sent the howling infant away with a smart slap, to be rescued by one of the large group standing wide-eyed at the end of the porch. Peggy's eyes were watching the mother, fascinated. There was in her face the remnants of a wild, dark beauty.

"Why, if it ain't the young Master," the woman said in a deep, throaty voice, "an' his bride, I'll be bound. Now I take this very kindly for you to come callin' on us. Help them out of their conveyance, Bumper, an' bring them up on the porch. You childer," she yelled with a sudden change of voice, "get them clothes an' stuff off the chairs so the company can set down. Come right on up but watch them steps. Bumper, he's been so poorly this summer, he ain't had a chance to mend them. My, you're pretty, little Missus!"

Jim and Peggy exchanged a look and then got out of the buckboard and carefully picked their way up to the sagging steps.

"Well, Mrs. Bumper, how are you?" Jim asked, holding Peggy's arm tightly as they passed over the rickety boards.

"Just middlin', Master Jim. You can see I got a lot of responsibility here. Hey, you," she interrupted to call to the tallest girl watching the scene, "take that squallin' brat out to the back so's we can hear ourselves talk. An' how do you like The Richlands, Missus Ryall?" she added in her company voice.

"Oh, very much," said Peggy, her lips twitching as she spoke. "You really must be kept very busy here."

"Lord knows I am, with this here flock to fend for.

Bumper, now, he was took terrible with his back — last spring —" She cast a side glance at him, to which he agreed with a heavy sigh, "I sure was."

"So," Mrs. Bumper went on, "everythin' just kinda falls on me." Her voice changed again. "Didn't I tell you to take that brat out back? Awwww — he wants his mummy, does he? Well, bring him over."

She took the dirty and unbelievably handsome child to her arms and prepared to nurse him. "If you'll just excuse me. He's on the bottle, of course, but I give him a treat now an' again. It keeps him healthy. Doctor says so an' none of my childer is ever sick. I'm tellin' you."

Jim rose abruptly. "We must be going, Mrs. Bumper. We only stopped to speak to you. I'm glad you are all well, except your husband here. Sorry you'll be laid up at cider-making time, Bumper."

"Now, now," the man said, hastily rearing himself to full height. "These last few days I think I've been a leetle bit better. I'll sure be ready for cider-making."

"I couldn't think of it," Jim said with mock gravity. "The risk would be too great after all these months of pain. But you've got a lad here I've been watching. I believe he would be the very one to climb trees and run some presses, too. What's your name, son?"

"Pete," said the boy. His eyes under the torn straw hat were eager. He had edged toward the front of the group of milling children and now stepped close to Jim. He looked to be about twelve, sandy-haired, thin-shouldered and with the amazing good looks of the rest of the children.

"I'd like workin' for you. I've often wanted to ask, but I was scared, sort of. I'll try real hard if you'll take me."

"It's settled, then," Jim said, giving no heed to Bumper's continued protestations. "Come up later today. You can maybe start picking next week."

"He can climb trees like a squirrel, that one," Mrs. Bumper called from the porch. "Will he be gettin' any wages?"

"We'll see," Jim answered. "He'll get three good meals a day for a starter. Can he stay up at the house, Mrs. Bumper? There's a little extra room there. And, of course, he could come home weekends if he wants."

"Sure, sure. In this mess of childer you'd hardly miss one. Pete's good about doin' little jobs, though. He may suit you. My oldest boy, Junior, don't take much to workin', somehow, but Pete here is different. Awful nice of you to come. An' good weddin' luck to you."

There were general good-bys, Peggy's being especially kind, for the faces of "the childer" of all ages haunted her. Before the buckboard had gone more than a short distance, Bumper came loping toward them. Jim drew up reluctantly.

"Jist forgot, Master Jim, to tell you there was a man nosin' round here 'tother day."

"What did he want?"

"Well, I didn't rightly know. He said he'd been in at the county seat and thought he'd look over this part of the country. Asked who owned this farm an' if I'd heard anything about sellin' it an' how many people lived up at your place an' all. I answered him short, you may be sure. He didn't talk like us. Had a sort of funny twang to him."

Jim looked annoyed. "If you are ever asked about The Richlands again, you can just say it's not for sale and then shut up."

"Looked like he might have money."

"He hasn't got enough to buy this farm. If any stragglers you're uncertain about ever come round again, send them up to me." He made a gesture for Bumper to stand back and then drove on.

"The queer thing," Peggy was saying, "is that I don't feel like laughing, even though they *are* funny. Where did they ever come from, Jim, and what do they live on now?"

"It's a queer story, all right. Years ago, my father kept a hired man who lived with his family in the tenant house you saw, only it was in good shape then. When this man's wife died, he wouldn't stay on, and just after he left the Bumpers came looking for work. Hard to believe, but he was a good, able-bodied man then and she was really handsome. Both very dark and swarthy. So much so, my father thought they had belonged to a gypsy tribe that had been camping along the old highway."

"Gypsies!" Peggy echoed.

"Well, my father was desperate for help so he decided to try them and for several years it worked all right. Bumper was strong and seemed to take to farming and Mazie — that's Mrs. Bumper — helped with the milking and cleaning the house and so on. Then Bumper found a place he could get whiskey and from then on he slackened off. Mazie had a baby every time the wind blew so she couldn't be counted on much either. But my father always said, 'How could I turn them out? Who would ever take them as they are now?' And I feel the same."

"But what do they live on?" Peggy asked.

"Oh, I guess we feed them, directly or indirectly. They

have a cow and we always give them a couple of pigs at butchering time — we never miss them — or a sack of flour when we go to the mill with any wheat. One thing they really do well for themselves, that is, gardening. That carries them through the summer. They make our garden, too, at the end of the meadow and those children all have green thumbs even if they have dirty faces. They are shy as fawns, though, and never bring the produce up to the house, at least where they will be seen. We find baskets of vegetables on the back porch but it's just as if fairies had left them there."

"I like this Pete," Peggy said. "He's got nice eyes but, Jim, he's no gypsy. He's not swarthy and his hair is almost light. Several of the children look like that. There must be a mixture of blood somehow."

"I like Pete, too. I've been hoping to get him. The older boy I wouldn't trust around a stump. But as to the mixture of blood, darling — the world's a queer place, but let's just take it as it is and keep very quiet about it."

Chapter III

The advent of Pete into the Richlands household was a
fortuitous one. It was surprising how many little odd
jobs he took over, apparently with pleasure, for his smile
was ready and so was his laughter. After the Sunday drive
and its confessions, his presence seemed to bring a certain
healing to the hearts still sore over Dave's leave-taking.
Jim had watched the boy's reception with interest. Tom
was an old friend, it seemed. "Well, if it isn't Pete," he
had grinned as the introductions took place. "I never
saw you outside the garden patch. So you're going to
stay with us for a while, eh?"

Duncan had looked the other way and sputtered something about a boy's being more trouble than he was worth
at that age. But after Jim had showed Pete the little room
just off the backstairs landing which would be his, and
had allowed him to glimpse the rest of the upstairs, they
came down to the kitchen to rich smells of chicken soup
with homemade noodles bubbling in it. The boy's thin
nostrils dilated. Duncan, looking up, saw and recognized the expression of eagerness.

"Come away then, laddie," he called. "Sit you down
and taste this good soup."

When they were all seated, Pete stared at the large dish before him and turned to Jim. "Is this all for *me*?"

"Every drop! And here is plenty of bread and butter to go with it."

There was pound cake to top off the supper, with some of the cream from a big crock in the springhouse to add to the delicacy.

"This cake is better than mine, Duncan," Peggy said loyally.

"Na, na, but it's no so bad. I thought you'd be needin' a bit of sweet after the soup."

"And I'm needing a second piece, Duncan," Tom said.

The boy's small plate was clean and Jim said, "Would you like a bit more, Pete?"

"Could I have it?"

"Of course."

When they were all finished, Pete made an observation. "I never knowed there was such good things to eat in all the world," he said.

He was on his feet quickly when the others got up and began to carry the plates over to the big work table. "I could wash the dishes," he said eagerly to Duncan.

"Aye. That you could, laddie, and fine help it would be. I'll show you tonight how we do it here an' then after this you can be on your own."

Later when they were all in the sitting room, Duncan handed Jim the big family Bible. "You'll be takin' the Book as usual?"

"Certainly," Jim said, though his heart felt sore even as did his body, still bruised from the fight. He thumbed the pages until he found his father's favorite psalm: "Lord, thou hast been our dwelling place —"

At the end they repeated the Lord's prayer together. Pete's eyes had been wide with interest during the reading but he bowed his head with the others. "I'd like to be learnin' what you all said," he whispered to Jim when they were talking again.

"Of course. I'll see you get a little Bible of your own. It's in that."

"An' the thing you read? I like that."

"Yes. That and a great deal more. What about your school, Pete? Have you learned to read and cipher?"

"Oh, yes. I can read a'most anything. My mother teached us all and I sort of took to it. My Pappy's good at cipherin' and he showed us how. We never went to no regular school."

Jim was thoughtful. "Farm work is slack in the winter. We might be able to send you to our country school here for a couple of months. You'd like that."

Before they went to sleep, Peggy touched Jim softly. She could feel his instinctive reaction of pain.

"It still hurts so?"

"It's much better."

"You were so good to drive out today. I wanted to thank you."

"As though you needed to!"

"When you left here, did you think then of asking Pete to come?"

"It hadn't entered my head. I have been watching him, though, when I would see him in the garden; and when I saw him in that crowd of slovenly-looking children, I just whispered to you and went ahead. I should have consulted you more."

"Do you know what I think, Jim?"

"What, darling?"

"I think Pete is going to be a treasure. He has already made a big conquest. Do you know what Duncan is doing right now?"

"No idea. I came up early."

"He's brought in the big tub and has the hot water ready to give Pete a real bath. Then he told me he was going to fit him out with one of his own body shirts and a pair of shorter "breeks" and clean up his coat. Did you notice how Duncan looked at the boy when he thought no one was noticing?"

"I did."

"Well, go to sleep now. I just wanted you to know I'm pleased about Pete."

As the weeks passed, a gentle merriment filled the stone house. It was different from Peggy's own brightness; this was a boyish glee which had its effect upon all, but especially upon Duncan. Just as Pete's thin frame filled out from the miracle of three good meals a day, so the deep lines in Duncan's face seemed to soften. And the sharp glint of his blue eyes more often became a twinkle. He made no effort now to conceal his affection for the boy, and no one was disturbed by it for everyone had the same in some measure. Pete now sat in Dave's chair at the table and seemed somehow to belong there.

It developed soon that Pete was taking over so many helpful tasks about the house and barn that Duncan was left free to take Dave's place with more of the regular farm work. Accustomed as the boy was to the mysteries of birth, it had not been hard to tell him of Peggy's pregnancy. Jim also spoke of it casually to Tom who showed no surprise.

"I've thought that might be the reason for the afternoon naps and the loose aprons. Well, that's fine, Jim. We'll all try to take good care of her."

"Good old Tom," Jim was thinking, "there were no wild fires burning in *his* heart."

It was decided that the trip to New Salem should no longer be postponed. Peggy, in a pleasant little flutter of excitement, often talked over its main events with variations before she and Jim went to sleep. These would be the calls upon the minister and on the doctor — if Jim insisted.

"I insist," he always said.

Then there would be the fun of shopping in the General Store, for Pete must have a decent outfit of clothes. His shoes were practically in holes, too.

"And there may be a few things you'll want yourself. You can look around," Jim always said.

"But it will be strange to be taking money from you," she mentioned once. At which Jim first laughed and then looked grave.

"Why, my darling little wife, it will make me proud as Punch to think I can give you money. Don't you remember what I had to say when we were getting married? 'With this ring I do thee wed and I all my worldly goods on thee endow?' "

"I don't think I heard. I was too excited."

"Well, it makes no difference. What ·is mine is now yours, too. I wish I always had more ready cash, though. To hand you a few bushels of wheat wouldn't be quite the same, would it?"

Then they laughed and made love and were deeply content.

Peggy woke him one night, apologetically. "Jim?"

"Yes, darling. Is anything the matter?"

"No. I couldn't wait till morning to ask. I was just hoping that when we go to New Salem I could go to the house of the lady who makes bonnets in her parlor. Could I?"

"Of course, you precious little goose. Now get back to sleep."

On the day of the trip, the sky was beautifully and intensely blue. Against it, the leaves of the sugar maple grove were growing scarlet, with here and there a larch rising like a slender tower of gold. Everywhere there was color and a soft sense of fulfillment in the air. The great fields lay as though satisfied, their summer work done. There was a delicate whispering rustle among the corn shocks as the pumpkins lay in lazy yellow opulence between them. Peggy sat in the buggy waiting for Jim and Pete to join her, looking over the wide expanse of The Richlands and exulting in her love and the joys that went with it.

It had been a little disappointment, Jim had admitted the night before to Peggy, that they could not set off alone, but if Pete was to have shoes and some sort of a suit he must be along to try them. Peggy insisted that nothing could change the pleasures of the day and when Jim and the boy came out she gave them both her smiling welcome. Pete was stowed away in the back of the buggy with Jim and Peggy settled in the front seat. Jim drove carefully over the patches of stony roads and loitered a little at Peggy's request along the smooth, wooded stretches.

At last the outlines of the town came suddenly to view. A small one it was but to Peggy's eyes, accustomed only to the Cross Roads church, blacksmith shop and tiny store, it looked quite like a county seat. Between the crest of the high hill where they now were and the low one to the west, the little village seemed to nestle with a comfortable finality. It had been there for a long time; it would probably stay for many more years to come without much change. As the small creek on the southern side wound its accustomed way without questioning where or when its waters would ever reach the sea, so Jim thought, with a flash of insight, would the citizens of the town lying before them go about the business of living as their fathers before them had done, with a quiet acceptance of joy and sorrow and the simple vicissitudes of life. "Well, don't we all?" Jim thought, and then shook himself lightly as though to stop his wandering mind.

"Now, let's wait here a minute while I point out some of the places of interest," he said, picking up the buggy whip to use as a pointer.

"We'll enter the town on the eastern end of Main Street. It's the one you can see with the big maple trees bordering the sidewalk. Most of the houses are there and all the stores. Look where the iron posts on down the street are connected by an iron rod to which the horses are tied. See the big building there? That's the General Store where you can get *anything* from a safety pin to a sleigh! The striped pole is in front of the barber shop and just across is the old Stone Hotel."

"Oh, Jim, I am excited to see all this!"

"Back on the side street you can see a large, red brick building. That's the church we'll be going to. There's another one near with a steeple, but it was considered too fancy for the old Presbyterians. Well, maybe we'd better be getting along. Let's make our calls first and then be free to do our errands and enjoy the day. Pete can wander around and have a look at the shops while we're busy. All right?"

"Only I'm nervous."

"Think about the new bonnet and don't worry."

Halfway down the street, Jim tied the horse to a stout stone block in front of a plain brick house with its porch, like many others, projecting inquisitively into the sidewalk. He dispatched Pete, ecstatically clutching a few small coins, and then with Peggy went up the steps to a door lettered: Robert Flemming, M.D.

"I guess we just walk in," Jim said, and did so. There was a small anteroom and beyond, a half-open door through which they could see a roll-top desk, its flat surface a mass of letters and papers. In front of it a strongly built, ruddy-faced man was busy spooning a white substance into small slips of paper which he then folded.

"Powders," Jim whispered. "Should we knock?"

Peggy nodded, and in a second the doctor had risen. "Come on in," he called gruffly.

Once before him, as the introductions were given and the errand stated, Peggy kept a nervous hold on Jim's hand. Then suddenly the doctor smiled, and it seemed as though the shabby office itself had visibly brightened.

"Well, well!" he said. "Now isn't that nice! Which would you rather have, Mrs. Ryall, a girl or a boy?"

"Could you tell?" Peggy asked, a little of her fear wearing off.

"Well, no, but we can all guess, can't we? I'm sort of

partial to girls myself, but I find I'm always safe to guess a boy. For the first, anyway."

"Oh, yes. I think I'd want a boy for Jim."

"Now," the doctor went on, "you take the county paper here, Jim, and wait out in the entrance there while I just check your wife and see if our new friend here is giving her any trouble. I won't be long. That all right, Peggy? I thought you looked a little scared when you came in."

"Oh, not now. Not when you smile."

"See, Jim, what a way I have with the ladies? Slip your dress down, Peggy, so I can listen to your heart better. See if it still beats for Jim, and all that."

The doctor was still jovial as he helped her up on a high chair, the back of which could be lowered.

Every little while as he proceeded he cheered her up with such remarks as "Very good! That's fine!"

At last he helped her down to the floor and went out to talk to Jim. "Is everything all right?" Jim asked huskily.

"She's in perfect health. I just want to mention one thing. She's small. You know the difference between a brood mare and a racehorse? Well, what I want to say is, when she finally has her first labor pain, send for me at once. I may know a few little tricks that will make it easier for her. You won't forget?"

Jim gave him a strange look. "Do you think I could?"

"Well, no, not with the first."

"Nor with any. Doctor, I do thank you. May I pay you now?"

The doctor waved his hand casually. "Oh, no. I will want to see her once again nearer the time. I've put the date in my book. Don't worry, my boy. Everything will be fine. I wish all the women would come to see me before the last minute. Will there be a woman there later on?"

"Oh, yes. Aunt Polly. I think you know her. She says she'll come over a week or so early."

"Good. Oh, here's your wife. She's a little beauty, Jim!"

There were friendly good-bys, and as she went down the steps Peggy whispered, "I'm so glad you made me come. I won't be afraid anymore."

"Now for the preacher and then we can enjoy ourselves," Jim said.

The manse stood farther up the street and though there was no reason one could clutch, it looked severe and, in a sense, melancholy. The first fallen leaves lay unswept upon the walk and the window curtains hung limply at the tall windows. A huge pine tree threw a sort of funeral shade over the house and the large side lawn.

"Well," Jim muttered as he pressed the bell, "let's get it over with."

A thin woman in a wispy, black dress opened the door and eyed the young couple.

"Are you wishing to get married?" she asked.

"We are already married," Jim said, grinning.

"Oh, in that case, I'll show you right into the minister's study. You see, when strange young people come, they usually want to get married and I show them into the front parlor. Just follow me, please."

The pastor's study into which they were ushered was a more pleasant place than the exterior of the house would have suggested. There was an imposing desk, many books and a few steel engravings on the wall. The tall man who rose to greet them had a long, ascetic looking face, but he smiled as he spoke.

"Dr. Knox?" Jim asked.

"Yes. A good name for a Presbyterian, isn't it? And you?"

"I'm Jim Ryall from The Richlands and this is my wife. We would like to join the church here."

"Sit down. I'm glad to meet you both. The Richlands, eh? A fine tract of land, that is. You didn't go to college, then? It seems I've heard Dr. Donaldson speak of you."

"No, I chose the farm. I have some ideas I would like to work out."

"Well, you know your own mind, anyway. Where have you gone to church up till now?"

"My wife belonged to the Cross Roads and I to Mount Zion."

"This will be farther for you to come, will it not?"

"By the main road, yes, but by what we call the lower road, it's only about two and a half miles. We feel it will be pleasant to get to know the New Salem people. Though," he corrected himself quickly, "we would not be coming just for that."

"I should hope not," said Dr. Knox. "However," he added, "there is 'the fellowship of kindred minds' mentioned in the old hymn we sing so often. The author evidently felt that church friends were important. When would you like to join?"

"As soon as we can lift our letters and get them to you."

"I would prefer you would be here to be publicly received. Could you come for the November Communion? We have the preparatory service as usual on Saturday afternoon, and since the Manse here is large and only my wife and I in it, we would be happy to entertain you overnight."

He looked admiringly at Peggy as he spoke and she looked back at him, aglow with pleasure.

"Why, how kind of you, Dr. Knox! We would be very pleased to do that, wouldn't we, Jim?"

Jim's eyes had caught those of the minister and, without being able to explain it, he felt a certain distaste. He added his thanks, however, to Peggy's and the matter was left that the letters would be forwarded and the new members would come, if possible, in late November.

"We have to consider the weather, you know," Jim explained and, blushing a little, added, "My wife should not drive over rutty roads just now."

"Oh!" said Dr. Knox, looking keenly again at Peggy's pretty face. "That's delightful news. We'll expect you before lunch that Saturday, then. Which will give you both time to meet the Session before the service hour. By the way, when were you married?"

"The twentieth of June," they answered together.

"And the child is expected?"

"The last of March."

"Very good," Dr. Knox said. "You must forgive my questions, but we've had so many cases of prenuptial fornication right in our own midst that the Session and I have been forced to treat the matter seriously."

Jim stood up. "I fear we must be going." His tone was cold. "We thank you for your time and helpfulness and we'll hope to get back in November."

"Before lunch. My wife and I will enjoy having some young folk in the house."

He showed them out over the leaf-strewn porch and they walked slowly along the street. A wide meadow lay just across from and beyond the Manse, and the houses began on either side.

"Well?" Peggy questioned. "Which did you like best? Doctor or preacher?"

Jim laughed. "You read my thoughts or you would never have asked that question. Well, I'll tell you. When the doctor smiles, his whole face wrinkles up. When Dr. Knox smiles, it never gets higher than his mouth; never reaches his eyes. Well, how do *you* feel?"

"I thought he was very nice, but I liked Dr. Flemming the best, too. I think Dr. Knox could be quite stern if he was set on something."

"I do, too. You still want to put our letters in here?"

"Oh, yes," Peggy smiled. "It may not sound very religious, but I think it will be exciting to come here and get to know new people —"

"And have a bigger place to show off your new bonnets," Jim put in, laughing.

"You're a tease," Peggy said. "But tell me what Dr. Knox meant by those long words, prenuptial something. I never heard them before."

"And you shouldn't have now. I was annoyed that he used them in front of you, and questioned us, too. I was angry."

"But what do they mean, dear?"

Jim looked puzzled as though planning the best way to explain. "Well, to put it bluntly, sometimes a young couple in love forget how to behave and a baby gets started before they are married."

"Oh, that!" Peggy gave a small giggle. "Of course

I know about that, but I never heard the name for it. Why would the minister and the Session make a fuss about it?"

"That's what I say. I think it's none of their business. And I thought it was pretty rude of him to question us."

"But he *is* hospitable. Won't it be wonderful to stay at the *Manse*. Aren't you pleased?"

"Yes, but I don't want to be 'beholden,' as they say. When we have to spend a night here, I think we'll go to the Stone Hotel."

Peggy stopped in her tracks. "*The Stone Hotel!*" she breathed.

"Why, yes. I'd always hoped we could go there on our wedding night only, as you know, everything was changed. But it's not so expensive. I inquired once when I came in to the mill. Why, darling, would you like that so much?" For Peggy's eyes were brimming over.

"Oh, *so* much. I'd feel like real city folk then. I just realize what a very quiet life I've always had, and now all sorts of things are going to happen. The best of all is what I have all the time. Can you guess it?"

All her beauty seemed suddenly to flow into her face. No one was in sight and Jim stooped to kiss her.

"You'll have me crying in a minute. Emotion," he added. "Well, come on now, let's have fun. I wonder how Pete has gotten along."

They found him a little way down the street and Jim caught his hand.

"Now," he said, "we had early breakfast, so I think we should have lunch right away. And I have a surprise. See that store just two doors down from here?"

Pete spoke promptly. "It says 'ice cream parlor.' I read it on the sign."

"It is indeed. Or it's being prepared for one. We're going to take our sandwiches and cookies and go there to meet Mr. Billy Wester, the proprietor. I know him well. I think he'll let us eat our lunch at one of the tables in the parlor and then we'll finish off with a dish of his new ice cream. How's that?"

"I can't believe it!" Peggy glowed.

They found Billy, rotund and beaming, his steel-rimmed spectacles as usual pushed down on his nose, while above them his bright eyes took note of everything about him.

"Jim Ryall! Now this is a pleasure even if I must tell you how I miss your father. He always brought the wheat to the mill himself, do you mind?"

"Of course."

"An' he'd come in for a little chat an' find out how I was gettin' on with my ice cream! Well, he's left The Richlands in good hands, Jim, and it looks to me as if you had some pretty news to tell me."

"I have. This is my wife, Mr. Wester, and if it would not be too presuming, I thought maybe we could eat our sandwiches here before we sample your new product."

"Now ain't that nice! I'll have a chance to serve the bride an' I'm proud to meet you, Ma'am. Who's the boy here?"

"This is Pete. He's living with us now and he's a good help."

"I'll bet he is. Well, come right into the parlor now an' get on with your lunch. I expect you're in a hurry with errands, ain't you?"

"We are, a little, and thank you, Billy. You know, this is an experience. We're not used to ice cream."

Billy ushered them through a door at the end of the counter into a room filled with small marble-topped tables and cane-backed chairs. "It's empty now," Billy explained, "but come evening when the beaux begin to call on their girls an' take them out for a treat, the place gets filled up. You'd be surprised! An' last winter in sleighin' time, by golly, they'd come here from five miles away in their spandy cutters to get a good warm at my open fire an' eat ice cream. I never hurry them. So you see, I wasn't so crazy to start this business. Well, now, just let me know your flavor an' I'll bring it in later. Chocolate an' vanilla is all I've learned to make yet."

"Chocolate!" Peggy's voice was amazed. "Why, I never heard of that!"

"I'll join her in that choice," Jim said. "And you, Pete?"

"Oh, me too, *please*."

The sandwiches were Duncan's best and the dessert exciting. Billy would take no money for it. "Can't you let me treat your bride?" he kept asking irritably. "Can't I give my weddin' present in ice cream? Don't listen to this fellah, Mrs. Ryall. He makes me mad, but I still like the stubborn mule." And the meal ended with second helpings and much laughter.

As they left, Billy jerked his thumb for Jim to wait a little after Peggy and Pete had reached the sidewalk and were scanning what seemed to them both a metropolitan line of stores.

"How's your little Scotty?" he asked.

"Duncan? He's fine."

"Him an' me are cronies, sort of. You see, Jim, a man can't live by ice cream alone an' in this confounded temperance wave that's hit the town, you have to play the sneak to get a bottle of whiskey. I manage, and when

Scotty comes in, we just bend the elbow a little together an' I always have an extry bottle he can buy."

"So that's the way he gets it!"

"Sure! What's wrong with that? But what I wanted to ask you was whether Scotty was ever married?"

"Not that I know of."

"Well, that boy. That Pete you have. It just struck me. One way he turns, he looks uncommon like Scotty. What's his last name?"

Jim hesitated. "B — Bumper," he said.

Billy stared. "Oh, my God!" he said. "I wonder!"

Jim looked anxious. "Listen, Billy, if you have any ideas in your head about the boy, will you please keep them to yourself! I beg you to do this."

"Now, now, what kind of an old gossip pot do you think I am? I've been round here for nigh on to sixty years an', bein' a bachelor, I've heard enough secrets to blow this town wide open. I've never told one an' I ain't beginnin' now. Get along with you an' tell Scotty — that's what I always call him — that I've got a new flavor in. That'll bring him fast enough. You know, Jim, that fellah can walk as straight after half a bottle of rye as most other men can after a second dish of ice cream. Good luck to you. Bring your pretty bride in again."

Jim overtook Peggy and Pete and proposed the plan for the next couple of hours. They would all go to the General Store, Peggy could look about and get what she had written on her list, then, while Jim saw to Pete's new outfit, she could call on the lady who made the bonnets. This arrangement seemed perfect and in a few minutes they were going over the wide, stone steps that led to the town's real emporium.

Inside, Peggy gasped at the size and the incredible amount of merchandise ranged along the sides, taking up all the room except for the small elevated office at the back from which General Welles, the proprietor, with a title left from Civil War days, could scan his customers and clerks. He was near the door now and came at once to meet them, tall and portly, his shrewd, steely eyes contradicted by a kind smile. His full cheeks had evidently lost a little fleshy support just as his black alpaca sack coat, spotted faintly here and there from good dinners, hung a bit more loosely upon him. His words came in a genial torrent.

"Well, well, Jim Ryall! This is a pleasure, but with sadness in it, too. A great loss! A great loss to all the community, your father's death was! Master of The Richlands he was in fact, and now you'll be the new one. With a helper at your side. Is this your bride?"

"My wife, Peggy, General Welles."

"And a little beauty if I may say so and avail myself of an old man's privilege." He leaned down and placed a kiss on Peggy's cheek. "You'll never miss that one, Jim," he added with a laugh that seemed to rumble through his chest like gathering thunder. "Come in, come in and let me serve you myself. Where will you shop first, dry goods or groceries? Oh, a fine little lad you have here!" He remarked as Pete stepped out of the doorway into view.

"Yes, Pete's a good helper and I want to get him some shoes and a suit for Sundays. Will you trust me to get the groceries, Peggy, while you look around? Then, General, maybe you'll tell us where the lady lives who makes the bonnets?"

"Miss Lucy? Oh, you have to call on her; then the

whole town will be satisfied. When a new woman comes to town and the busybodies find out she makes all her own bonnets, they look down their noses at her a little. But I'll tell you, child, they'll never look down at you, for the Ryalls of The Richlands are *gentry* in these parts. However," he added, winking at Jim, "it won't do any harm to have a boughten bonnet and I'll point out the house when you go."

They all met again after Peggy had examined the dry goods section with care, and then left Jim to get the groceries and Pete's new outfit while she went with a fast beating heart to the tiny house the general had indicated, with its front window filled with bonnets and a box of ribbons and flowers.

When she returned to the store to join the others, she wore a beatific expression and carried a bandbox.

"Ha!" beamed the general. "She's got it!"

"I'm afraid it cost too much," Peggy said as she looked shyly at Jim.

"Listen to her! Lookin' like a rose an' talkin' about cost. Now I'm an old bachelor, unfortunately, but if I had a little wife like Peggy here, I'd never begrudge her a new bonnet. Would you, Jim?"

"Never!" he said stoutly. And then added, "I would like to go over our accounts next time I'm in town, General. Father was perhaps a little lax about keeping his books, so I'd like to check with yours."

"Very right and proper. I'll be at your service." All at once his countenance changed, as a swarthy man with a faint swagger entered the store. He had a black mustache that concealed his mouth completely, and eyes below his slouch hat that did not look too candidly upon the world and the people in it.

"Ah, General Welles! Don't let me detain you from your other customers." He looked keenly at Peggy, and Jim glared back at him.

"Not at all! Not at all! Glad to introduce you, Mr. Watson, to Mr. James Ryall, the new Master of The Richlands, as we call him. Also the young Mistress, his wife, and the boy here who lives with them."

The man called Watson removed his hat and metaphorically licked his lips. "Ah, The Richlands," he repeated. "Now there's a farm in a thousand. Never saw anything better, even a big plantation. I'm from Virginia, sir, but everything's done for down there. A man can hold plenty of land but he can't get the —" He checked himself and looked at his listeners. " — the help to work it. So I sold out an' come up here to look around. Well, glad to have met you, Mr. Ryall, an' you, ma'am. I'll wait at the back, General."

The general's brows were drawn as he looked at Jim. "Can't get a majority vote in my own mind about that fellah. Back county's not heard from yet," he chuckled.

He held Peggy's hand tenderly and hoped to see them all soon again, then waved them off from the front steps. With their packages in the back of the buggy and Pete between them on the front seat, and with the precious bandbox at Peggy's feet, they started up Main Street, settling themselves to talk things over.

"We really met a good many of the important people. Not bad for one day, is it? Tell me how you liked them," Jim urged.

"The doctor best of all," Peggy said. "He's so kind. I'm not a bit afraid now. Dr. Knox *wants* to be kind, I think, but he can look pretty stern. Billy Wester at the ice cream parlor and General Welles are both jolly. They make me feel I've known them always and oh, dear little Miss Lucy who makes the bonnets! Wait till you see mine, Jim. I really think —"

Jim pulled on the reins as a slight man with white hair and burnsides came hurrying down the walk from the house above the manse, waving to them.

"Why, that's the Squire! What do you suppose he wants?" Jim said.

The man approached the buggy.

"Hello, Jim!" he began. "I heard you were in town and I was watching for you. Is this the little bride?"

"Squire Higgins, how are you? Yes, this is my wife. I've had a good many errands today or we would have stopped to see you."

The squire waved a deprecating hand. "No need! I can always keep track of you. Everybody knows just where you've been today. I just want to give you a little advice. Look through your father's papers and see if you can find any paper or deed about the ownership of The Richlands. There's a man who says he's a Southerner snoopin' round here —"

"We just met him now in the General Store."

"The devil you did! Well, he looks shifty-eyed to me. He's just bought the Harbison place!"

"No! Why that's only two farms away from our own! Why did they sell?"

"Oh, I think he drove them into a corner! I wish they'd come to me first. They got a lawyer in the county seat who I think is in cahoots with Watson. He made out there was something wrong with their deed, so I just thought I'd tell you to look over your papers. Don't be scared. I've got a cousin in Virginia and I've written him to see if he can get a line on this Watson. I think he's a crook. Well, nice to meet you, Ma'am. Jim sure done well for himself. 'Bout that deed, Jim; don't be surprised if it reads 'a parcel of land from the black oak tree on the northeast corner to the big boulder,' etcetera. Well, the Ryalls have been there long before and since the oak tree. Good luck to the two of you."

The Squire hustled back up his walk, his white hair still blowing.

"That doesn't mean trouble, does it?" Peggy asked anxiously.

"Oh, no." Jim said. "But I'm glad he gave me a hint about this Watson. I'll look up our own deed tonight, if there is one, and then I'll dismiss him in short order if he comes nosing around The Richlands. You must get to bed early tonight, darling, for you've had a full day and more now to come. Cider-making and corn-husking and butchering, no less. Big days at our house. I hope we can get Aunt Polly over for them. She likes the excitement."

It was a short but happy evening. Pete showed his new clothes, while Duncan kept saying in a throaty voice, "Aye, laddie, but you're braw!" Then the boy was allowed to take some candy and go home to treat his family and exhibit his new elegance. Peggy went early to bed and the others discussed the day's experiences, expressing the deepest interest over the sale of the Harbison farm.

"Why do you think they sold?" Tom asked. "They're not so young but the boys are plenty able to take over. Maybe they just got the itch to move to New Salem?"

"Na, na," said Duncan decidedly. "If you ask me, I'd say that foxy Watson got round them some way. I seen him once on the street an' I didna' like the cut of his jib. Did you hear where he comes from?"

"From Virginia, he says."

A change came over Duncan. All at once his face grew less ruddy and he picked up his candle and started for the stairs. "I'll bid you good night. It's been a long day."

When the stair door had closed, Tom looked at his brother. "Why that's a pretty howdy-do. What struck him all of a sudden?"

"Dear knows!"

"Well, he's right. It has been a long day. I think I'll follow his example and go on up, too. Coming?"

"Not just yet. I want to look over some accounts and things in Father's desk. I didn't mention it, but the Squire came flying out to speak to us as we passed and he said every farmer ought to keep his records in good order."

Tom stood holding his candle, ignoring the records. "Did Peggy see the doctor?"

"Yes, and he says she's fine, only she's small-boned and girls like that have a little harder time."

"And what else?"

It was a strange comfort to be able to talk about anything to Tom. "It's quite a way off, as you know, but he said at her first labor pain we were to send for him and he'd come at once and make it easier. He's going to see her again, too."

"We'll certainly remember that, and you know I can get to town faster than anyone else. I'll bring the doctor back on the horse behind me if it's necessary. Get to your records, then. I'm off to bed."

Jim went into the sitting room, set two extra candles on the small table beside the desk and sat down. It was a handsome piece of furniture, as his father had often pointed out, made two generations before by a master carpenter in New Salem. The beautiful, grained walnut was from a big tree on the farm, cut by a former Ryall and planed for the carpenter's use. Now it stood close to the ceiling, the upper half a bookcase behind doors, three small, square drawers across the space just below and three long, deep drawers down to the floor in which Jim remembered his mother had kept her best tablecloths and linen sheets.

He stared at it now, his eyes moist. It seemed a part of his father's very being, for he had loved this desk. Jim opened the doors to disclose the neat shelves of books, many of which he had read himself, but more had been his father's constant companions. "A bookish farmer," the Squire had once called him. But now Jim closed the doors quickly, for his work was with the three small, square drawers beneath. A polished knob at each side could pull out a flat surface for writing. Clever workmanship! Of this Jim now availed himself and carefully spread upon it the contents of the first drawer.

Letters chiefly, he saw at once, kept for reasons unknown, a few dating back to the day when the first Ryalls took up the great tract which was to be later called "The Richlands," a few more recent. But in them all only family items were discussed; no mention of purchase or sale of land. Instead, he read here and there:

Weather cold and windy and difficult to keep even kitchen warm. We buried little Carrie last week. Strange are the ways of Providence. Yesterday shot two wildcats. Last week after hard labor, Martha delivered of a son.

So it went: birth, death, sickness, occasional merry-making and the exigencies of farm living. Jim read each letter with care and then put them back in the drawer. All but one. This one was sealed and unaddressed, with a small bulge inside. It had evidently been put with care under the others to insure its not being found. Jim fingered it, feeling he was doing wrong to expose some secret to the light, but he finally broke the seal. Into his hand fell a small, pressed, pink rose with a faint hint of past fragrance exhaling from it. There was a paper in his father's fine writing. Jim recognized the words from one of Shakespeare's sonnets, for they had studied it at the Academy.

Shall I compare thee to a summer's day?

His father had apparently underlined certain lines he particularly liked.

Rough winds do shake the darling buds of May . . .
But thy eternal summer shall not fade . . .

Jim stood, astonished, touching the paper and the dried petals of the rose. His mother had not been a romantic person. He could remember well her somewhat caustic remarks about his father's sitting up late to read "poetry and things," as she put it. The contents of the envelope had been inspired by someone else. His father, then, had doubtless given up not only his chosen career but his true love also in order to be faithful to The Richlands.

Jim put the envelope tenderly back underneath the other letters and shut the drawer. "I've got to make the most of my inheritance," he thought. "A lot of sacrifice has gone into it. But I must get on now with my search."

When he emptied the middle drawer onto the writing space, his spirits rose. The papers, some yellowed and kept for sentiment, probably, and some newer, were certainly records of importance. Two long foolscap sheets with red wax seals, he opened tremblingly. They both proved to be wills: "In the name of God, Amen." But neither had to do with the land itself. It was evidently assumed that the son would succeed the father in that regard. What the wills dealt with was the disposition of household goods. The wife was to keep the four-poster bed and the room she had always slept in and the son was to see to it that she always had wood chopped for her fire. In the other will, the wife was to have the china dishes and the daughter-in-law, the second best set. So it went.

Jim folded the old wills, which someone had deemed worthy of keeping, and turned hopefully to the other papers beside them. These he saw at once were about sales and purchases, and his heart beat faster. But, again, they did not refer to the land. In careful detail there were set down transactions in connection with animals or furniture, important, evidently, to the recorders. Twenty lambs bought, one young bull sold, three Jersey milk cows purchased. From the many papers, one stood out to Jim's eyes. It stated: "One horsehair rocker for Mother's birth-

day." He turned his head. There it stood, still sound
and comfortable, designed with homely grace to fit every
curve of the body and relax a weary head. The chair that
was his great-grandmother's! Evidently the Ryall boys,
as they came along, had not been allowed to harm it by
rough usage, for though the horsehair was now browned,
it was intact with its old dignity.

The fourth drawer was filled with his own father's neat
account books, down to the present year. Jim realized,
though, as he scanned them that he must soon have a settlement with General Welles who served, in a sense, as the
banker for the farming community; and then see that his
own records were kept straight.

His heart sank with something like fright as he closed
the desk, knowing now that *there was no deed*. But when
he picked up his candles and went to the kitchen, standing with, his back to the fire to warm himself, he began to
take heart. Even though no legal paper affirmed it, the
Ryalls had held this land for generations. It wasn't as
though it were now lying unclaimed and fallow. It was
lived on, worked and productive. How could even an un-
scrupulous man do harm to its ownership? He decided
to speak to the Squire again and, if need be, to a lawyer,
but meanwhile he would put aside the uneasiness and
enjoy the richness of the days as they came. He thought
of Peggy, lying sweetly asleep, all warm and lovely, in
their bed upstairs and all his blood rushed hotly through
him. He loved her so terribly, so completely, that he could
not now imagine life without her.

Then, because of this, and above it came the thought of
the sealed envelope in the drawer, the secret of which he

himself had broken. His own sire, then, had also known
the tumultuous pangs of love, but not, it would seem, their
crowning fulfillment. Jim turned and looked at the chair
at the head of the table as a rush of remembrance of things
past swept over him. There was much of his father's gentleness and kindness to recall, and pride, not in himself,
but his sons. Some of the memories brought tears to
Jim's eyes, but his last thought was of the sonnet and the
little crushed rose. He knew that in all his life he had
never loved his father as much as in that moment.

Chapter IV

The air those last October days was still mellow with a faint, golden haze pervading it, and the color, which before had run suggestively through bush and tree, now had become masses of reds and yellows, flaunting its glory to all eyes before the fall rains drowned it. So now the world looked bright and gay and at The Richlands hearts were happy, too, for this was apple time and Aunt Polly was coming over to help.

She arrived, driven by Dave, one afternoon in her black bombazine, plaid shawl and summer bonnet, displaying, after she had kissed the young people tenderly and shaken hands with Duncan, a spandy new apron.

"You see," she said proudly, "I'm all spittin' ready for work. And while they may not have told you, Peggy, I'm supposed to make the best apple butter in the county. Not that I should say it. 'Let another praise thee and not thine own lips,' Mr. Solomon wrote and he was a wise man, but the fact is, it's the truth no matter who says it."

There was hearty laughter as Aunt Polly winked at Peggy and promised to tell her the secret, then looked up as Pete came into the kitchen laden with two big baskets of apples.

"And this, I suppose, is your new boy," she said calmly.

"But how did you know about him?" Jim asked in surprise.

Aunt Polly pushed her glasses farther up on her nose and motioned to Pete. "Come over here, my boy, and let me look at you."

Pete obeyed and she looked him squarely in the eyes as he returned her glance. She patted his shoulder. "Good eyes," she pronounced. "Looks straight at you. Do you think you could call me Aunt Polly?"

"I'd like to. I haven't got no aunts."

"Not *any* aunts."

"Yes'm, that's what I said."

"We'll get to the grammar by slow degrees," Jim laughed, "but you haven't told us yet is how you got the news."

"Ask him," Aunt Polly said, looking at Dave.

"It was Tom's idea." Dave returned.

As the two brother's eyes met, Jim was suddenly aware of how much each had missed the other. "As Duncan would say," he thought to himself, "I'm very slow on the uptake."

"Well," Aunt Polly was beginning brightly, "if they won't tell you, I will, for I'm mortal pleased about it. One Sunday afternoon, Tom, here, rode over to check on Dave an' when he left Dave rode back with him as far as Middling Hill and they made it up that they'd meet there every Sunday and exchange all the news of both houses. So it's as good as a telegraph."

"Why, that's capital," Jim cried. "That means we're not isolated any longer!"

"Iso — what?" Dave teased in his old fashion, and the constraint was lifted as they all made plans for the next day's work.

It was decided that Aunt Polly and Peggy would start at once, paring apples for the butter. The great copper kettle, in which they would ultimately be boiled, was brought in to show how beautifully clean and shining it had become after Pete's hard work on it. The long-handled wooden stirrer, too, was displayed, scrubbed and ready for use. Then, as in other times, Tom and Dave went out to check on the cider press and Jim and Duncan stayed to watch the apple-paring in which Pete had already joined. The great baskets were set within easy reach and also the pans and crocks needed for the work. Aunt Polly was easily the champion. With an apple poised in her left hand and a sharp knife in her right, she started to pare until, in an incredibly short time, an unbroken, long, spiral curl cropped into the pan. She quartered and cored the apple quickly and went on to another, saying as she did so, "Now I want all the news of your trip to New Salem. Are these Northern Spies, Jim?"

"They are."

"Good. They make the best apple butter. Ramboes are a little too soft. Well, tell me what you did!"

With many promptings and questions, the day was rehearsed as Aunt Polly listened greedily. All at once Peggy wiped her hands.

"Oh, I can't wait to show you my new bonnet. It won't take but a minute to get it!"

When she came back she was wearing it, a straw with white ruching around the face and tiny rose buds peering from it here and there as though to enhance the charm of the bright cheeks beneath it. There was about it, along with the elegance, a sort of seductive lilt which became more apparent as Peggy turned this way and that to show it off. Aunt Polly's apple and knife dropped into the pan as she looked.

"Bless me, child," she said, "that's the prettiest bonnet I've ever seen in my life. If you wear that to church, not a man there will hear a word of the sermon."

There was laughter until the door suddenly opened and Tom and his brother came in. Dave looked across at Peggy as she faced him and his eyes devoured her beauty with such a burning light that, for a second, no one moved or spoke. Then Dave himself broke the silence. "I'll go out and bed down the stock for the night, Jim," he said huskily, and went out. Tom followed and behind them in the kitchen there were only aborted sounds: Duncan tried to hum a little tune, Peggy's feet clattered over the backstairs, and Jim kept remarking to Pete, somewhat at random, on the different kinds of apples. Only Aunt Polly was strangely silent and her hands idle. She finally began muttering softly to herself and once Jim caught some of the words. "So that's the way it is with him, and I never fully understood it. Poor Dave. Poor Dave."

Very soon the room settled into its former activity, except that each one knew that something like a flash of lightning had crossed it swiftly and had gone. Duncan sang "Hunting Tower" and "The Crookit Bawbee" because they were Aunt Polly's favorites, and the big crock of pared apples was filled and another set out.

"Now, child, I'll tell you my recipe for apple butter. Most people boil the cider down till it could almost stand alone and then cook the apples in that till you have a thick, sticky mess you can hardly get a spoon into. Now my way is to boil the cider a little first, then put in the apples and then — here's the trick — add *sugar*, with some cinnamon and nutmeg toward the end. Keep stirring and simmering and adding cider and sugar time about till you have a nice thickness like jam, and then dip it into crocks. It will stiffen up a little, but still be easily spread and *sweet*, the way it ought to be." Aunt Polly looked proudly at Peggy.

"Oh, I'll do it your way, you may be sure, and thank you for telling me. I'll be helping you tomorrow and see exactly how it's done."

"Pete here has all the jugs washed an' ready for the cider," Duncan said.

"And I might as well confess," Aunt Polly put in with a twitch to her lips, "that I always let my jugs stand a while till they get a bit of a tang!"

Jim saw to it that the old lady got early to her room where, on a feather tick, she insisted she was as cozy as by the fire. He and Peggy went early also, and although she was asleep almost at once, he lay listening for Tom and Dave to come in. He heard them at last on the stairs, then entering the room across the hall which had always been theirs. The door was shut and for a time there was quiet, then murmurs and once a sound like a sob. Jim sat up, startled. It could have been the dog, he decided, who had followed them up. He had always been Dave's special pet. But he was shaken by it nonetheless.

The weather still held the next morning and the household was early astir. Duncan was busy frying sausage and piling stacks of buckwheat cakes on a hot platter, when

Bumper, in patched pants and a reasonably clean shirt, entered the kitchen.

"How are you, Scotty?" he began airily.

"Don't call me Scotty!" Duncan flared. "I'm Mister to you. I thought you'd be makin' it round this mornin'."

"An' if you knowed how my back's hurtin' me, you wouldn't be so grulchy. Here I come out of kindness —"

"Yes, yes," Jim intervened. "We understand, Bumper. Sit down over here and have a good breakfast and then we'll all get to work."

"An' I sez to the Missus, I sez, here they are needin' me with cider-makin' an' then corn-shuckin' an' then butcherin' the hogs comin' on, an' who am I to leave them in the lurch, as it were. Master Jim's a good —"

"Here's your breakfast, Bumper," Duncan said, "Eat it an' mebbe it will stop your clackin'."

The table was once more full and Jim would have surveyed it with pleasure if there had been no undercurrents of pain in the night. In the bright morning, however, with hot food bracing the members of the household, there was again conversation and light teasing. Peggy sat at the end of the table close to Jim, and Dave flanked Aunt Polly at the opposite end, so there were not even glances exchanged between them as Tom and young Pete kept the laughter going.

"You can go ahead when you're through, Bumper, and get the cider presses set up," Jim told him, "and we'll be ready for work in a few minutes."

Aunt Polly and Peggy would pare another basket of apples and by then there would be plenty of cider in the big buckets so that some could be boiled for the butter. Pete's job was to build a small log fire upon which the iron ring would rest to hold the big copper kettle for this boiling. A tricky business, this, but under Jim's supervision it was done. Meanwhile, Bumper, with the annoying competence which he was mostly too lazy to use, had set up the two cider mills, run a few apples through each to clean them out after their long lack of use and then began emptying the baskets into great piles near by. Jim, coming over to him, was still chuckling as he remembered overhearing Aunt Polly's advice to Peggy when he was going out.

"Now, just attend to our own work and don't look too hard at the cider-making. You know men. They're not too fussy. They'll put a lot of apples through those mills that aren't just *sound* inside, if you know what I mean. A woman would pick them out. But when they're all made up into cider, it's as sweet as sugar, no matter what's in the apples. So just let the men alone, enjoy the cider when it's done and ask no questions."

In another hour, everyone was busy. Dave and Tom worked the two presses as Bumper lifted the apples and fed them in, Duncan caught the cider in the buckets, Pete fetched and carried as he was told while Bumper watched him with apparent pride, and Jim stayed close to the big kettle over the fire after he had brought out the pared apples from the kitchen. There was cider boiling now and soon Aunt Polly pronounced it time to put in the apples. Then, with the end of the long stirrer in her hand, she presided like a high priestess over the simmering mass in the kettle.

"Keep your distance from the fire," Jim warned. "It gets hot. I'll bring a couple of chairs for you to sit on. You don't have to be looking into it all the time."

"This stirrer is so wonderful," Peggy said. "We never had one like this. It's so long you can stay back from the heat and the cross piece at the end goes right to the bottom of the kettle. Oh, Jim, I'm going to enjoy this. Aunt Polly, isn't this a lovely day?"

It was. The faint chill of morning moved into a gentle warmth by noon and the blue of the sky intensified. There was plenty of loud chaffing and laughter among the cider-makers with Aunt Polly and Peggy calling back to them with their own brand of humor. No one stopped long for lunch, for Duncan brought out thick sandwiches and tin cups so they could dispose themselves on the ground or, in the women's case, on the chairs, and eat the food with the fresh cider to wash it down and lose little time at work. Jim came over to the kettle and took the stirrer. "This is a long, slow business," he said, "and you musn't get too tired, either of you. Pete will take over now for a while and you can rest your arms."

By three o'clock, the mound of apples on the ground had been transformed to a pale, sweet liquid filling endless great jugs which sat now on the porch. The apple butter had been slowly thickening with sugar, cider and spices added to it alternately, and now, after much tasting from the spoons and saucers Pete supplied, was almost done.

"I'd say fifteen more minutes," Aunt Polly pronounced judicially, "and it will be perfect. It's just a thought thin now around the edges. Our fire's getting low, Pete. Could you get us a good quick one for this last bubble?"

Pete flew to put on more light sticks, then ran to help his father and Dave clean the presses, while Tom was raking debris beyond and Jim and Duncan were busy in the kitchen fixing a basket of food for Bumper to take home along with his cider. Everyone was busy and suddenly quiet when the cry rang out.

"I'm going to have one more taste while you stir," Peggy said to Aunt Polly.

With her spoon and saucer she ran to the kettle and leaned a bit toward it just as the dry wood Pete had deftly placed beneath it burst into sudden flame. The sparks flew and the red tongues leaped out until, in the fraction of a second, they had caught Peggy's long skirt and were licking their way swiftly over her body.

"Jim!" she cried in terror. "Jim! I'm on fire!"

They all came, terrified, but Dave was the nearest. With two great springs which his body could not have made merely by an act of will, he had reached her, was striking out the fire with his bare hands, was tearing off the blazing clothing and fending the flames away from her face.

"Bring water!" he called. "Bring cider!"

They brought both until Peggy stood drenched, the fire out, and her small form clad only in her thin undershift. She leaned, moaning and shuddering, in Jim's arms, her hands, burned from her own efforts to fight the danger, outstretched as though the air might ease them. All at once she looked up.

"Dave!" she cried to him as he stood there white with pain, "oh, Dave, your poor hands! You saved me and I can't ever thank you enough. Oh, your poor hands."

And Dave managed to smile at her through the anguish. "It was nothing," he said.

Then quickly, recovering from the first shock, Aunt Polly took charge. "Help them both into the kitchen, boys. Jim, do you have any sweet oil?"

"Yes, we always have it."

"Get it out in a hurry, Duncan, and some cotton wool. We'll do our best to take care of this. You, Pete, just let the kettle simmer away and rake the fire out. I don't feel like seeing apple butter for a while. Let's get on out of the air."

Tom helped his brother, an arm about the sagging shoulders. Jim carried his wife, and Bumper, with unbelievable gentleness and care, took Aunt Polly. In the kitchen, Duncan already had the work table cleared and the big bottle of sweet oil in place with cotton and old linens beside it. Jim ran to get a quilt to wrap around Peggy and, seeing Dave shiver, brought an extra one for him, being careful it didn't touch his arms. Aunt Polly, her lips set tight, her eyes at times beclouded so that she had to wipe her glasses hastily, set to work.

"Peggy first," Dave said, still thickly.

"Oh, no! Dave's so much worse. I can stand it."

But Aunt Polly bent quickly over Peggy, pouring on the sweet oil and gently putting thin strips of linen over it. Jim hovered over her, almost beside himself. When the old lady got to Dave, she caught the back of a chair to steady herself. Dave was white and he had difficulty holding up his head.

"Duncan," Aunt Polly said sharply, "he's nigh to a faint. Get him something to brace him. An' after that I'll have a cup of tea and Peggy will, too."

It was only a minute until Dave was drinking thirstily, sputtering a little as he did so. But whatever had been put in the tin cup, it seemed to quiet him and soothe him a little. Then there was tea for the others with a "wee bit

of something in it besides sugar" for Aunt Polly. Jim
held Peggy's cup tenderly to her lips and brought pillows
for the hands of the patients to rest on; then Aunt Polly,
her face set as they had never seen it before, began to put
the sweet oil on Dave's hands and arms. It was then that
they missed Tom. No one had noticed him leaving or
heard the quick hoof beats of a horse, but they all knew
now that he had gone for the doctor and a wave of relief
seemed to sweep the room. But someone else had quietly
slipped away also. This was Bumper, but little notice was
taken of his absence.

When he did come back, though, he was not alone. Mrs.
Bumper was with him and they walked into the kitchen
with a small air of assurance.

"This is Mrs. Bumper, all. She's great at burns.
Learned it when she was a girl. Even if Tom's gone for
the doctor, he may be far enough on his calls afore Tom
catches up with him, an' meanwhile there's mortal suf-
ferin' here. So let her go ahead."

"Jim!" Aunt Polly cried. "You're not going to have
this woman —"

"I'm going to have anything done that will help these
burns. Go ahead, Mrs. Bumper."

"Give me the shears, a tin cup and two heavy towels to
lay his arm on, Duncan," she said with a faint smile. Then
she cut the tops of Dave's shirt sleeves, which no one else
had thought to do, slitting them down until they would
come off without touching the burned flesh. Very gently,
she removed the strips of linen Aunt Polly had laid there,
then, after doing the same to Peggy, she came back to Dave.
"He's the worst," she said to Jim, "but I'll be to her soon.

I'll work fast." She began dipping cupful after cupful of the brownish liquid she had brought in a jug and poured it slowly over Dave's arms and hands as they rested on the towels Duncan had found. At first there was no sound in the kitchen and Jim, his heart beating wildly, stood smoothing Peggy's hair and wondering if he had done a foolish or even a dangerous thing in allowing this woman to do whatever it was she was doing before the doctor got there. Then as he watched her, steady, sure of herself, concerned for her patients, he began to feel a certain faith. The secret of the brown liquid might have been learned beside a gypsy campfire and guarded from all but those who had Romany blood in their veins.

All at once there was a long, almost hissing sound from Dave and then faintly the words, "Oh, that feels good."

"It'll feel better yet when the fire's all out of it, but this will hold you while I fix up the little Missus here."

In a second she had placed Peggy's hands on the extra towels Duncan had brought and was pouring cupfuls of liquid over her hands and wrists. In only a few minutes Peggy raised her eyes to Jim who had been wiping away her tears of pain at intervals. "It's stopped hurting," she breathed.

"That's the girl!" said Mrs. Bumper. "Now I'll see how this fellah over here is gettin' on an' I'll be back to you."

Dave was completely relaxed, as one is after the cessation of extreme pain. Duncan had brought a cushion and placed it under his head so he leaned back in a half-daze. As soon as he felt the cooling liquid again upon him he roused at once.

"Mrs. Bumper, I can't thank you —"

"I don't want no thanks. Just rest yourself an' be comfortable. Before long you can go to bed an' sleep it all off."

"Won't I be awfully blistered?"

"Not after the last dose of this," she replied.

"Well, now that things are takin' a good turn," said Duncan, "I'll just stir me stumps and see if I can rustle us a bit of supper. Mebbe just soup for Dave an' little Mistress, but the rest of us will be ready for more seerious fare. You'll stay for a bite to eat, Mrs. Bumper?"

"I don't mind if I do," she answered in what Peggy had, at their last meeting, thought of as her "company voice."

"An' Doc may need some vittles by the time he gets here," Duncan added.

"Didn't I tell you," put in Bumper, "that he might be to hell an' gone off in the other direction afore Tom ever caught up with him? Well, I must say a little food for all will be welcome. I think I sprained my back again over that cider press."

The patients, now drowsy with relief, were lying down, Dave on the lounge and Peggy on Aunt Polly's bed in the room off the kitchen. Jim hovered over her, still anxious, but found himself outrageously hungry as the good supper smells reached his nostrils. Mrs. Bumper sat like a large queen bee devouring all that was set before her, the expression on her face like that of Pete's at his first meal there. "And yet," Jim thought, "they can't be actually hungry. They have a cow and chickens and plenty of vegetables. The trouble probably is sheer laziness. She sets down anything on the table that doesn't take much cooking and just lets the children do their best with it." While he mused on the strange woman, trying to mingle his distaste with thankfulness for what she had done, Bumper kept up a steady lament about his back, Duncan kept his eyes on the stove as far as was possible, Aunt Polly sat silent over her cup of tea and Pete's bright eyes took in all the scene.

It was an hour later when they all heard the quick hoof beats, and in a minute Doctor Flemming came hurriedly into the kitchen. When he saw Mrs. Bumper he gave a laugh that was a mixture of mirth and irritation. "So you beat me to it again," he said.

"And a good thing I did. This was a bad business. No one knew when you'd get here an' Bumper, my husband, knew what I could do so he brought me over. That's the amount of it."

"And your cure worked again?"

"Ask Mr. Dave here. He had the worst lookin' arms I ever seen."

Dave was up now and listening to the dialogue. "It was like a miracle, Doctor, they way that stuff worked. Aunt Polly had put sweet oil on but this stuff washed it off and then began to take the fire out. And before you'd believe it I got relief. I can't ever thank you, Mrs. Bumper."

"What about your wife?" the doctor said, turning abruptly to Jim.

"I'll get her and you can examine her hands, too." For the doctor was carefully inspecting Dave's arms and hands, now sometimes emitting a low whistle.

When Peggy came out she held out her hands. "What Mrs. Bumper did with that liquid was beyond belief, Doctor. The pain just left like magic." She gave a little giggle. "I think that must have been it."

"Not magic, my child," the doctor said gravely, "but a

secret from the medical profession." He examined her carefully. As with Dave, there was now just the smooth, reddened skin. Then he turned to Mrs. Bumper.

"It's a wonderful job. I would be the first to tell you that. I can see what it has been. But now, I ask you again to tell me what is in this brew — this medicine — so that I, too, can use it to help suffering. Better still, won't you make a large jug of it for me to keep in my office and I'll pay you well for it. You can set your price, indeed. Will you not do this?"

"I will not," the woman said calmly.

"But why not?" he urged.

"Because the secret was showed me when I was a young girl and the charm was taught to me if I'd never tell a livin' soul. If I ever did, the virtue would go out of it."

"Now, that's ridiculous!" the doctor said angrily. "The liquid is made, I'm sure, from certain roots, like sweet myrrh and sassafras and all the rest, but we don't know what or how much. If you told that or made it up for me, how could it hurt the results?"

"I'm takin' no chances," she answered. 'You'll just have to take no for an answer. An' then," she added, "you once saw yourself how it works. When the Harbison barn burnt, their boy was in a bad way an' they sent for you, but the girl come over to me first an' you saw when you got there how my brew, as you call it, worked, didn't you?"

The doctor nodded. "Yes, I did, but I was puzzled."

"All right, then. Just leave it at that an' thank you kindly for the supper, Mr. Jim. I'd better be goin' before the childer pulls the roof down over their heads."

Jim handed Bumper some money and suggested he use the buckboard to take his wife home along with his allotment of cider jars. Pete could ride in the back with a basket of eatables for the "childer" and come back in the morning. Then Aunt Polly did a strange thing. She rose and with great dignity approached Mrs. Bumper and held out her hand. "I want to express my thanks to you for what you did this day for my grandchildren. You're a fine woman."

Mrs. Bumper, overcome by this tribute from one she had always held in awe, said good-by hastily all around, meeting Duncan's eyes for a fleeting second and then, after heartfelt renewed thanks from all the family, left the kitchen, taking the precious jug with some of the brew still in it.

When the Bumpers were gone the doctor sat down at the table, admitting he had had nothing to eat since breakfast, and the talk went from one to the other, but always about the wonderful cure. "Did her lips move when she was pouring on the stuff?" the doctor asked.

"Yes, they did. I noticed," said Jim.

"There! You see, some sort of incantation goes with it. She learned it as a girl and while, of course, it has no possible connection with the effect of the liquid, you'd never make her believe that. It has all come down from the old gypsy tribe and so, while she's not really a Romany now, she clings to it."

The talk went on, gossip about New Salem people in which they were all interested. Dr. Knox was a little stern with the young people and pretty set in his opinions, the Session thought. The general had had to stay in bed a day with what he called just a summer cold but he wouldn't take anything for it so he had to behave himself at the last. Billy Wester was off to Pittsburgh to visit his cousins and learn more about making this ice cream. It was from them he got the first idea and the recipe. He was bent on fixing up his parlor and people did seem to be taking to it.

Then the doctor would come back to Mrs. Bumper. "That night the Harbison barn burned they sent for me as you heard, but she got there first by a few minutes and I let her go ahead. I stayed until I saw how her brew worked and then I stayed on to help quiet down the women if I could. You see, there was one horse they couldn't get out. All the men said the roof was just ready to fall and it would be death to go in again and you could hear the poor thing calling and whinnying and even the men had tears on their faces."

He paused a minute as though hearing it again and then went on. "Well, all of a sudden this Bumper woman ran toward the barn and right through the flames and came out with the horse. Then the roof fell. The men yelled and shouted and she stood there out in front, her arm around the horse's neck, smiling and talking to it — some sort of gibberish — but it seemed to understand and it quieted down. But the thing you won't believe was that as she stood there — it was moonlight — her face lifted up sort of triumphant over what she'd done, she looked actually beautiful!"

"Wasn't she burned?" Dave asked quickly.

"Oh, terribly. And here is where I feel pretty small. There was some liquid left in the jug after the boy had been treated and she asked *me* to pour it over her. I did and saw the results. Well, I don't know when I've ever talked so much but that woman certainly interests me.

Not one man would go back for that horse the way the roof was burning and yet *she* did. There was never much said about it, either. I think the men were ashamed, though I didn't blame them. Quite a story. I must be getting along and I certainly enjoyed my supper."

After his good-bys, Jim followed him out to his horse.

"Do you think this will hurt my wife's pregnancy in any way?" he asked anxiously.

"No," the doctor said slowly, "I don't. She's well along toward her fifth month and that's a fairly safe point. I checked her heart and blood pressure before I left as you may have noticed. Just let her take things easy for a week or two and I think she'll be all right."

That night the house grew quiet very early. Jim got Peggy to bed and saw that Dave was still comfortable. When he came down, Tom was out at the barn and Duncan was busying himself on the porch. Aunt Polly looked tired and old. Jim felt a pang of sympathy for her. She had been accustomed to being the manager in any time of crisis. This time her leadership had been swiftly taken out of her hands. And well it had been so, but the old lady would feel it a little. It had been good of her to thank Mrs. Bumper, but now she suddenly looked as if her strong position as the matriarch of the family had been shaken.

"Well," Jim began, as brightly as he could, "it's been quite a day, hasn't it? Your sweet oil certainly helped until the other stuff got working."

"Is she really a gypsy, think you?"

"I don't know," Jim said. "I'm inclined to think so. They maybe got tired of the wandering life. When Bumper asked for farm work my father took him on, as you know. Now I'm stuck with all of them. But maybe, like today, there's a blessing in it."

"That Bumper, he's pretty slack in the twist, isn't he?"

Jim laughed. "He's all of that. He's always sick when the heavy work's to be done, but when he does exert himself he's a very good helper. So I just go along. But, Aunt Polly, you must get to bed. I'll help you — Oh, here's Duncan! He'll want to do the honors."

"I want to tell ye your's is the best apple butter I ever tasted. An' if you're botherin' aboot it, Pete an' me dipped it all out into the crocks while you were finishin' your supper an' they're on the porch now, covered with plates. In the mornin' we'll be sealin' them. But come now, Mistress Polly, I'll gie ye a hand to your bed."

"Ah' I'll be takin' it, Duncan. I'm a bit dodderin' the night."

When all was quiet, Jim lay reviewing the events of the day. Peggy was comfortable, he could see, with even the redness of her hands growing less. He was exhausted himself from the excitement, the anxiety and the vicarious pain before relief had come, but he could not sleep. The big clock downstairs had struck twice before he turned drowsily on his pillow. But his last thoughts had been of the doctor's story and of what he had seen for himself of the woman, Mrs. Bumper, and how strangely that day she had come into their lives.

Chapter V

Outwardly, the next days at the farm moved on in their normal routine, though now and then, like the ripples a stone striking still water makes, a sudden word brought back the tension of the cider-making day. Dave had decided unopposed, one morning, that he would drive back to give Uncle Charley a hand with his own small crop of apples and leave Aunt Polly to round out her visit and be driven home later when Uncle Charley could come for her.

"A good idea," Aunt Polly siad decidedly. "I'll stay till after butchering. You know, Jim, you always count on me to sample the sausage for seasoning. A little too much sage and you've ruined the lot of it."

"Now I do feel safer about it," Jim said, laughing, "and it will be good to have you here longer. It will be good for Peggy, too, for the doctor says she must rest up a good deal for another week or so. I think she's still asleep now."

"Good. I've got a new quilt all ready for the frame and that will be nice sittin' work for her. What about your corn-huskin'? Can you spare Dave for that?"

Jim glanced about to be sure Pete was not in the kitchen. "Yes, I think we can. It's a queer thing about Bumper, but he's the best husker of all of us. I think we can do the job. I'll tell you what I have in mind, Aunt Polly. I want to build a new corncrib, a bigger one. We've a big crop now but I'm planning on a still bigger one next year. If we get stuck, Dave, we'll send for you."

"Not to build the crib. I think the one we have is big enough and so's the crop. Well, I'll be on my way. Good to see you all." He glanced toward the stairway.

"It certainly is good to see you, and thanks beyond words for what you did for — for — at the fire. Come back when you can," Jim said.

The words were stilted but the best he could manage. Tom went out after Dave and Jim hastily climbed the stairs. He found Peggy still asleep as she was now each morning when he himself quietly left the room. He studied her face. The color was coming back a little to the pale cheeks and she lay relaxed from all the tensions past. Oh, she was lovely! What wonder the beauty smote Dave's heart? How innocently young he himself had been to bring her here to live in the house with his brothers without a thought of dangerous consequences. He kept on staring at her, anxious for her safety and that of the child she carried, thinking of the doctor's last words. He had started off as Jim waited on the edge of the porch, then reined and came back.

"As I said, I think she'll suffer no harm if she rests a great deal for a couple of weeks, and for at least that long she should have no emotional strain whatever, if you get what I mean."

"I do," Jim had said, and thanked him.

Now he went back down the stairs and began to organize the day's work. "It's early yet, so we can get a good start.

Aunt Polly, can you keep an ear open for Peggy and be sure she's all right? She'll maybe just want a cup of tea when she wakes up."

"I'll fix her a nice little breakfast when she's ready. I'm not beyond *that* yet, I hope."

"An' I'll gi' you a hand in the corn now, boys, but I'll be in at noon to fix us a few vittles," Duncan stated. "I believe, Master Jim, I'll just check the corncrib for mice, drat them. You'd think five cats at the barn could take care of them but still they get in. They tell me if we had enough camphor we could scare them out but it would take too much 'siller' to do it."

"Oh, the mice and rats have always been at the corn and always will be," Aunt Polly told them. "You're not as bad off here as if your farm were small and close to another; then they *do* run you a race. Well, now, be off and do a good job. Bring me up a few ears, Jim, and I'll shell them and parch them in the skillet."

"Your father isn't coming?" Jim asked Pete, who turned red at the question.

"He says his back was hurtin' him something turrible but he might make it here by afternoon."

"In time for some vittles, I'll warrant," Duncan muttered.

The work with the corn was, like all at The Richlands, done with habitual system. Now a workhorse and wagon stood at the end of the field near the barn. Pete was left in charge of it while the men fanned out along the rows, quickly, even roughly, pulling off the ears and dropping them into the bushel baskets they moved along as they went. When a basket was full, it was emptied into the wagon and the work went on again. By noon the wagon itself was piled to the top, and Tom drove it up the slope to the barn floor on the upper level where the ears were dumped down to await the time for husking.

When the men came in to get something to eat, Peggy was there to greet them, looking refreshed and happy over the propect of work on the new quilt. Since the frames were still up before the west window, the work in the fields would be seen as she and Aunt Polly set their tiny stitches.

Duncan had been right. Before the fried mush and bacon had been finished, Bumper came hobbling in, holding his back as though in extreme pain when he could remember to do it.

"Well, Bumper, have some fried mush and syrup and then we'll all get to the corn field. I want to finish stripping the ears off today if we can."

"That's an awful big field, Master Jim," Bumper lamented.

"I know it, but if we all work hard I think we can clear up the first stage today. Then for the husking! You were always good at that, Bumper."

Forgetting his back entirely, Bumper spoke with pride. "Yes sir, I allays took to huskin' some way. I can beat any of you here at it, that's a fact."

"Well, you'll get your chance tomorrow. Let's be off now and clean the field," Jim said decidedly. "We're only half through."

It was a hard afternoon for them, for the day was unseasonably hot. Aunt Polly and Peggy, sitting quietly beside the quilting frames, could feel the heat of the sun as it must strike the corn pickers. Suddenly Aunt Polly got up, took a large pail and filled it nearly full with spring water. Into this she poured two cups of vinegar and two of sugar and stirred it well.

"A little vinegar sling will cool them off a bit. I'll ring for Duncan."

She shook the big hand bell that always stood on the porch bench and, at once, it was Jim who came running, his face white. Aunt Polly waved and smiled and held up the big tin dipper. Jim reached the porch, breathing heavily. "You did give me a scare. Is everything all right?"

"All but the blazin' sun. I made some vinegar sling for you in the big bucket. Take it along with you and don't jibble it. If you need more, you can send Duncan back for it. Now mind, there's another day to come so don't kill yourselves. Here's the dipper."

"Thanks, Aunt Polly. Peggy all right?" he asked again.

"Oh, go in and give her a kiss and you'll work the better for it. I'll look at the pasture field while you're at it."

Jim laughed and complied, then loped off with his bucket and dipper.

Supper was late with candlelight showing the men's tired faces, the satisfaction on Jim's smoothing out the strain to some extent. Aunt Polly eyed them keenly and spoke her mind as usual.

"I don't think farm work should be rushed," she said. "The sun an' the rain take their own time about things and farmers ought to do the same. I'm afraid you'll go at it hammer and tongs, Jim, just out of pride maybe. Now on a farm you have to work steady, everything done at the right season and all that. But you oughtn't to wear yourself out. You know, even fields have to rest sometimes if they're overworked."

Bumper, having eaten, was preparing to leave. "That's what I say, Mistress Polly. Never overwork nobody. My back, now, an' one leg are aching something turrible. Mind, I ain't as young as you boys."

"Of course," Tom observed wickedly, "if you aren't able to do any husking tomorrow, we could —"

"Not do huskin'? I'm the best of the lot of you at that and you know it. I'll be here in the mornin'." And he went out the door. But in a minute he was back.

"You know this here feller — Watson, his name is — sort of snoops in an' out. He allays seems to keep an eye on Duncan here. I don't like him. When he thinks Duncan's in the taproom at the hotel or mebbe in at Billy Wester's, then he goes there, too. He says he's headin' out for Canada soon as his leg is well. He sprained it."

"He's a stranger, Bumper, and I wouldn't talk too much with him," Jim said sharply. "Well, get along now and have a good rest for tomorrow."

Jim began at once to discuss the matter of seed corn. It had always been carefully selected from the rest so that perhaps a couple of bushels of the most perfect grains could be used for the new planting. There was a certain demand for it from other farmers and New Salem townsmen who had extra ground to be planted. This year Jim intended to have more available for selling. He had a dream of making his seed corn famous. In the farmers' catalogs and advertisements. "Richlands corn! Richlands wheat! Something special! Something fine!" And better than the long-time best.

Everyone was tired, and soon after supper eyes began
to grow heavy. Duncan helped Pete up the stairs for he
was half-asleep. "This bairn mustn't work so much
tomorrow." And Jim agreed remorsefully. He hadn't
watched the boy carefully enough.

At last Jim and Peggy were alone on the back porch in
the soft darkness, enfolded in each other's arms.

"Aunt Polly was right," he said. "I believe I am too
proud. I've always had that feeling about The Richlands
but now, when in a sense I'm Master of it, I'm planning too
much. Maybe I've too much ambition."

Peggy's reply was on a different subject. "Jim, why
does Duncan seem angry and scared when that man or
even Virginia is mentioned?"

"That's what I'd like to know. I've been upset thinking
about it. This is only surmise, but we know nothing
about Duncan's life before he came here one winter wanting work. My father needed help and, being a trusting
man, he took Duncan and asked no questions. From
that day on he's been one of the family. Ten years it's
been. But I've wondered —"

"Yes? Tell me."

"It's only a guess but he could have been brought over
to Virginia with a born Scotch family as their servant.
Then gotten into some trouble and run away, finally getting up here, of all places."

"It just might be," Peggy said slowly. "I feel a bit uneasy. Could I tell Aunt Polly? She's so wise."

"Suppose *I* tell her when I think it's best, and meanwhile let's just forget all about it. Duncan's pretty able
to manage his own concerns. And you, my darling, must

go right up to bed and go to sleep. I'll sit here and watch the stars a few minutes and relax."

"You're not coming up right now?"

"For a while longer, dear, it's better for you if I don't." He laughed a little as he held her again in his arms.

When she was gone, Jim walked to the orchard path and stood looking across to the great field of cornstalks standing like sheeted ghosts in the pale moonlight. There had been a huge crop this year, but there would be still larger ones. The soil of The Richlands had responded well to those who had worked it, but it would do still more. He thought how little did the old fields know what new richness and even fame itself lay within them to come forth at his own bidding. His eyes roved over the fresh ploughing, the young wheat, the fruitful orchard, and with each new glance his weariness seemed to lessen and his vigor returned. He looked up at the stars as though to meet a challenge, speaking to them as though they could hear him.

"I was right," he cried aloud. "This is the way for me. I was right to choose the land."

The next day brought another early morning but Jim said at the breakfast table that Aunt Polly had given good advice and they were going to take two days at least for the husking. "And we'll set two chairs at the side of the barn floor so she and Peggy can sit there and boss the rest of us while we work."

The women each carried a small bucket for choice kernels they would select themselves for parching in the skillet that night. When the real work began of stripping the husks from the ears of corn, it became evident at once that Bumper was the master hand. His long, bony arms shot out, he grabbed a couple of shaggy multiple husks and in a minute had two, clean, golden ears in the bushel basket beside him. Before the other men, with Pete doing well himself, had filled their own baskets, Bumper had three to his credit.

"Will we just empty right into the corncrib, Master Jim?" he asked.

"I think so," Jim said, "until we get halfway through, whenever that time comes, today or tomorrow. Then we'll start shelling to put into the bins. I think we may have quite a good sale this year. We'll check on our seed corn then."

Aunt Polly and Peggy sat comfortably out of the way of the hard workers, enjoying the mild breeze that swept through the big barn doors and husking a few ears occasionally just for the fun of it and also to fill their buckets with especially nice-looking grain which would, that evening, brown itself in butter in the big skillet. Duncan brought out some food at noon: great slices of bread spread richly with butter and Aunt Polly's apple butter on the top. Jim took large bites of his first piece and then waved his free hand.

"Why, this is elegant, Aunt Polly. It's elegant! It's delicious! I hope you brought out plenty, Duncan. Only have a care about the cider. Some of it may have quite a head on it by now."

"It's arranged, Master Jim. The jugs are for the menfolk who I think can handle it wi' no difeeculty. The bottles with the sealing wax are for the ladies and Pete. Here are the cups," he added, jingling a half dozen on a string. "Gi' me a hand, Tom."

In a few minutes they were all supplied. The men ate and drank as they stood about to stretch their legs, but from the smacking of lips as they drained their tin cups and re-filled them, there was no doubt that the "head" on the contents of the jugs was fully appreciated.

"Listen to this," Tom called out once as he raised his mug. "Who would ever have believed that a nice little Maiden-Blush apple would have had this much alcohol in her! It just goes to show —"

"It goes to show," Aunt Polly broke in decidedly, "that you've had quite enough hard cider, Tom, and I might say the rest of you as well don't look too steady on your legs. Mind, this stuff has plenty of authority if you take enough."

Jim laughed. "Now, Aunt Polly, we're not really stag-gering around as you suggest, but it might be well to save some for later in the afternoon. We'll be thirsty enough by then. What do you say, Duncan?"

"Me? I'd say it's about as strong as mother's milk. I could finish the lot of it an' never know I'd had a drop. But I'll be settin' it in the shade an' you can help your-selves. Unless," he added slyly, "you'd all prefer *vinegar sling.*"

The meal ended in a roar of laughter, and then Jim picked up the buckets of shelled corn. "It's about time for ladies' naps," he said, smiling at Peggy, "and I'll carry your loot up to the house for you."

He walked slowly, half-listening to Aunt Polly, but most of the time looking full in Peggy's face with a light in his eyes that made her blush. Once in the kitchen, he saw that Aunt Polly was comfortable, then hurried up to help

Peggy into her wrapper, draw a light comforter over her, take a sweet, passionate kiss and then run whistling down the stairs and on out to the barn floor.

The men were wickedly talkative after Jim came in. "Course, Mistress Polly's an old woman an' she would ought to be put to bed careful-like," Bumper observed.

"Aye, you're right. I've heard of an old lady breakin' a leg just getting into bed for a wee bit lay down," Duncan added.

"Now a young lady," Tom went on, "that's different. You might suppose she wouldn't need much help just to settle for a nap. But you can't be too careful, even if it does seen to take a —"

"Stop it, you rascals!" Jim broke in, grinning. The truth was he liked any tender jibes directed toward Peggy and himself. "If we hustle up, I believe we can half-finish filling the crib by evening and then be all ready to start shelling tomorrow. Hurry up, fellahs! Let's get a move on!"

They did well, and by late sunset the corncrib was full enough and some extra piles of unhusked ears waited for the shelling when it would begin the next day. There were always two calls for meals: one by bell, either from the "farm bell," as it was known, large and elevated on a high, gallows-like structure and pulled by a rope, or from the hand bell on the porch bench if the men were nearer at hand; the other call always came from Shep, the dog, who added his considerable voice to the tone of either bell. The combination carried over the farthest fields, for Shep always knew when he was hungry and delighted to join in proclaiming it by a mixture of deep, throaty barks and curious, high, falsetto whines. When the men came in from work he circled around them, eager for praise as though he alone had got the message to them.

"As a matter of fact," Dave had often said, "I could hear Shep better than the bell when he gets into that high key of his."

There was no question but that there was a special rapport between the dog and Dave. It was Dave who taught him all his tricks: to sit up, to shake hands (always with the *right* paw), to say his prayer standing on his hind legs and leaning his head and front paws on the low back of a kitchen chair. This was the favorite trick, though Dave was always inventing new ones. Jim tried his best to take Dave's place and the dog seemed to feel a new closeness between them, though of course he was the pet of all.

As they gathered at the supper table that night Shep made his rounds, sitting for quite a time beside Peggy who was inordinately fond of him, then quietly going to Jim to lie at his feet.

"I declare," Aunt Polly said, "that dog's all but human. I know he misses Dave. That night when he brought me over I heard him an' Shep go up the stairs together — last ones up. I'd give my word he slept in the room with him."

Bumper, who had been served early and was now about to leave, gave a great guffaw. "That just minds me of a story," he said. "There was these two men wanted lodging an' they was told there was just one bed for the both of them an' the one fellah said no, he'd as lief sleep with a wet dog as with another man."

Bumper laughed uproariously, Tom with a sudden

burst, Aunt Polly giggled, Duncan worked over a basket of food, Peggy blushed and Jim looked angry.

"All right, Bumper, you can get started. You did a fine day's work and we'll look for you tomorrow."

Bumper took the basket and Duncan received the thanks while his mouth still twitched at the corners.

"The children, they allays expect a bit of cake or sumthin'. You hadn't ought to spoil them, Master Jim," Bumper said, peering eagerly under the covering tea towel. "Now 'bout that story; you looked sorta glum, an' it was just about a dog so it sure was all right to tell in front of ladies. 'By all and thank you."

"Good night, Bumper. See you tomorrow."

After Bumper was gone there were still a few giggles from Aunt Polly smothered by small coughs and then Tom's loud burst. "Come on, everybody. Have a good laugh and be done with it and then let's get on to the parchin'. What do you say, Jim? You don't have to look so sanctimonious."

"Oh, I just don't like Bumper to start on his stories. One brings on another and you never know what he *could* say. But now, I'm all set for the frolic. Had we better have the biggest skillet, think you, Aunt Polly?"

"The very biggest! We'll all help clear up so we can get at the corn, and put your apron on, Peggy, for it sputters."

In no time the work table was clear, the big table was laid with bowls and plates and dish towels to wipe buttery hands.

"It's a hard job, this. You'd better let us do the stirrin' an' you can boss us," Duncan said, taking the large spoon from Aunt Polly's fingers. Peggy sorted out the very finest kernels and then Aunt Polly pronounced all was ready.

"I can always tell by the *smell* when the butter's just hot enough. Crisp and not burned, that's the secret for parchin'," she added.

The great mound of butter was soon melted down as the kernels turned and swirled within it, and a rich fragrance like to no other filled the kitchen.

"I think it must be done by this time," Tom said as he approached the stove with his bowl.

"Go awa' wi' ye," Duncan said, giving him a friendly shove. "Ye'll get none till the young Mistress is served, that's for certain. Gi' this a good whummle round, Aunt Polly, an' see if it's done enough."

Aunt Polly stirred assiduously and then declared every corn was browned and never a one burned. "Bring up your bowl, Peggy, and get the first sampling. It's hot, mind, so get a teaspoon, too."

As they all crowded about with their pans and bowls, Duncan could be seen carefully spreading a thin layer of the corn on a tin plate. Shep stood near enough, licking his lips, to catch the fragrant, nutty flavor but as Duncan moved he hastily retreated while everyone laughed. Poor Shep! His first experience with the delicacy had given him very sore lips; now he always waited wistfully until he was sure there was no danger of pain, and one of the family always made sure there was not.

It was a jolly evening. They all agreed there had never been such delicious parched corn. Indeed, a second skilletful was needed to supply the demand. There was a nice warmth from the big, log fire, just enough to be cozy in the chill of the first fall evening. If one of the family had enjoyed these simple rituals of the parching of the corn, it had been Dave. When Tom mentioned it, Duncan joined quickly in.

"Aye, he was the one for it. We'd be shellin' away, fit to take the hands off us an' he say 'But just think of the parchin' we'll have to make up for it.' Aye, he was the one for it, he was. As bad as Shep."

"Oh, Master Jim, couldn't you make Shep do his tricks tonight? I've never seen them yet," said Pete.

"Now that would be an entertaining way to end the evening," Aunt Polly affirmed.

"Oh, do!" said Peggy. So Jim whistled and Shep came out from behind the stove still munching on his last grains of corn. While he was peculiarly Dave's dog, Jim had done well in taking his brother's place. Indeed, he had found a sort of comfort in teaching some tricks, new ones, and polishing up the old ones.

"All right, Shep, could you go all around and shake everyone's hand? Start with me."

Shep, with dignity, presented his paw — always the right one — to each person in turn and was loudly praised. Shep enjoyed the praise and sat waiting for the next command.

"Oh," said Pete, "make him sing, Master Jim, please."

"Duncan took part in this trick," Jim said. "I never would have thought of it. Go ahead, Duncan."

"Sit up nice, Sheppie, me laddie," Duncan began. "We're goin' to do our duet. Are you in good voice, mon?"

Duncan cleared his throat huskily and Shep gave a raucous growl.

"Fine, laddie. We'll start now. Sing out now when I point up my finger. Ready."

"Sheppie's all *weet*." The finger pointed up and there came at once from Sheppie a high, shrill, dog soprano note. Then the song went on:

> Sheppie's seldom *dry*
> He's draggled all his bushy *tail*
> Comin' through the *rye*.

At each accented word and upward pointed finger, Shep uttered his shrill note.

When the song was over, the audience was convulsed while Sheppie had his treat of tidbits as a reward.

"How did you ever think of having him do that?" Jim asked between laughs.

"Well, you know that high screech he gives when he calls us to dinner? That put it in me head. He's a nice dog, that one."

The corn bowls were empty and Jim said, "One more trick and then we must go to bed. We've heavy work tomorrow."

"His prayers! Make him say his prayers, Jim, please!" from Peggy, and the others joined.

"All right. Come on, Sheppie."

He set a low kitchen chair with its back to the dog. "Sit down, Sheppie. Now say your prayers like a good fellow."

Jim sat down on his own chair and put his hand over his eyes. At once, Sheppie stood on his hind legs, put his paws on the back of the chair in front of him and laid his head upon them. He held the position until Jim removed his hands, and then with joyous barks showed he felt he had done well and ate his reward greedily while Aunt Polly laughed until her sides shook.

"Oh, I've never seen that one before. That caps the climax."

Everyone gave way again to mirth, had a last drink of cider and prepared to say good night. A knock on the kitchen door startled them. When Jim opened it, the man Watson stood there.

"Excuses for disturbin' you this late, but I heard the laughter and it sounded pretty cheery to a lonely man. Is your servant, Duncan, here?"

"He's not our servant," Jim said sharply, "but our good friend. No, I'm afraid he has already retired."

"Never mind. I'll see him again. I like to hear him talk. I'll be getting along and thank you, sir. Good night, all," and he left.

"I don't like the way that man keeps turning up," Tom blurted out, "though the roars we made over Sheppie's performance must have sounded over quite an area."

"I think he's bought the Harbisons' farm and now he doesn't know what to do with it. That's my idea," Aunt Polly pronounced.

And then, filled with different dreams, Duncan's strangest of all, the old farmhouse grew quiet in sleep.

By the end of another week the corncrib was filled with golden ears of corn, the bins were filled with the shelled kernels, the seed corn was placed in tight burlap bags, nothing was left in the fields but the bare stalks jostling each other in the wind, and the piles of pumpkins were ready to be sorted and put where they would keep until Hallowe'en would convert them into pies.

A little hiatus occured here while the men scanned the almanacs and Aunt Polly, looking up from her quilting, said over and over that it was good luck to butcher in good weather.

"What does it signify if it gets a bit warm?" she asked. "The hams and flitches will be smoked and will keep no matter when you smoke them. The sausage can be put in crocks with melted lard over them and sit in the spring trough or in the cold cellar you boys made and right you were to do it. Besides, I ought to be gettin' home soon. I've left Charley too long."

That settled it. Tom passed the word to Dave at their Sunday rendezvous and it was arranged that Uncle Charley and Dave would both drive over for the high sport of butchering and then Aunt Polly would go home.

When the day came it was cool and cloudless. All the machinery connected with the last rites of the three pigs was kept carefully away from female eyes. Aunt Polly went into the front parlor and drew Peggy with her so they would not hear any sounds that might distress them.

The men had long been experts and worked fast. In a few days' time the great hams, lesser shoulders and flitches were all treated and in the smokehouse; the smaller delicacies were put carefully aside, especially the strip along the back that the boys had always called "the turkey meat" and of which they made a feast.

At last came the time for sausage-making, usually done in one end of the big kitchen. The grinder was set up, pans and dishes arranged and crocks made ready for the packing. Tom fed into the grinder mouth pieces of the meat. Aunt Polly, wearing a huge Mother Hubbard apron above the elbows, stood ready to receive the long, thin strips from the end of the grinder and mix them with her own hands in the great tin bucket for the first testing, with Jim helping as he always did.

"Easy with the salt now, Jim. You can put more in but you can't take it out. Some pepper now and the least bit of sage. I'll mix this first batch and then try it."

Duncan was ready with his skillet, into which Peggy laid small rounds of the meat, and all waited nervously. The rounds cooked quickly, cooled and were passed around. Aunt Polly smacked her lips. "As I'm a livin' woman, I never tasted better sausage meat in all my days!"

There was loud acclaim from all the tasters. "If we can just make the rest to taste like this." Jim said.

Aunt Polly winked. "We can, for I measured every spoonful we put into this batch. Now let's get it all. Duncan, you can render down the lard — and keep back the rest of you, for it's hot stuff, mind. Then I'll let you fellows pack the crocks and seal them up. And be sure to keep a good lot out for supper. In spite of the handling, I can relish a good smart bit of it."

Before supper the untidy mechanics were put away, the kitchen cleaned and the table set, with good rich odors filling the air. Aunt Polly and Peggy had been ordered to rest about four o'clock, when it was seen they were growing too tired, and now the dinner bell woke them and a chorus of voices raised the usual cry of "lazy bones."

There was laughter and clatter at the table for Uncle

Charley had come to take Aunt Polly home. "It's been just a beautiful visit," she kept insisting, "but if I don't go home, I can't come back, as the Quakers say. I planned to go back after butcherin', and you see so I will."

Dave had come to help with the work that day but now, after putting Sheppie through his tricks for Uncle Charley, he finished his supper, waved a "good-by all" and quietly rode away. The old people stayed the night and then left after early breakfast.

"And now," Peggy said wistfully, "it does seem as if all the fall excitement is over, doesn't it?"

"Well," Jim said, "if the weather holds, we do have an invitation to the Manse for overnight!"

"Good heavens! There's been so much going on right here, I had forgotten the big occasion."

"We'll wait and see how the roads are. You're doing well and we won't take any chances. If we shouldn't be able to make the trip, would you be very disappointed?" He held her close, his lips on her.

"When I have you, I don't believe anything else could *really* disappoint me." He drew her to him again.

Duncan, coming in from the back porch, took one look and broke into one of his raucous couplets:

> The greatest kisses ever seen
> Were in this very house I ween.

"Get along with you, Duncan, and tend to your business. Mind, we've got plenty of shelled corn yet to bag."

"Just a wee bit of song," Duncan responded airily. "I feel sort of down since Aunt Polly left."

"So do we all, but work will help cure us. Fill up the

bags of seed corn first for I've an idea we'll soon have buyers for that."

He was right. Even in the sparsely settled farms the news spread that Jim Ryall had made a specialty of seed corn and for a good price was selling it. For more than a week the wagons came, the farmers demurred at the price and finally left with their golden bounty. Jim had within him a great air of elation. His plan was going to work.

Meanwhile, a remarkable mildness of weather still lay upon the quiet fields and hills. The leaves dropped softly; many, besides the oaks', had not yet fallen at all. The farmers read their almanacs, consulted and drew various conclusions. Most of them felt that the present, slow coming of winter meant that the following one would be a bad one. Jim, at the blacksmith shop early the next morning, heard the dire predictions and laughed. He was not given to superstition. "Yes. sir, I'm tellin' you. We'll have an easy time this year and the devil will buckle on his horns next year. You mind me, now!"

Jim was pondering on the trip to New Salem. This would be a perfect day. It *would* be nice. Just he and Peggy alone in the buggy this time, the reception into membership and Communion itself, as well as meeting many new friends. If they started early — say today — they could reach New Salem by early lunch time, and the following day could make it home by dark. There seemed to be no risk.

Jim hurried the horses back when they were shod and burst in with his news to Peggy who started at once to pack their small valise. Duncan watched the sky and proclaimed it perfect. He put some scones and cookies in a bag just in case, Tom hitched up the rig, the last admonitions were given, and before they could believe it Jim and Peggy sat side by side as the horse trotted over the farm roads and onto the open pike. All was quiet. No other conveyances were in sight. If Jim and Peggy had been happy before, they were even more than ever now. The rich quiet of the Indian summer enfolded them; the nostalgic breath of summer's sweet fragrances floated in the air. They sat still for a long time, drinking it all in, and then began to talk of the pleasures still to come and the new experiences.

"To visit in a strange house and the *Manse*, at that. What if I'm scared, Jim?"

"How could you be? You live in a house much bigger than it, don't you?"

"Yes. You're comforting. But Dr. Knox rather gives me a shiver when he looks at me. What if he would start in on the catechism? I wouldn't remember a single thing."

Jim laughed. "Neither would I. He'd never take a chance like —" Suddenly he slowed the horse. His ears had caught a soft, steady beat of feet not shod with iron. He looked back quickly. There was *Sheppie*, doing what he had never done before, what had been carefully guarded against over the years. Shep had followed, slipping carefully behind the buggy after all the careful restraining efforts had somehow become loose. He never followed a rider, but a buggy or buckboard just fitted his stride.

Jim stopped the horse and he and Peggy both got out and looked at Sheppie who now, conscious of his guilt, cringed at their feet and wagged his tail for forgiveness.

"How could he get untied? I fastened him up myself."

"Where?"

"The wagon shed."

"I'll venture Bumper has borrowed the buckboard for the day or maybe Pete was sent for it by his father and, in the effort of getting it out, let Sheppie pull himself loose. But what will we do now?"

Jim thought. "It's too long for you to drive back again after the long trip here, and we're so close now —"

They both looked at the church steeple of New Salem in full view and the outlines of the quiet village with its Saturday morning shoppers holding their baskets on their arms. No, it was too late to turn back now.

"*Bad dog!*" Jim said to the culprit which made him hang his head in distress. "We'll just have to get him somehow into the back of the buggy and that will make him less noticeable as we get to the Manse. Then Heaven help us if the preacher doesn't like dogs. He doesn't look like a dog man to me," siad Jim.

With lifting and pushing, cajoling and scolding alternately, they managed to get Sheppie into the back of the buggy and put the light cover over him. This he resented but finally arranged his various members in a way reasonably comfortable. Jim drove on, his face grim except when he looked at Peggy, whose face was piteous.

"Never mind," he kept saying. It may work out all right, if you just *smile*."

They drove up to the Manse where Dr. Knox hurried to help Peggy from the buggy. As he did, Sheppie joyfully leaped from his prison and joined them.

"What is this?" Dr. Knox asked in a heavy voice.

"Oh, Dr. Knox, it's a beautiful dog that's come with them. Oh, how I'll enjoy taking care of him!" his wife exclaimed.

"I would like to explain everything," Jim began.

"I think an explanation is due," the preacher said. "Will you come with me into my study, Mr. Ryall?"

Sheppie was following closely behind.

"Not in the house. I don't care to have animals in the house. I have always thought the saint who made the statement 'Without, are dogs' was quite correct. Well, come along, Mr. Ryall and let's hear your story."

Jim told it simply, and at the end Dr. Knox said, "Well, what are we to do with him now?"

"There are two choices," Jim said rather icily. "We can start back home and take him along, or we can tie him in your stable very securely."

Dr. Knox looked grim while his wife patted Sheppie's head and muttered soft endearments. Apparently she didn't agree with the Scriptural quotation.

"Well," their host said, "if you'll come down to the stable, we'll arrange for the dog while Mrs. Knox is showing Mrs. Ryall her room."

The guest room was large and empty of all decoration except a dull quilt on the double bed. It had the look of being seldom used. Mrs. Knox bustled about admiring her young guest's clothes, especially the bonnet.

"You should get one at Miss Lucy's, too. She has lovely ones!"

"Oh, Dr. Knox would never allow it. It would look too frivolous for a preacher's wife. Now I'll look to the lunch and you just come down when you wish."

The men were rather silent when they came to the table, for an occasional soft bark could be heard from the stable.

"As to the proceedings," the doctor said. "We do not have the new members come to the front today. Instead, they just rise in their places as their names are called. It is really tomorrow at the Communion service that they come forward and are formally received before the pulpit. More impressive this way, I think."

The lunch was cold meat and potato salad, both served sparingly as evidently was the custom in the house. There was tea and a sad-looking pie at the end. It was clear that Mrs. Knox was not gifted as a cook even though her kindness was unlimited. Her face broke into smiles as she watched Peggy and Jim and also glanced toward the stable.

"I hope," the doctor said, as they rose, "that you'll make sure of that rope, Mr. Ryall. I still have a feeling of uneasiness about that dog."

"I'll check again. Ther's a chain there, too. Don't worry, sir. It's been an unfortunate thing, but I do hope it won't disturb you."

There was quite a little reception as they all entered the vestibule. Peggy's face was full of pleasure and excitement as she was introduced as Mrs. Ryall, the wife of the new young Master of The Richlands. It was all as she had pictured it, and if the women eyed her new bonnet and the men the face under it, there could surely be no harm in that. By the time they had met all the Elders and their wives, Dr. Knox said he thought it was time to be entering the Sanctuary and told Jim and Peggy that for this service they should sit just where they pleased and Mrs. Knox would accompany them.

The tall church windows were open enough that the soft threnody of the cricket's song came in with the autumn air. It was a peaceful scene, Jim thought, and he was happy to have his wife and unborn child under the blessing of the holy place. The church filled quickly, for the preparation service on Saturday afternoon was considered important. Dr. Knox rose in his place behind the pulpit, made a few general remarks as to the reason for their presence, read the names of the new members and after a brief prayer announced the opening hymn. As they stood to sing, Jim's quick ear heard something above the notes of the reed organ and the song. He detected the soft, steady pad of paws coming ever nearer, and an occasional break in the voices behind him. Before the hymn was over, Sheppie stood beside the pew waiting to get closer. Jim instinctively did the best thing. He moved a little, allowed the dog to get over his feet and lie down between him and Peggy. There Sheppie stretched comfortably and went to sleep through the rest of the service.

There was a sermon, short prayers from the Elders, a few more words of instruction from the minister about each one's preparation for the morrow and then came the ending which wrought havoc in the solemn atmosphere.

"We will now bow our heads to receive the benediction," the minister intoned.

There was a general shifting of bodies, and Sheppie woke and looked about him. Jim had leaned his head against the back of the seat before him and shaded his eyes with his hands, completely forgetting the signal for the famous trick. At once, Sheppie rose up on his hind legs, placed his front paws on the same seat — just the right height for him — and laid his head on them in a truly devotional attitude.

It was too much for the younger members even in that solemn moment. There were choked sounds and smothered giggles, and the aisle was almost blocked as Jim undid his gesture at once and with a firm hand on Shep's collar tried to get out as soon as he could. But this was not easy. Dr. Knox had waited to greet the new members who had been sitting near the front, and did not know the cause of the sounds which seemed to break involuntarily from the throats of those who should have been quietly leaving. Also, his own eyes having been dutifully closed, he had not seen Sheppie's devotions. It was when he reached the outer walk where he usually greeted his congregation that, amid laughter and repetition and more and more mirth, he heard what had happened. His face became white.

"In the House of the Lord!" he said, brokenly, "as though it were a *circus!*"

"But it was *so* funny!" a boy's voice insisted.

"It was not funny. It was blasphemous. I urge you all now to go home and concentrate on thoughts of the morrow and forget what unfortunately happened today. I can assure you it will not do so again." The minister turned toward the Manse.

Everyone else turned, too, and followed the streets home in silence, with only now and then a child's laugh quickly subdued by his parents.

Jim, with a tight grip on Shep's collar, was waiting in the yard and began his explanation before the minister could start.

"I haven't words to tell you," he said, "how utterly ashamed and miserable I am over what happened. Somehow the dog broke loose. He walked quietly up the aisle to me during a hymn and lay down and went to sleep in the pew. I think if that had been all, there would really have been no disturbance. But he has been taught a trick and I was nervous and anxious and so, without thinking, gave him the signal which he is used to."

"What was it? I demand to know!"

"When I bowed my head and put my hand over my eyes, he stood up on his hind legs, put his paws on the back of the seat in front and laid his head on them." Even in the exigency of the moment, Jim found it necessary to cough for some minutes while the minister seemed actually shocked out of speech.

"But one thing I've decided," Jim said, "after I've already had a word with my wife. The best thing for you and the church and everyone is for us to leave at once. We can squeeze Sheppie into the back seat of the buggy and put the cover over him until we're past the main part of the town. You see," ever warming to his subject, "you know how small boys are. If we stay here as intended, there will be a steady stream of boys coming either over your sidewalk or into your yard to get a look at the dog. Their reports will stir the story all up again. Now, if we quietly leave at once, everything will settle down and you'll see that there will be peace just as you wish for your sermon tomorrow."

Jim stopped for breath and Dr. Knox drew a long sigh as the color came back to his face.

"Your dinner?"

"We have a hearty lunch with us. Our man at the farm always puts that in, wherever we go."

"I'm ashamed to break our invitation but, oh, my dear Mr. Ryall, you can't imagine my relief. You couldn't have been more kind than to suggest this immediate leaving."

"Let's get ready at once, then."

They found the two women in the kitchen where Peggy was trying to comfort her hostess.

"I've looked forward so to having you," Mrs. Knox lamented. "It would have been a bright spot in our lives. It's so lonesome living right next the gray church and the old stones. My husband says we should be always reminded of our mortality, but I'd like a bright red rose arbor all along our lot. Oh, you're like a red rose yourself and I hate to let you go."

"Come, come!" the doctor spoke sternly, but Peggy broke in at once. "Why, we'll still have our visit only it will be at our house instead of yours. Oh, we'll show you all over the place, won't we, Jim? Everything, and you'll love it. We'll write an invitation soon so a time can be set. Won't you come?"

Even Dr. Knox had a smile. Peggy and Jim both had a quick perception that perhaps the minister and his wife were not invited out often. The guests were speedily gotten into the buggy. Peggy in her second best bonnet in case of rain was now felt to be less conspicuous. Sheppie, though crowded, managed to get himself into the back of the buggy under the cover and with a very bare soup bone seemed to feel content.

As they turned the corner from the left which was usual,

Jim whispered to Peggy, "Darling, don't cry out if you wonder where we're going, for we aren't going home today."

"But where then, Jim?"

"Now don't say anything until I'm done. We're going the back way to the old Stone Hotel. All I told Dr. Knox was exactly true. We had to get the dog and, of course, ourselves off his premises or he would have been overrun by small boys and some big ones, too. It's too late to start back to the farm tonight and thirdly and lastly, I'm *starved*."

Peggy said nothing but her face was one smile of rapture. She leaned far back in the buggy seat, though, as they reached the big back lot of the Stone Hotel. Jim knew both Mr. Hartman, the proprietor, and Jake, the man who took care of the horses as they came, so when they stopped and got out with Shep happily at their heels, it was Jake who spied them first and sent them in the back way to greet Mr. Hartman.

"Mind you, there's a crowd there already tellin' him all about what happened in church. Don't I wish I could a' seen it. I'll bring your satchel in. You'll be stayin' the night?"

"It's a little too late to get home," Jim said, while Peggy gave his arm a quick squeeze. "Should we take our dog inside? Down, Shep, until we decide about you."

Jake whistled and Shep knew the sound of a friend. "I'll look after him," Jake said. "When we get the horse fixed up, I'll get the dog here a nice, juicy bone. You two just get away in."

They waited in the shadow of the big dining room until the talking and laughter had all subsided around the high desk where Mr. Hartman sat to keep his books. Then, holding Peggy's hand, Jim advanced to speak to the jovial man who was still chuckling. "We crave sanctuary, Mr. Hartman," Jim said, "my wife and I."

"I'll bet you do! And haven't I heard rumors of a *dog*?"

At this, mine host leaned over to kiss Peggy's hand and shake Jim's and then give himself up again to roars of laughter. "I don't go to church much, but I always get all the news and never has there been anything like to-day's. For the good laughs you've given me after an unusually dull stretch, you are all my guests. The best room is vacant and the dinner is always a little extry because some folks usually drive over from nearby towns for a little change on Sundays. So the hospitality is all yours, my dears. Could I see the dog?"

"Of course, but we really can't accept all your kindness. We will stay and be glad to, as regular guests. As a matter of fact, we've been planning to come over for a night before all this came up today!"

"Your dog paid for every cent. Could you bring him in?"

Jim went to the door and gave his own whistle. In a minute, Shep was beside him, all wagging eagerness. Mr. Hartman had come from behind his desk and he and Shep eyed each other with mutual satisfaction.

"Now, Sheppie, could you sit down? And shake hands with this good gentleman?"

Shep promptly sat down and extended his right paw, nodding his head slightly as he did so.

Mr. Hartman was overcome. He patted Shep and sent for Jake to give him new instructions for his care.

"And the satchel, sir?"

"In the best room of the house, you might know. Now, my young friends, you've had a very tiring day. Wouldn't you like to go up and rest from all the excitement? Jake, tell Kitty to take up milk and pound cake to stay them till dinner time. And thanks again."

As the young people climbed the stairs they could hear their host muttering, "If I could just see him say his prayers — If I could just —"

In the great square room above there was an elegance from older days which they had not dreamed of: the big four-poster with its white tester, the comfortable chairs, a tip-top table with a fluted rim and a low chair and footstool covered with chintz just meant for a pretty lady. First of all they fell upon the pound cake and milk and consumed it to the last crumb; then after speculating on the people who had slept in this room before them over the years, they undressed and were soon fast asleep.

When they woke it was dark and Jim jumped up to light a candle. Before he did it, the voice of Kitty, the maid, was heard, together with a gentle knock. "I was just told to tell you you needn't hurry for we serve on pretty late, but dinner is ready any time you care to come down. Mr. Hartman is having you at the table with him for there's quite a many folk here tonight."

They hurried into their clothes, refreshed from their nap. Peggy wore her red dress and Jim a fresh stock and each looked long into the eyes of the other.

"Are we really here?" Peggy said.

"It would seem so, darling. Oh, you're so lovely!"

The scene below was enough to thrill their eager hearts:

tall candles lighted the dusk, and the big dining room with its crossed beams over the stone seemed a soft blaze of fairy fire as the shadows retreated before the candle on each table. Mine host looked the full part with a swallowtail coat and fresh stock and a nice air of gallantry as he handed Peggy to her seat. There were many tables occupied, and the soft buzz of conversation along with the voices of those who called out orders in the pantry made it all exciting to the countrydwellers. And never had they been so hungry or had such a fine dinner! Mr. Hartman was interested in Jim's ambitions for the farm. "And three brothers of you to work on it. Wonderful piece of land!"

When the meal was ended, on pretext of checking on Shep who had evidently been content with his quarters, Mr. Hartman took Jim outside.

"It looks like I just sit at my desk here and keep to the hotel but I know all that's going on just the same and I can always smell a mystery. Now this Watson that bought the Harbison place and still says he had an eye on yours — I don't think it's the farm he's interested in. I think it's your man Duncan. He's let slip one or two things when he was in here. Once he said, 'We always called him "Sandy."' And I said quick, had he known him then at one time. And he said, 'Oh, no, we always called every Scotchman "Sandy" down where I come from.' But it was a slip. Just thought I'd tell you to keep your eyes open and maybe talk to Duncan and get his story. He did just land here out of nowhere, didn't he?"

"Thank you, Mr. Hartman. I'll watch out, and I'm glad you told me."

It was decided that since the news had quickly spread

that Shep and his owner were at the Stone Hotel, it would be wise if they left early in the morning so their departure would not be noticed. Mr. Hartman did make a hesitant request. There was a small room back of his office. If he invited just a very few of his choice friends who were there tonight from a distance, could they have the dog in for a few tricks? He would promise there would be no undue noise or sounds unsuitable for a Sabbath eve. Could this be done?

Jim looked at his host's kind face, the gray eyes set well apart, the wide smile — a face to trust and yet that of a man who could manage business affairs shrewdly and honestly.

"If you keep your guests from laughing too loud I guess we could try it, but only with some of your friends from a distance. I wouldn't want Dr. Knox to think we really had a performing dog with us here."

It was settled. Peggy stayed in the ladies' lounge, little thrills of happiness still running through her blood. Here she sat with all these fashionable women while she could study them, hear them talk and talk with them! It was beyond believing.

"I wonder what those men are up to?" One woman asked as a burst of undeniable laughter came through the walls.

"Oh, some of their old jokes probably," said another.

But it was better than that. Happy to be with his master and warmed by a good dinner, Shep was outdoing himself with all the tricks he knew. The guests restrained themselves with difficulty but Mr. Hartman stuck to his promise not to keep the dog too long, so Jim took him out to his kennel before any locals had discovered what was going on.

The next morning their host was up to greet them with a good breakfast and start them on their way, though when Jim tried to settle his bill there was none.

"My boy, I haven't laughed as much for twenty years. I'm the one who owes you. But come back, come back; I'll treat you like regular boarders with maybe a little discount for Shep," he added.

It was pleasant driving through the early mists of the morning and Jim didn't hurry the horse. Shep now sat on the floor between them, giving small barks of satisfaction as they went.

"What a strange Sunday this is," Peggy said, "for us to be riding back home with Shep and thinking of all that happened yesterday, instead of going to church today. Do you think we've committed a terrible sin somehow?"

Jim was grave. "We couldn't have. We've done nothing wrong. But I feel, too, that it's all strange, and the worst part is missing Communion when we won't get there for a long while. The service was so solemn yesterday until —"

And then, because they were young and so in love, in spite of qualms and cares and fear, they laughed and laughed and kissed beneath the newly risen sun.

Chapter VI

There was fun that night around the kitchen table as the travelers unfolded their tale. Jim led up to the scene in church with the suspense of a good storyteller, and when at last he reached the climax of Sheppie's prayer there were literally howls of laughter. Oh course, there was Peggy's description of their wonderful night at the Stone Hotel and everything told over again from the time they had first discovered Shep following the buggy to Dr. Knox's expression as he realized the dog would have to stay with them.

"Aye, he's a great theologian, they tell me," Duncan said, "an' a very good man, but a wee bit *set* about things; stern, sort of, an' from the way he acted with Sheppie, I'll say he hasn't a drop of humor in him."

Tom had made his usual rendezvous with Dave and brought back all the news of Aunt Polly. They all felt that next week, by way of Tom, Dave would be the ideal one to recount the story to Aunt Polly and Uncle Charley.

Jim was slow "takin' The Book," as Duncan always called it, but when at last all the risibles were quelled, the family settled to quiet as Jim slowly read a psalm, and the prayer together followed, Pete joining in. Then the good nights of the strange Sabbath were said and soon all was quiet with Shep enjoying the freedom of the back porch or the warm spot under the walnut tree as usual. Peggy was almost instantly asleep and Jim sat in the dim candle's glow watching her beauty as he often did. He felt sure she had taken no harm. Her warm sense of humor and her calm acceptance of events even though unusual, like their stay at the Stone Hotel, had been sources of pleasure and did not leave her unduly excited.

But after the candle was out, Jim still lay thinking of Mr. Hartman's words. There was, indeed, a mystery about Duncan. Aunt Polly's remark had often come to him as questions rose in his mind. "There's nae lips tighter than a Scotchman's." He knew his father had put out gentle feelers once or twice as to Duncan's former place of living and his reason for leaving it and had received only a most courteous refusal to give any explanation. Now if this Watson knew something, if he had indeed wanted to locate Duncan rather than any good farming country such as The Richlands and had found the two quests in one, then something must be done and carefully. He tossed and turned. They all loved Duncan like a brother. No harm would come to him if he could help it! He decided at last to start with the Squire. He wanted reassurance about the ownership and that could be the excuse. Other questions could follow. If a lawyer was needed, the Squire would know the best.

It suddenly turned into a wet November. The leaves lay stricken on the ground and most of the branches, except the oaks', were bare. Jim told them all at breakfast one morning that he thought there was enough to keep the rest busy if he made a little trip himself into New Salem to do a few errands.

"And not take me?" Peggy said piteously.

"Not this time, darling. You'll have three stout men, counting Pete, to watch over you and see that you're cozy and comfortable and I'll be back before you know it." He held her face against his coat as he finally said good-by, for he knew her eyes were wet. Then, with a final embrace and a wave to the others, he put a lunch in his saddle-bag and rode off on Beauty. "I had to do it fast or I could never have left her," he said to himself.

His intention was to see the Squire first and, while the roads were damp from the rain, they were not muddy and Beauty cantered easily. Before he thought it possible, Jim was at the Squire's gate, had tied the horse and hurried up the gravel path. The Squire himself, long white hair flying about his face as usual, his keen blue eyes giving the lie to old age in spite of the hair, greeted him.

"As I live, it's Jim and I've just sat down to a good dish of lentil soup. Come in, come in, and join me. Nothing gives strength to the bones like lentil soup. *Come in*! Don't stand dodderin' on the step. It's raining."

There was no dissuasion possible and after the good thick soup and slabs of fresh bread and butter, the Squire led the way to his "office," as he called the book-lined, paper-strewn cubicle, and there bade Jim sit down and tell what business brought him.

"It's just this, Squire. As you know, the Ryalls have held The Richlands for generations, son after father. The land has all this time been under cultivation and care.

But there's no deed nor scrap of paper to prove this. It's probably all safe as it is, but I'd feel better if I had some proof in my hands. Is there no way?"

The Squire's head bent in thought for some minutes. Then he said, "Well, there is a way though I must say it always has a queer sound to me. It's old and established and right, though you'll need a lawyer. Tom McKelvey could do it up like a whistle for you."

"What is it?"

"Well, he would take a proceeding to establish title by adverse possession. He would prepare the papers. It's a mouthful to say, isn't it?"

"It sounds all wrong."

The Squire laughed. "When McKelvey gets through with it, old George the Third himself couldn't take it away from you. Now, see here —"

The Squire unfolded his plan. Just now they were only nine miles from the courthouse. Why not go there straight away and have McKelvey hear the story? He practically lived in the courthouse, so they would be sure to find him. "Did you bring any identification, Jim?"

"I brought the old family Bible and a few letters that go back quite a bit, and my own marriage certificate as the present owner."

"Good boy. What do you say?"

"It's a fine plan if it doesn't put me away from home too long."

"A lot less than if you went back and took a new start, don't you think? There's a nice, cheap little hotel we can hole in at, if McKelvey says it may take long. Unless he's in court, though, I've a feeling he can get a start on your problem right away. At least enough that you can leave for home tomorrow. If you have to come back again, you're still one leg up, as it were. Will you take a gamble?"

"I will," said Jim, with a sudden decision. "Will you ride, too?"

Miss Higgins, the Squire's sister, who kept house for him, approved the plan. "It'll do the Squire here good to see McKelvey and get the smell of the courthouse again. Get along, Mr. Ryall. Good luck to you. Of course he'll ride."

Jim was awed by the courthouse with its gilded dome and its stone walls and passages inside. A heavy smell of defunct cigars and "Five Brothers" was noticeable, but he felt he could well stand it if only the strange document were finally in his hand.

The Squire came back to the bench where Jim had been sitting accompanied by an exact opposite of himself. Mr. McKelvey was tall and stout with neatly trimmed brown hair and mustache. His eyes were keen and black and he shook Jim's hand with a strong grip.

"Your luck always holds, Squire. Court just out and I have a little time on my hands. There's an empty room back here. Come along and tell your story, young man. I knew your father. Fine person. Now, go ahead."

Jim gravely, and with great care, gave all the facts and explained his desire somehow to prove ownership of The Richlands.

"Any brothers?"

"Two. Younger."

"Well, while not exactly a law, the rule here is still of primogeniture. Any proofs?"

Jim laid what he had brought on the table before him, while Mr. McKelvey scanned them and made some notes.

"Now," the Squire broke in, "what I suddenly thought in this case was that you could take a proceeding to establish title by adverse possession. It wouldn't be such a big job to prepare the papers, would it?"

For answer, McKelvey slapped the Squire's back as he gave a loud chuckle.

"You old groundhog!" he exclaimed affectionately. "You know more law than I do. Why, that would just fit the case. Tell you what I'll do. I'm just finishing up this thing I'm on; then I'll be ready to take a proceeding on this and prepare the papers. When I'm done you can either come in to sign or I'll pick up the Squire and go out to see you. On the whole, it would be better for you to come here in case other matters might need to be talked over. All right, Mr. Ryall?"

"More than all right. I've been uneasy and this will calm me down. I do appreciate the kindness of you both."

"Wait till you get his bill!" At which the Squire laughed heartily.

"Well, let's start with a bit of a snack. It's your turn to flip, Squire."

The grave ceremony ended with heads for McKelvey who professed great depression. "He always gets the best of me one way or another. Well, let's get on with it. A nice cup of tea or coffee and a bit of pie to hold us together till supper time. Sorry I can't ask you for a real meal then, but my wife's at a big meetin' of some kind and I surmise the pickings will be slim. But the little Wasp's Nest just back of the courthouse will do, won't it?"

Jim smiled as they entered, for some wag with a gift at molding wet paper had made the decor all too realistic. Women would surely have cried out, but the occupants were all men. It was easy to see that McKelvey and the Squire were favorites with the other lawyers. There was much badinage passed about and much interest shown in Jim as the new Master of The Richlands. Every once in a while at a story McKelvey made a note of it, such as, "Yes sir, my grandfather always bought his wheat at The Richlands, and I guess his father before him."

The tiny hotel was clean, if certainly devoid of anything like luxury, and Jim slept with a sort of exhausted relief after the night's discussions, until the thought of his next day's travel woke him up. The Squire was ready soon and after some breakfast they set off. It was as they were turning the corner that Jim suddenly pulled on Beauty's reins and stared back at a man loitering at the side door of the courthouse. It was Watson! What need had he of a lawyer? He put the question to the Squire who rode on undisturbed.

"Can't tell! Farm deed maybe. Snooping round your property rights and so on. Mebbe just makes him feel biggity to walk round the courthouse. I've known men like that. Guess I'm kinda one myself. I always wanted to be a lawyer and now the very smell of a court chamber puts new life in me."

"Squire."

"What's up?"

"We stayed all night at the Stone Hotel when the episode of the dog kept us from going back to church next day."

The Squire roared. "Had you heard of it?" Jim asked.

"Heard of it? There wasn't a man, woman or child who didn't hear about *that*. And I can tell you, it gave the town just the shakin' up it needed. We'd get pretty stodgy without knowing it and pretty over-religious, *I* think, and a good shakin' laugh from hill to mill will do us more good than a sermon. Well, what's on your mind?"

"Mr. Hartman has theories about Mr. Watson."

"I'll bet he has. He ought to been a detective. What's he come up with now?"

"He thinks Duncan ran away from some sort of crime in Virginia and this Watson plans to get even with him. It's not a pretty thought. I'm worried."

"Well, now, if Duncan wanted to show his hand, he's been a long time doin' it, hasn't he?"

"I've thought of that. He's been with us fifteen years."

"And what good's a lawyer goin' to do him here? He couldn't practice in Virginia. I think there *is* a mystery of some kind, Jim, and I never have liked this Watson. All the same, I think we should all just keep quiet until the dust settles, whatever it is, and keep our eyes open, of course. Well, there's New Salem comin' into view, still laughin' over Sheppie's prayer, I'll bet a dollar. It's a long ride home, Jim. Stop and have a bite. You'll go the faster and let Beauty have time to eat her oats.

"Thank you, Squire. I'll give Beauty a rest, but I've got a good lunch in my saddlebag and," he smiled, "I've a pretty good reason to hurry on home."

"That you have, my boy, so go your own gait. Just don't worry too much about your man Duncan. You're fond of him?"

156

"Like a brother!"

"And don't forget, if you ever need a place to keep your dog, he'll be welcome here and I can tie a special knot. I'm pretty tender over dogs."

It was lovely dusk when Jim rode up toward the house, gloating as he did so over the wide, wide fields of cornstalks representing their recent yield, dreaming of the beauty of the wheat which was the greatest harvest of all. The wheat, so tender and green and then, at last, so ripe and golden. It was the wheat which put the real cash in their pockets, though he was determined to make the corn another great market.

As he neared the house he could see Peggy at the front waving the little shawl she had just taken off her head. He dismounted as he came close, let Beauty go her own way toward the barn and caught Peggy close in his arms. The endearments poured from his lips. "Our first night apart," he whispered.

"I thought I'd *die* without you!"

A strange chill ran through Jim's body. He spoke quickly. "One more kiss and then we must get in. It's cooler than it seems out here."

When they reached the kitchen door, Duncan was already there, his face white.

"So that's why the horse came in riderless! I might have guessed it. But don't the two of you scare our wits out of us that way again. Come away in, then. We're glad you're safe back, Jim, an' now Mistress Peggy there will mebbe smile a bit for us."

"Oh, Duncan, I didn't mope, really. Mind I baked you a pound cake and made ginger cakes —"

"With the tears droppin' in the batter! I seen it." Pete added to the mischief.

"Now, now," said Duncan, "suppose Mistress Peggy was never lonely for her husband, we'd all say:

> Sic a wife does Jimmy hae
> We wouldna' gi' a button for her!

After the general laughter and the reports of the day which could be translated, they all sat down to the hot, homely supper waiting for them.

"I believe it tastes as good as the one at the Stone Hotel," Peggy said, her cheeks now all dimpled and rosy.

"Hear the young flatterer, would you, Duncan?" said Tom.

"Ay, have ye never heard it's the bonnie face makes bonnie food?"

It was a jolly meal. Jim's return after two days' absence with Peggy's glow at his place beside her sent a rush of pleasure around the table. Pete had developed amazingly in the short time with the family and now, with quick wit and ready farm knowledge, was never at a loss for words.

But after the baked apples drowned in sugar and fresh churned butter and the ginger cakes had been disposed of, there was a general feeling that the day was done. Jim was unusually weary after his long ride, the men had been busy in the fields and Peggy's eyes looked heavy.

"I'm having another apple," Duncan said, "an' I'll warrant Pete here will join me. So the rest of you get yourselves on up to your beds. You'll be tired. Get away now. Pete an' me will clean up when we're done."

They needed no second urging. Tom said good night quickly and his heavy shoes sounded on the stairs. Jim went to pet Shep who now stuck to him as though his usual routine had again been established.

"A noble beast," Duncan kept muttering as he selected some special tidbits for the dog. "I'm tellin' you, there's no other like him!"

At last Jim and Peggy said good night to those left and went quietly up to their room.

"I put roses in the vase there, so we could smell them while we sleep. That little climber will keep us supplied till the frost, I do believe. Jim dear, I've something to tell you."

"Anything wrong, darling?" His anxiety made his voice break.

"No, not with me at all. Just something odd about — about Duncan!"

"What is it? Please tell me all of it."

"Well, Tom took the work horses to the Four Corners to be shod yesterday and of course waited as the men all do in the little store where the post office is. And just for fun Tom went up to it and said, 'I'll just take my mail while I'm here, please.' Everybody laughed and then didn't the postmaster hand him out a letter and before he handed it to him he read it aloud. The address, I mean. It was to Mister Duncan McPhee, in care of Mister James Ryall, The Richlands, Westmoreland County, Pennsylvania. And before Tom could get the letter from the postmaster this Mr. Watson was waiting there, too, and he had grabbed it out of his hands. Tom said it was a pretty sight with the postmaster and Tom holding Mr. Watson down while the postmaster got the letter. Then he gave it back to Tom and told this Mr. Watson to keep his hands off other people's mail or there'd be a fight for sure."

"That's all pretty queer," Jim said, "and I don't like it. What did Duncan say when Tom gave him the letter?"

"He looked sort of white and scared, I thought, and then he began to whistle and went on about his work. I did hear him say one thing. He said —"

"What?"

"It was something about, 'You'll sing small, my larkie, before I'm done with you,' but it was in Scotch and I could hardly make it out. Can you?"

"I'm afraid so," Jim said. "I think he's pretty mad at Watson for trying to get the letter and I don't wonder. But I think I'll talk to Duncan and maybe I can make it all right. Let's forget all about it now, since we're safe back together!"

They lay close, forgetting Duncan, as the soft night air enfolded them. Jim heard the squeak of the old backstairs and the pad of Duncan's stocking feet as at long last he climbed up to his room. Jim's former forgetfulness of Duncan as he had clasped Peggy in his arms was gone. He thought of the story of the post office all over again. A danger somehow lurked here, linking Watson and Duncan, hidden all these years and now suddenly bringing itself to light, culminating in a *letter*! It was not just a memory, then, that rankled. There must be a living connection. A message written on palpable paper by a human hand. There was something here that must be thought of and judged, and somehow he felt it would not be for the Squire or a lawyer to settle, as was the title of adverse possession. The one man he longed for to help him was his father. The man who had pressed and kept the faded rose.

Jim withdrew his arm from Peggy's side and moved softly until he sat up in bed, his feet on the floor. The thought that had struck him was that the trouble that had driven Duncan to make that incredible and perilous winter journey all the way from Virginia to the place he now found himself had been in some way connected with a *girl.* The idea seemed absurd on the face of it, but *was* it? When he had first come to them, Jim remembered, his thick, curly, sandy hair, his wide smile that showed his white teeth, the broad shoulders and strong arms. Even the "bandy legs" he was always joking about were not so unusual and certainly not when covered with trousers. "Why," he thought, "Duncan must have been good-looking in his late twenties and with his charm —"

Jim felt sure he had known appeasement of the flesh at least once with the gypsy woman, for a glance at Pete confirmed it, but this he was also sure was a strange accident unrepeated. There was something steadfast and immovable about Duncan, whether it was the way he hoed corn or perhaps the way he loved. "I'm a stubborn Scotchman," he had once said, Jim remembered.

As he climbed once more wearily into bed, Jim could not untangle a thread in the web. He could only mutter as he fell asleep, "It might have been, of all things, a girl — about a girl," and the problem faded and he dropped all cares for the time.

In the morning Duncan was bright and brisk, the only change being that he hustled them all through breakfast

a bit early and asked Jim if he could spare a horse and himself for the day, as he would like to ride into New Salem
and do a few little personal errands.

"Why sure, Duncan," Jim agreed. "Would you like me
to ride in with you? I always have a few leftovers to do."

Duncan's face suddenly turned grave. "Thank you,
Master Jim, but I'll not be needin' you."

"If you ever do, let me know," Jim answered and hurried
on with his breakfast. He walked to the end of the farm
road with the rider, though, and his face, too, was grave.

"I don't know what problems you may have, Duncan,
but if anything ever comes up to trouble you, remember
we are all behind you. And one thing I want to ask. This
Watson bothers me. I heard what happened at the post office and I don't like it. Does he hold anything against you?"

Duncan flung up his head. "Oh, he'll sing small, that
larkie, afore I'm done with him." And, giving the horse a
short slap on the rump, he cantered on out to the open road.

Jim was deeply worried. He and Tom discussed earnestly together what they should do. They had once seen
Duncan's anger raised in a white fury when Bumper was
beating a jaded horse he owned at the time. Before they
could stop him, they feared for Bumper's life. So they
had deep anxieties to share.

"I somehow can't picture Duncan mixed up in any girl
trouble," Tom said as they stowed the hay more evenly in
the barn loft for the winter. "Since we've never seen him
angry again — not like that," Jim responded, "I wonder if that might somehow give us the clue to the mystery?"
He spoke slowly and Tom stopped his work and looked
back at him.

"If he ever committed a crime down there wherever he was, they're taking a long time makin' any fuss about it."

"I know," Jim said. "The other queer thing was this Watson suddenly appearing on the scene. Did he look mad when he grabbed the letter from the postmaster?"

"He looked funny," Tom said. "Sort of as if he'd at last got what he was waiting for. Sort of smart-alecky. But determined, you bet."

"Well, we may get something out of Duncan when he gets back, if he isn't too close-mouthed. I don't like a mystery hanging around. It makes me nervous."

That night it was late when the sound of a horse's hooves came along the farm road. Peggy had cooked the dinner, Pete had cleared up afterward, and now they had gone to bed and Tom and Jim were trying to concentrate over a game of checkers.

When Duncan came in, they looked up in apparent surprise. "What are you doin' up at this 'oor?" Duncan growled with a strong flavor of his native tongue. There also exuded from him another flavor still stronger, of which the new temperance movement would not approve. He had a black, half-shut eye and a long cut on his chin. He glared at them as though daring them to make comment.

"Get on wi' your game," he said.

"Oh," Jim said easily, "we'd a lot rather hear the news of the town. Who all did you see?"

"Weel," said Duncan, "as you might expect, I goed first to me old friend in the ice cream store an' we had a wee crack. He telt me he signed the pledge this morning for some pretty lassies come askin' him an' he done it to please them, but tonight he tore it up an' would I care for a wee drop? So we had a one or two. Then when I got me warmed up to it, I sez, 'there's a mon I'd like to knock into kingdom come if I was just sure he would light in the right place there.' " Duncan slowly drank a dipper of water. "Sae me friend sez it's quittin' time an' he can kick anybody into the right spot an' he'll come wi' me. Sae he got his horse an' buggy an' a little refreshment for the way an' we went to Watson's."

"You didn't!" said Jim."

"Sure an' awa' we did, an' got him oot o' his bed an' pasted the wits out o' him. An' I sez, the thing is to put him in the buggy an' take him to the Squire. He's a good friend o' mine an' he can't abide Watson."

By this time, Tom was rolling with laughter and Jim making queer, choking noises of his own.

"Sae we got to the Squire an' a couthy mon he is an' all. I just sez, 'Squire, you can see this Watson mon here isna' fit for a civilized community. He ought to be sent awa'.

" 'You're frae the south,' the Squire sez. 'Why dinna' ye no go back to it?'

"An' Watson gie me a dunt in the ribs an' sez 'I'm fol-lerin' this man till hell freezes over.'

" 'An' it just might,' the Squire sez. 'It does that here sometimes. Why don't you get away south for the could weather an' come back later on? Besides, if you stick around you'll be into a lawsuit about that farm you bought. There was cheatery in that an' the Harbisons want it back.' An' here he winked at me an' gi' a nod to the door an' I left."

"How did you ever stick on the horse in the condition you're in?" Tom asked.

"Aye, ye may well speir at me about that. All the way I kep' thinkin' that in the mornin' you'd all be singin',

> Toom hame came the saddle
> But never came he.

"Only you wouldn't know the words belike. Ach, it's a weary mon I am the night."

Jim propelled him over to the bench where the wash basin stood. He reached for the arnica and witch hazel bottles and the roll of court plaster. Then gently he wiped the sore spots with the home remedies.

"But, Duncan," he kept repeating, "if Watson goes off and sells the farm back to the Harbisons, won't you be relieved? Won't you be safe, then, from whatever has been troubling you?"

Duncan's head fell upon his chest. The words came hard. "Oh, laddies, you dinna' ken the half of it. I was no better than a bairn for keepin' out o' trouble. Watson was the only man who knew I was innocent but he swore he'd track me down no matter where an' then he'd never tell the truth. Oh, he's like a curse on me."

"Duncan," Jim said in a low voice, "had this trouble anything to do with a *girl?*"

Duncan rose unsteadily and started with many fumblings for the stairs.

"I'll be biddin' you good night the noo," he said, "an' thank ye."

When his unwieldy gait had at last reached the top of the stairs, Tom and Jim eyed each other for a moment.

"And that," said Tom, "is all we'll get on *that* subject."

"And somehow I respect him for it," Jim finished.

The next morning the strains of "Hunting Tower" rose as usual as a tocsin when Jim was dressing, and when he reached the kitchen he found Duncan, his hair neatly brushed, his bruises much eased and his general demeanor blithe. There was already a good smell of cooking breakfast in the air and Jim drew a breath of relief. The strange events of the past night had evidently changed color by the alchemy of sleep.

"I'm hungry as a hunter, Duncan," Jim began, "and a very good morning to you, by the way."

"Good mornin' to you, Master Jim, an' as to hunger, I'm thinkin' I could eat a boar meself. It just struck me when I woke up that last night I had no dinner, so I started early on the flitch an' corn bread an' I'm what you might call half-filled up now. Sit you down an' have a try at them."

As always it was tasty with the corn bread light as a feather and Jim was well on his second plate when the others appeared. Peggy had been coming down to breakfast since all danger from her burns was evidently past. Her eyes were sparkling as she sat down beside Jim.

"I've just been *thinking*," she began.

"Now would you think it possible?" Tom murmured.

"Don't tease, Tom. This is serious," she said. "You know, it will be Thanksgiving before long and you said you always have Aunt Polly and Uncle Charley over. Well, we promised the Knoxes a day's visit and they seemed *so* pleased. Do you suppose, Jim, we could ask them, too? I have an idea they aren't asked out much."

166

There were a few seconds of quiet consideration and then Jim said, "I think it would be a real act of kindness and we might find we got some pleasure from it, too. What do you all say?"

Tom was a little dubious but assented and Duncan was already considering the size of the turkey they would need. So it was settled and a note was dispatched by the first rider who went to New Salem, that Mr. and Mrs. James Ryall would be happy to have Dr. and Mrs. Knox come for Thanksgiving dinner, at three, and spend the night if convenient.

The reply was returned by the one who brought the message. It was written in thin, nervous, spidery penmanship, but its meaning was very clear. Dr. and Mrs. Knox would be pleased to enjoy Thanksgiving dinner at three with the Ryall family and with many thanks would come prepared to spend the night.

This plan suddenly took precedence over everything else in Peggy's mind. Her full role as the Mistress of The Richlands would now be exercised. She got Jim and Duncan, as they had time, to put in the big boards in the dining-room table; she measured the long tablecloths that Jim's mother had kept in the big secretary drawers; she counted napkins and knives and forks.

"Now don't get too tired, darling," Jim would adjure her often. But she only laughed at the thought. She was enjoying the first real taste of preparing for hospitality. As the time drew near, even the men took on an added excitement. For Christmas they always went to Aunt Polly's but Thanksgiving had always been the Ryalls' day. Duncan moaned a bit over Dr. Knox's Temperance principle.

"We'll not get even a wee nip when he's around. Uncle

Charley always sneaks a swallow himself. Well, well, the *barn's* a cozy place for a few men to discuss the crops sometimes." He winked at Jim who appeared not to notice.

Jed Burke, the carpenter, dropped in often after his early supper to show designs he had made for the new corncrib and also the granary, separated from it, where Jim was planning in his own mind to store the wheat. For, with new fertilization and working, he was sure the old fields would produce twice as much or more than they were now doing. Jim studied the plans carefully. He wanted the old crib put in better condition, the walls made safer from rats and, in the new one, large bins, more than they had ever had, for the wheat. Without knowing it, his face took on a strained and then, at times, a dreamy look. He was feeling himself Master of The Richlands more than he had ever done.

The mellow autumn days drew on through November as the work outside took up its usual routine. Inside, Peggy was full of plans for Thanksgiving. She and Duncan, who enjoyed it, collaborated on ideas like spiced peaches — or would spiced pears be better? There must be cole slaw, of course, and the bread for the turkey stuffing must not be too fresh.

"I'll bake us a good big batch in the outside oven some days before," Duncan said, "an' don't you fash yourself about a thing, Mistress Peggy. Mind, I've done big dinners before."

It was Peggy, though, who made the guest room ready for the Knoxes and smiled as she thought of the little woman's wistful face. "She's going to have one good visit, anyway," she murmured.

T.R.   M

When Tom was next at the post office, he brought home a legal-looking letter for Jim and another for him also with the squire's address in the corner.

Jim took them with unsteady hands and sat down to read. The squire wrote:

McKelvey may call me a hound dog, the old skunk, but we're good friends and he got right at preparing the papers I asked for. In the big envelope you will find the "Title by Adverse Possession" which ought to satisfy anybody. Next time you're in, stop in and bring contents of other envelope with you and you can sign and pay McKelvey if he puts in a bill. Then you can have an easy mind. I don't think you really needed any of this but I think McKelvey had a good time working on it.

Watson's no good and I scared him out, I think. He's got some money and he's left for Virginia or wherever. I think he had something against Duncan even before the bloody nose. Duncan was likely in some trouble and this dog may bark again. But so far, so good. Respects to your pretty wife.

Your friend,
Squire Higgins

The other envelope had the title and papers of possession. The strain all went out of Jim's face. He took the two envelopes to the old secretary and put them with relief into the inner drawer next to the one in which lay the crushed rose.

All that day, Jim laughed and sang like a school boy. Peggy couldn't believe it and rejoiced, for he had seemed somewhat worried and anxious of late. Each time he came into the kitchen to a meal, Tom sang out, "Behold, the bridegroom cometh," with a few extra lines of his own.

The great day came at last, bright, crisp, just cool enough for a few glancing snowflakes. The great turkey was stuffed and trussed and Peggy looked on it with pride. When she came to the farm, she had taken over the care of the chickens and turkeys and even in June the turkeys led precarious lives since they could not survive wet feet. The chickens paddled and splashed in the rain puddles but the turkeys had to be gathered in to the dry. Peggy had proved a skillful and patient hand. Now, although she had lost some, this magnificient creature, along with many others, had survived by her efforts.

The long table was laid as it had been for the wedding feast, the kitchen was redolent with the beautiful smells of good cooking, the pumpkin pies lay side by side, the turnips and potatos were both being mashed by Duncan's strong arm and over all was the rich, pungent odor of baking turkey and gravy.

Aunt Polly and Uncle Charley got there by two o'clock and sniffed the kitchen air appreciatively. Aunt Polly kissed Peggy on both cheeks and then Jim.

"You got yourself a fine wife, Jim, and no mistake! Duncan, if you don't behave, I'll kiss you, too."

"I'll beat you to it, Mistress Polly," and, with a quick turn toward her, he gave her a hearty smack. Meanwhile Dave stood for a minute shyly and then, muttering something about looking around the barn, went out, with Tom following.

The Knoxes arrived, as though by careful timing, just a shade before three. Little Mrs. Knox, as Peggy and Jim met them at the front steps, kissed her hostess and told again, with moist eyes, how pleased they were to come.

"Did we really understand you that we are bid for overnight?"

"Absolutely," Peggy said. "I have your room all fixed."

"It's a real visit," the little woman said, "and I haven't had one for so long!"

When they were all at the table with the turkey before Uncle Charley, who was a master carver, and Aunt Polly opposite him, Jim said courteously, "Dr. Knox, will you be kind enough to say grace."

"Gladly. Let us bow our heads." Then followed a rather lengthy dissertation on the spiritual grace and the need on all occasions to mortify the flesh. The young men squirmed in their chairs and Duncan, who had already brought in the turkey, looked at it anxiously and curled a bitter lip. The prayer went on. When the Amen finally came, Aunt Polly's voice, crisp and firm, was heard.

"As the oldest here, Jim, may I add a short grace to the doctor's?"

"Of course," Jim said, surprised.

Aunt Polly spoke.

"Let us give thanks! We give thee thanks, O Lord, for every mouthful of good food we'll eat today. It all came first of all from Thee. We thank Thee for the kindly fruits of the earth and all the good men and women who work with them in fields and kitchens. Bless us all as we sit around this table. May we know love and joy and good appetites. Amen." Then with a swift change of tone, she added, "Now get right at that bird, Charley, or it will be too cold to eat!"

There was no doubt but that Aunt Polly had broken the ice. While Dr. Knox looked first a bit shocked and later dashed at her prayer, he was soon swamped in the loud merriment that surrounded him, and most of all with the smell and the delicious taste of the viands with which Duncan heaped his plate.

"Really! This is far too much! Really — you must not — remember I'm — really — I mean — I —"

Duncan kept on and after he had seen the good doctor put away his third plate, Jim decided the mortification of the flesh was easing a bit. When the pumpkin pies came, there were groans of repletion and yet no one refused. "Who ever made these?" little Mrs. Knox said, her eyes shining as they had not for many days.

"I did them all myself. Duncan can do them as well, but he let me because I have a very special crimp I put around the edges. Do you see, Dr. Knox?" Peggy asked.

"I do, indeed. I'm afraid to eat it because it's so pretty."

His wife spoke low to Peggy. "He's so different just now. I suppose he'll go back to his old self tomorrow, but oh, my dear, we've had one wonderful day and even if he's stern and lost in his theology again, I'll always be able to remember this."

There were cracked black walnuts at the table after it was cleared, largely by Pete who had borne a good basket home for the Bumpers before the big family feast, just as he had also shelled the walnuts from the big tree outside the kitchen window a week ago, as his stained, brown hands showed. There were also riddles and old stories before the low glow of the big fireplace and, of course, Duncan entertained them with songs and Scotch anecdotes.

Though declining more food, the boys were ready for a bedtime snack and everyone followed after Dr. Knox's long "worship prayer," for Duncan had guessed the weight well and there was plenty of what he called the "bubbly-jock" left over.

By the time the fun, the food, the general happiness had lessened Dr. Knox's sternness a little bit, his wife's eyes were bright and her whole face had something on it like a flush. It made her look like a desirable little woman.

"I know you must be very tired and if you would like I'll show you up to your room now," Peggy said later on. "I think we'll be going up soon, too."

The pale little flush on Mrs. Knox's cheeks actually became a blush. "Why, my dear, that would be so kind if you would. Wouldn't it, Dr. Knox?"

So they went up to what Peggy and Jim wickedly hoped would be complete forgetfulness of the mortification of the flesh and very kindly hoped the old room would hold a renewal of love.

When the Knoxes left the next morning, their thanks was almost pathetic. She, especially, had actually changed. She whispered to Peggy, "Oh, my dear. You wouldn't believe what this has meant. I mean I couldn't tell you all that happened — it's been so long —" Her voice trailed off in an embarrassed smile.

Aunt Polly and Uncle Charley left in a few days taking with them a little basket of what Duncan called very good "leavin's." Dave seemed eager to get away. "I can't understand this fellow. He seems to like us. You'd think he'd like the more excitement you have here. Well, so be it! We're glad to have him. It won't be long till Christmas, an' then, Duncan, you can fatten up the biggest bird for our house. Are you well, child?" she added to Peggy.

"Couldn't be better!" Jim answered with his arm around her.

No one would believe how many pieces of work there are to do on a farm as the winter gathers in. Jim had decided to leave the new corncrib and the other granary until spring, but there was wheat to be taken to the mill in New Salem with its rich, creamy odors and great rolling belts; there were trips to the Four Corners and days when Peggy felt compelled to go to her father's to clean his house and, as she said, "cook up" for them a little. Inside at home, she used the last of the cucumbers and some pumpkins to make pickles and preserves, and added these to the rows of jellies and jams already on the pantry shelves.

Outside, the men prepared bags of seed corn and bags of regular corn for buyers, they went over the fields, they mended holes in the chicken house and built a large new hog trough when, to their horror, they discovered that the young bull had broken his chain, gone on a rampage and kicked the old one to pieces. His getting loose was a serious matter and Jim talked it over with the others. "Of course, he's young now, but you can see already how much ginger is in him. I'd sell him to the first bidder. We don't need him. We have all the cows we need."

"I'll tell you who would like him. That's your carpenter man. He spent a lot of time leaning on the fence watching him. He is a pretty beast for a bull," Tom said.

"A carpenter wanting him! Why on earth?"

"Well, you see, back of the Four Corners he and his brother's family have a nice piece of land and this fellow is interested in cattle. I'll bet he'd buy the young bull. What would you ask?"

"I'd sell him cheap before he gets any bigger. I don't know; I guess fifty or so. Why don't you ride over and strike a bargain and keep your winnings?" Jim laughed.

"I'd like that," Tom said. "I may just do that," he added.

In the fields there was discussion of sorts. The cornstalks were cleared and it was decided to sow oats there. The greatest wheat field was carefully raked and spread with lime. One bare field was to lie fallow with the red clover in it, perhaps. There was to be one field of barley, for Duncan begged for it.

While the men were discussing, finishing up the fall ploughing, harrowing, putting seeds where it was time for them to go, Pete was making a mountain of corncobs to start the winter fires. The men between jobs chopped and sawed wood until the pile of it looked as though it would never end. But they knew no amount was enough.

Peggy, with deft fingers, designed tiny christmas gifts for all, knitted ties, a pen wiper for Jim who had to do a good deal of writing and a soft knitted scarf for Aunt Polly's neck. They went in two conveyances: Jim and Peggy in the buggy as the easiest, and Tom and Duncan in the spring wagon along with the great turkey all ready for the last hour in the oven. There were pies and jellies which Aunt Polly professed to scorn.

"Bringing food in to us as though we were starvin'," she said. "You can just take it back with you, unless," she added to Duncan with a sly wink, "you could just leave the turkey, just for the beauty of the bird!"

Dave seemed to relax there more than he had before and the snug old kitchen with some pine in the windows gave the familiar, homely setting that seemed indeed to make it Christmas. They were close with no strangers. Even Peggy's father and uncle had declined to come. "We'll just roast a fat hen, mash some taters and turnips an' then smoke our pipes an' have a quiet nap. Thank ye, Aunt Polly, but we would rather be to ourselves today."

They ate an early dinner and left soon after so they could make it home by early night. The little gifts were all received with delight and a last thanks and surprise, for Aunt Polly had knitted a tiny hood and jacket and from old bed clothes had fashioned a little blanket and two tiny night-gowns with stitching around the collars. When displayed, there was laughter from the men, even from Jim, at the smallness of them all. But also from the boys there were half-shamed tender exclamations as though for the first time they realized the vague miracle in their midst was a real identity and would prove an actual little living crea-ture one day among them all.

The men sang in the crisp air as they all drove along toward home. Aunt Polly had sniffed the clouds from her front door as she saw them off and did not give the heavens a good report.

"No smell of snow in the air yet and last year it was skimpy. I like a good snow before Christmas. Good for the fields and for the rest of us, too."

"Wait for February and you'll get it," Tom sang out. "Keep well, Aunt Polly!"

When they got home, the men found that for once Bum-per had done what he was told. The cows had been milked and all the stock bedded. After bowls of Duncan's good soup reheated, everyone said "Happy Christmas" again and went to bed.

Peggy spoke before she slept. "The doctor himself isn't quite sure, but he thinks it won't be until May. Could be last of March or first of April, he says, from what I told him. Wasn't this a nice day?"

"Lovely. You saw the letters from the Knoxes? I left them for you but someone moved them. I found them later. We did a wonderful thing for him but he sounded as stern in a way as ever."

"Yes, I read them. She's the one, though, who has the twinkle in her eyes, now. Jim, do you think a boy or girl would be best for the first?"

Jim rolled with laughter. "You're speaking of the Knoxes, I presume?"

"Oh, you tease. As if I would ever — as if — you know perfectly well I'm asking *you*."

"What would you like?"

"Oh, a boy first for you and then next, oh Jim, a little girl with blue eyes and curls. Wouldn't you?"

"Darling, if I just have you I don't care too much about anything else.

The winter months moved on. Aunt Polly, exhorting the elements, still did not get her snow, only little, light, promising falls which disappeared in a few hours.

The men mended harness in the barn, enlarged the sheepcote, mended leaks here and there and finally scattered the manure and lime over the fields in case Aunt Polly's petitions for snow were suddenly answered.

But the quiet, even weeks advanced. The touchy little

bull was led away one day by his new owner, showing Jim's wisdom in getting rid of a later danger when there might be children around. "Children," he often whispered to himself, smiling.

They didn't try to go to the New Salem church again because, after rains and several freezes, the roads were too rutty but Jim and Tom often went to town and brought home all the news, that of Duncan being saltiest of all. It was Jim, of course, who thought of the hat. Into the spinster's genteel parlor he went one day after signing all his papers and bought for his wife a little blue velvet concoction which tied under the chin with one, lone, winter rose as added beguilement. He carried it home in triumph and gave it to Peggy with unsteady hands. Aunt Polly was already there and was speechless even as Peggy. Then the latter bore it to her own room, Jim following, to try it on and after set it on one of the great posts of the bed.

"So I can see it, even at night!"

By mid-March, spring was apparent to all the senses. After days of fairly light snow, the ground was bare, and from the great fields seemed to rise up a strange, earthy fragrance. It could not have been named. It was delicate and rich at the same time; there were early flowers, too, surprising one suddenly by their definite perfume as they bloomed here and there along the farm paths. By April a pulse of awakening, of soft excitement, stirred in the big orchard, even in Peggy's body.

The early May blossoms had flowered when one day Peggy gave a short scream, quickly hushed. Tom was on his horse in a moment and was gone for the doctor. Jim was white and terrified. Aunt Polly kept uttering

platitudes and making great pretenses that men were only
in the way at a time like this. But her face looked drawn
before the doctor came and Peggy couldn't bear Jim out
of her sight.

"I never thought it would be so — so bad," she kept
whispering.

"Nor I," said poor Jim, despairing.

Then they heard the quick hooves and in a minute the
doctor's hearty voice as Jim went to meet him.

"Now, keep your head on and all will be well," he said,
washing his hands at the kitchen bench. "Take me to her
and we'll see what we can do. Aunt Polly here? Good!"

Once in command in the bedroom, he had Aunt Polly
his slave in a minute.

"Get out, Jim," he said. "You're in the way now, but
Peggy will be seeing you soon."

Jim went down and shook hands with Duncan not
knowing what he did. He would have chopped wood if
Tom had not stopped him for the noise. He hurried to the
barn and raced back again to see if there was any word yet.
He ate Duncan's soup automatically. He listened and
groaned at the foot of the stairs. Near night, Aunt Polly
brushed past him, teeth gritted. "They ought to chain
every husband to the outside of the bedroom door," she
said sharply, "that's what!"

The tears rolled down Jim's face. Tom and Duncan
kept watch in the kitchen through the strange night.

In the gladness of the spring morning, a tiny cry was
heard, and finally the doctor came down and slapped Jim's
shoulder.

"Well, there's a new Master of The Richlands just

arrived. Make way for Aunt Polly now. She'll be coming down like an army with banners to show off the baby."

"But — but Peggy, will she be well?"

"Fine, when she gets two or three weeks' rest. Just take good care of her."

"And she'll be all right again?"

"Yes, she will!" Then he added, under his breath, "The question is, will *you* be." To Jim he said aloud, "Stop in next time you're in town, and congratulations now on a fine little son!"

Chapter VII

Everyone said there had never been such a baby! Aunt Polly said it and she was grudging in family praise. Tom and Duncan acted as though they had never seen anything so little and bewitching before and made strange awkward overtures to attract its attention. Dave and Uncle Charley rode over to behold the wonder but would not venture into Peggy's bedroom. Aunt Polly brought the baby down clucking her lips with pride as she did so. And Jim! He sang and whistled every day at his work, and when he could he rushed upstairs to hold the wee one against his breast before he laid it back beside Peggy.

"We must name him soon," she said, "and I insist upon Jim."

"Another Jim?"

"Well, Duncan says we could call him Jamie for short. He says it's a nice Scotch name. James and Jamie. Let's call it settled."

"You look so pretty lying there with the baby beside you. If I'd lost you —"

"I guess there was a good deal of trouble. I could hear the doctor talking low to Aunt Polly. Oh, well, it's all over now, and you have us both."

Peggy was a long time, it seemed, getting back her strength. Pete, whose mother had babies like kittens, watched with concern. He spoke of it once to Jim out in the wheat field. "I don't understand about Mistress Peggy being still so weak. Now my mother just goes to bed and gives funny grunts and my father gives her drinks of water, and all at once she gives a *big* grunt and then we hear the baby crying. My father brings the big tin washbowl and he an' my mother washes the baby and the next day she's up and around as usual."

"I know, Pete, but you see, your mother is a big strong woman and she's had many babies and Mistress Peggy is young and small and this is her first child. That makes a big difference. She'll be all right soon."

Pete seemed satisfied though still a bit puzzled. Jim was right on all counts, however, for there came a day when Peggy looked rosy again and began to trip around the house as she used to do, only now with proud new little tasks connected with Jamie in his cradle. The day even came when Aunt Polly reluctantly left, pausing and peering with moist eyes at the baby. Then she kissed Peggy and said good-by to Duncan, Pete and Jim, for Tom was to drive her home. She kissed Jim last of all, drawing him aside. "Now mind, Jim, you lie on your own side of the bed for a good long spell. That sweet child has been through something."

Jim promised, grinning, and put a little purse in her hands. When she demurred he said, "Just for love and good luck, and thanks for little Jamie."

They missed Aunt Polly's keen, sharp bits of wisdom and humor which seemed, as Duncan put it, to tone up the spirits like a drink of hard cider. But there were many things to take up their minds. For the great spring awakening of the fields and woods had come, sending waves of quickening new life abroad. There was an orchestration of sounds, too — the doves in the early soft break of morning and the first birds, the faint bleat of sheep from a farther field, the whinnies of the horses, the muted moos from the cow stable, with Shep's soft first barks greeting the rising household. And oh, the other sounds that made Jim's heart turn over with thankfulness and joy, the little hungry cries of Jamie waiting to be nursed.

Pete was delegated to help Peggy with the household tasks and the three strong men began the work of the spring, heavy, even though the winelike air buoyed them up. As they bent their backs to the ploughing, Tom growled, "We need Dave. What the devil is he staying away now for? Uncle Charley just has one small field ploughed for potatoes and a garden spaded up and look what we have. And we can't ever count on Bumper. Why don't you ask Dave to come back?"

"You ask him," Jim said.

So, on a gentle spring evening, Dave walked into the kitchen. Peggy was sitting by the table, nursing Jamie and Dave's eyes swept past her to the baby. There was no lightning flash as there had been before. Instead, Dave said, "Hello, Peggy," in his natural voice and bent over the better to see the child.

"So what have we here? He's a good one and the very spittin' image of you, Jim."

"Isn't he, though?" said Peggy proudly. "Feel how heavy he is already, Dave."

So Dave awkwardly held him and gave him hurriedly back.

"He's a big fellow, all right," he said.

And in the moment, the old scars were miraculously healed. Dave sat comfortably now among them, not looking at Peggy with burning eyes but watching every movement of the little child with something like reverence.

"I got Uncle Charley all fixed up and then I had a feeling he liked to do his own bit of work from then on, so I figured you could use an extra pair of hands here."

"And just couldn't we!" Jim said. "We're certainly glad to see you, Dave."

As in other times, the three brothers ambled out through the farm paths, discussing the way they should apportion their work, estimating the apple crop from the blossoms, and pronouncing upon the weight of the old sows and the young piglets.

"I'm still sort of set on the corncrib idea," Jim said hesitantly. "There's a carpenter been out and can fix up the old one, enlarge it a bit and then build a sort of granary beside it."

"Well, I'm all for that," Dave said. "From all you've told me about fertilizing, if the fields don't produce a bumper crop of wheat, too, then I'm mistaken. What made you think of the manure, Jim? Father never used it."

"I know. But it struck me we might have a sort of gold mine going to waste in that huge old manure pile. And lime is cheap. So we spread it all on."

Tom laughed. "Yes. A savory bit of work, that, but look how things are sprouting up already. Jim, here, read about it in the *Farm Journal*, so of course he couldn't rest till we'd tried it. He's got another bee in his bonnet, too."

"How's that?" said Dave.

"Oh, this is just a crazy idea but I thought it might be nice to put an ad in the Farm paper under the Western Pennsylvania heading: 'Fine wheat and seed corn for sale by the Ryall brothers, The Richlands,' etcetera. Look pretty, wouldn't it?"

"By golly, it would," Dave said. "Father would have liked that. He was always talking about the success of the next generation and now it's here. Little Jamie," he added softly and then, almost in a whisper, "It's good to be back."

They sauntered as they always used to do to the back porch with Sheppie at Dave's side, wiggling· into knots with the pleasure of being close to his favorite master, and Duncan, in high feather over the turn of events, greeted them and set a bedtime snack before them.

"Mistress Peggy left her good nights to you and ʻhas taken Master Jamie up to bed. She's still a wee bit doncie but getting stronger by the day. Pete has carried the candles an' gone to his own room, so sit you down now like old times for a bite and a sup."

The next day, since Dave's strong arms were on one of the ploughs, as he reminded them his furrows were the straightest of them all, Jim decided to ride into New Salem, get a few things Peggy needed for little Jamie and herself and, while in the big General Store, settle the year's accounts with the General there. Then he would have a chat with the Squire and perhaps, most important, stop in to see the doctor as he had been requested to do.

He explained all this to Peggy when the baby woke early, and then, with his arms about her during a rapturous kiss, urged her to take things easy as Duncan could get dinner now that Dave was in the fields. He told the boys his plan during a quick breakfast and then cantered off down the farm road, whistling as he went. The day was bright with a bracing snap to it that added to the pleasure of riding into the small, steady breeze. Jim made good time and by ten o'clock was tying his horse to the long, iron hitching poles which ran between wooden posts in front of the store. When he went inside, the General himself met him, full of congratulations and good wishes.

"Ah, that pretty little wife! And now she's brought you a fine little son! Well, well!" He shook hands over again. "The Ryalls produce good men! Good men! Father to son! Allow me to send a small gift to the child. Just come this way."

Jim was led to the far middle counter and a large box was lifted from the shelf. "This is so very kind of you, General. I want to buy a few things which my wife has listed here."

"We'll get to that later. Now," fumbling with his big hands among soft little garments, "this little 'sack,' they call them, wearable up to a year, is my small gift. Now what else, Jim, on your own list?"

He was deeply touched by this kindness of the General's and made his purchases quickly with a glow in his heart. "Now — I thought — for my wife —"

"The very thing! Just come in by stage from Philadelphia." Another big box came down and from it the General drew two, soft, fleecy nightgowns. "Just right for a nursing mother. Open down the front, you see."

"Expensive?"

"Well, in a manner of speaking, but mind, you have a pretty little bride who's given you a son. Is anything too good for her? This trimming round the neck is called 'rickrack,' blue on one, pink on the other. These are warm and cozy, mind!"

"I'll take the two," Jim said recklessly. "A box of saleratus and six yeast cakes from the other counter and I've finished my list, General. And thank you again for your gift. If you can do everything up in a small package, I'll be obliged. I'm riding and it has to go in a saddlebag."

"Very good!" said the General.

"Then," Jim went on, "I thought if you had time we might settle our accounts today. The New Year weather is so precarious."

Then, for the first time, the General's ruddy visage clouded, as though a chilly draft had passed over it.

"Settle accounts *today?*"

"If you are ready. It's just a year since I left the Academy and from then on I've taken over all the farm accounts. I look for heavy crops this year and I'd like to do my bookkeeping as well as you do yours. Of course, if it isn't convenient today and you'd like more time —"

"Well, I must say, you took me a little by surprise. Your father and I never had any trouble about accounts —"

"And I'm sure we won't," Jim put in. "Shall we say, I'll come in again in about two weeks? If that would suit you? The reason I feel strongly about not waiting for

New Year's was this paper.'' He held it out to the General.
"My father's last comment:

> 'Did not get settlement with the General as weather too in-
> clement at our usual time. General suggests we wait one
> more year.' ''

"Yes, yes," the General said, lacking his bombastic
voice. "Very moving. In two weeks I'll have my books
in order for you, Jim. You may be right. My regards
now to your wife and the rest."

"And many thanks to you, sir."

Jim untied his horse and rode slowly up the street. He
had a feeling the accounts had been loosely kept with his
father always coming out at the little end of the horn, so
to speak. His own report would be accurate but he hoped
there would be no hard feelings in the reckoning. He
reached the doctor's and found the front door open and
the doctor visible making his endless little papers of
powders at his desk. Jim walked through, smiling, and
the doctor looked up and grasped him by the shoulders.

"Well, Jim! I've been expecting you. Sit down. I
need to have a little talk with you. How is your family?"

Jim glowed. "Peggy is quite chipper now and Jamie,
as we call him, is as healthy as can be."

"Good!" The doctor stared at the ceiling so long that
Jim was frightened.

"Is anything wrong you haven't told me? With Peggy,
or the baby?"

"It's a hard thing, Jim, to break this to you, but I think
it's got to be done. When you first brought Peggy in here
I told you she was very small-boned and a birth would be

hard for her. How hard I didn't realize until this child came. Now, I feel bound to say this to you, though it all but kills me to do it. I could be wrong but my experience tells me that it would be very dangerous for her to have another child."

"You mean she might not live through it?"

"I feel it would be taking a great chance."

Jim sat very still, his face white, then he brightened. "But, doctor, when I have my wife and my fine little son, I can be content without more children. Don't look so sad for me."

The doctor laid his strong, bony hand, which nad ushered so many babies into the world, on Jim's knee. "My dear boy, of course you could, but do you not realize that you will have the hard part of partial continence to play in keeping Peggy safe? You are young and strong and virile and desperately in love with your wife — I've watched you. Now, I know a few things, not too many, but everything I know that will help you, I'll tell you. Now let's talk the thing over. And this time, don't *you* look so sad!"

They talked man to man, of intimacies too precious to be shared under other conditions. Sometimes Jim blushed, but the doctor persisted. Together they tried to build a wall of safety around Peggy.

"Now," continued the doctor, "perhaps the best help I can suggest is this: There are times in a woman's cycle when it will be reasonably safe to continue your marital relations. Make the best use of them. There are times when she is most sensitive. Avoid these. I will explain both as well as I can. One or two other little suggestions I have already given you. I may say that nature is stronger than we are and nothing you can do or refrain from doing will be completely successful, but you will at least go a long way toward keeping your wife safe."

"But — but won't she think it strange if I — neglect her?" Jim asked in embarrassment.

"Not if you take my advice. Give her plenty of kisses and caresses. Some women would rather have that than the other anyway. Besides, after a hard day in the fields, you won't need much excuse."

When Jim left, the color had come back to his face though his eyes looked strained. The doctor went with him to the post while he untied his horse. "This is not the end of the world, Jim. I know other men who for other reasons have to keep an extra bed warm. Good luck now! And I think all will be well."

Jim had expected to make a few other calls, but in view of his mental state he decided to get on to the Squire's and eat his lunch with the old bachelor there, perhaps a cup of the famous soup which his sister always kept bubbling, French fashion, on the back of the stove.

He found the Squire as always eager to receive or impart news, his white hair like a tousled halo around his face.

"Come in! Come in! Now, Jim you never need to bring any lunch along with you *here*. Come sit down. I'm just at *my* soup."

The hot brew, better even than Duncan's, revived him. "Oh, that's what I needed!" Jim replied. "There's sort of a spring chill in the air." And before he knew it two tears had appeared. He wiped them quickly away but the Squire had seen them.

"Hear you have a fine little son out there. Everything

all right with him and Peggy?" His sharp old eyes looked hard at Jim.

"Why, they're both just fine!" Jim countered.

"And what else is on your mind? I'm an old bachelor but I've seen an awful lot of life. Have some more soup and decide whether you want to tell me your problem or not. Nothing told me in confidence ever goes any further. Heard anything more about Watson?"

"Not a thing. Duncan seems more at peace, too."

The Squire leaned back from the table and laughed until he shook. "I swear the night the three of them were in here, I thought they'd lift the house from its foundations. I wouldn't have missed it for the world. When I'd got rid of all the noise, Watson was meek as a lamb. I'd put the scare of hell into him. Then Duncan preached a sermon. Did he tell you? That was when I rolled off the chair. The Harbisons are getting their farm back, for Watson cheated them right and left. They're both old and they want to end up on the old place."

"You think, then, we've got rid of Watson for good?"

"Well, I mightn't just say that. As Mr. Shakespeare puts it, 'We've scotched the snake, not killed it.' He's still got something in his craw about Duncan. If you only *could*, Jim, get him to tell you the real story of it. And now, what's your own? If you care to e-lu-ci-date?"

Jim smiled for the Squire was noted for his big words but the blue eyes under the wild, white hair were very kind and tender.

"If you never tell anyone. The doctor had just broken it to me before I came here that Peggy could never have another child. That is, it might endanger her life. You can draw your own conclusions around that."

The Squire went over to the small fire that he kept burning except in extreme heat and stood with his back to Jim.

"Dear boy," he said at last, the words coming strangely from his lips, "long, long ago I had a pretty wife. I lost her and I've been a bachelor all these years. Any sacrifice is small compared to keeping your wife. God bless you!"

Jim rode on at last, strangely cheered by his visit with the Squire and glad to get home and find Dave's hearty strength taking over much of the work as the routine of the summer advanced. By the end of June, the oats were two and a half feet tall and the corn four inches. It should be knee-high by the fourth of July, the boys reminded each other, and they mowed the first crop of hay with pride for it was a big one.

The christening of Jamie was the high spot of the summer for the family. In a long, tucked, white muslin dress, with infinite rows of fine stitching, and a little bonnet to match, he was borne up the aisle of the New Salem church one bright Sunday on his proud father's shoulder. There was a full half-circle of parents with babies before the pulpit and Jim stifled a smile as he overheard the General whispering in the vestibule to another Elder, "Well, a good crop this year!"

The baptismal ceremony was lengthy in the extreme. Dr. Knox rolled his remarks unctuously and made the questions as long as possible. By the time it was ended all the babies were crying. "And no wonder!" Jim said as they started back home again with Jamie in his mother's lap, pacified by a bottle. "That man, that Dr. Knox, takes all his duties pretty seriously, I'd say."

"I wonder if the visit to us didn't change him a little."

192

"Maybe, but I think we'd better have them back again."
At which both laughed.

And the months rolled on. By August, the corn was starting to ear and there was another big hay harvesting. This, Peggy particularly loved. The fresh smell of the sunny field, tinged faintly with clover, stored in the great hay mow.

By October, the corn was in the crib and the new granary ready for the next year, with the late September planting of wheat already showing green.

And the winter came and the big fire roared and the men relaxed a little from the summer's strain. The feast days came as usual and before anyone could believe it, the baby, Jamie, looked like a little boy, toddling among them, making sounds like words as each one called to the other to comment on how unbelievably smart he was. And May, with all its springtime beauty, brought his first birthday. It was like a summer day, with a warm balminess that stirred the senses, while riding over the heavens as if to waken cravings in all lovers was a full moon.

Duncan had baked a special little cake for Jamie, Dave and Tom who were both clever at whittling had, with their skillful knives, achieved a little horse from a block of wood, and Jim himself, some time before, when he had, with tact and firmness, settled his account with the General, had also bought a toy against this day, a tiny wagon. So, the birthday supper, the first one, was a delight to them all, not only to the child. At last, with his new treasures, he gave them each a kiss and went to bed.

Peggy came down again when he was settled, for the night was still warm and sensuous. She and Jim sat in a close embrace on the porch while the boys checked the barn again and Duncan and Pete played one of their endless games of checkers. At last they had all gone upstairs.

"Don't stay up too long, you moon-gazers," Tom called. "We've got work tomorrow."

"It's so beautiful tonight," Peggy said.

" 'Ah, moon of my delight, that knows no wane,' " Jim quoted softly.

"What was that?"

"Oh, some poetry we had to read at the Academy. I can't quote any more, but those lines always stuck in my head."

"I suppose we should be going up," she said hesitantly.

"I'm sure of it!"

There was a long, last embrace and then he put out the candles except her own and the one with which he guided her. He stopped outside their door. "I'll go into Father's room," he said, as he kissed her, and went next door quickly. But he couldn't go to sleep and he knew by the sounds Peggy was also awake. At last he heard her voice.

"Jim! It's so lovely! Can you hear me?"

"Of course."

"The moon is just sailing right past my window."

"Silence!"

"It's all so beautiful tonight, but I'm so alone." There was a catch in her voice.

For a year, Jim had used every suggestion the doctor had given him and all his own iron will. But this was too much. He leaped out of bed and in a few moments, was holding her close in his arms. Ah, moon of my delight —

It was only two months later that she looked at him, half-proudly, half-shy. "Jim, I'm pretty sure I'm pregnant. From that night — you know, Jamie's birthday. When the moon was so lovely and I called to you. I'm a little ashamed about that."

For a moment Jim could not speak. Then, "Are you *sure?*"

Peggy giggled. He had kept all fright from her. "Well, I guess as sure as a woman can be. You look so strange. You're not *angry* about it, Jim?"

He put his arms around her. "Good God, no! I'm not angry. I'm just a little afraid you're not able for another birth so soon."

"It will be nearly two years. That doesn't seem so soon."

"Well, darling, I'll go in to see our good friend the doctor. He may have some little powder he will want you to take, or even see you. I'll find out all his ideas, and meanwhile let's just keep it our secret. Agreed?"

"Of course."

The other boys teased Jim about his dark spirits when he was in the fields, but they stopped when they found he couldn't talk at all about Peggy. They sensed there was something wrong, but saw that when he was with her, if anything, he was more tender and free about his love than when alone with them. It was serious, then; something he was keeping from her.

When Jim walked into the doctor's office one August day, he didn't speak, but his white face told his story.

"I had really thought you might come before this," the doctor said.

"I was sure I had myself completely under control. I slept a lot in my father's old room next to ours. I made all sorts of excuses. But that wonderful night in May when the moon was full, she called to me. She was lonely and it broke all my defenses down." He leaned forward, the tears running down his cheeks.

"You're only human, Jim. You've done your best. And bear up. Don't despair. I'm not God. I make plenty of mistakes and I hope this will be one. With Aunt Polly we ought to be able to bring this one through safely. Think about that. Say your prayers and keep her happy. That will have an effect. I think you'd better bring her in soon so I can see how things are going."

After that visit it was decided the baby would come the last of February. Aunt Polly, scanning her almanac, predicted that her long-awaited snow would come then, too, though no one paid much attention. Peggy, buoyed up on that trip by a visit to the ice cream parlor and lunch, actually, at the Stone Hotel — for Jim insisted upon this — made some small purchases happily from the General who now kept his accounts with The Richlands carefully and treated Jim with a wary respect.

As the fall turned into winter and the dark days began, there was incredible laughter and song in the big kitchen. Jim had finally shared his secret with his brothers and Duncan and with their arms about his shoulders they had brought him cheer. "She'll be fine, Jim! Never you fear. And we'll all try to keep her spirits high."

So, with games and the parched corn in the evenings and old riddles and stories and all the best of Duncan's songs, you would never have guessed that a cloud hung over the old rafters and a moaning was at times in the chimney wind.

As February began to close in, it was thought wise to bring Aunt Polly over so she would surely be on hand. They were all waiting to greet her, but when Dave returned he did not have Aunt Polly. Instead he had a young girl whose braids of hair wound about her face showed when she laid aside her bonnet and stood shyly before them. Jim's face was white. Without Aunt Polly was there any hope?

"I'll tell you all about it." Dave began. "Aunt Polly's been sick. She says she's fine now and can do just fine for herself and Uncle Charley, but she hasn't enough strength to come over and — and help here. So she's sent this young girl, Phoebe, who Uncle Charley found up at the Four Corners post office one day looking for some work. He was awful glad to get her, for Aunt Polly was at her worst then. Now she's sent her over to us." He introduced them all, and when she smiled at Jamie the child ran straight into her arms. "I — I like children," she said softly, "and I'll be glad to help you all. You must be very disappointed about Aunt Polly for she's so good at birthing. But don't be afraid, Mrs. Ryall; I've had some experience, too, and know how to work with a doctor when the time comes."

Peggy looked at her, the fright in her eyes lessening. "It will be nice to have a young girl to talk to. There are so few around here. I'm sure you will help me, Phoebe. Let's see about her room, Jim."

So Phoebe was quietly established in the small spare room and also in the household. Jamie was at once her slave, and the others, saying little, still looked on her with favor and, in a sisterly way, Peggy talked with her at the upstairs grate which Jim insisted must be lighted in the evenings. They spoke of intimate things until they heard Jim's feet on the stairs.

One night toward the end of February, the snow began to fall. By early morning, the ground was covered and the white showers continued. Tom leaped from his bed as did the others, for they had all heard Peggy's first small cry.

"Bring him back, Tom, as quick as you can. Who would have thought of this last night with stars in the sky. I don't like the look of it now. Ride hard. She's started already."

"I'll get him quick if I have to carry him," and Tom rode off at a gallop.

And the snow kept falling.

Phoebe stayed close to Peggy and, strangely, Jim did not resent her presence. She had learned small tricks to ease the first pains temporarily. At each little surcease, Peggy would hold hard to Jim's hand. "I'll try so — so hard to be brave," she said with difficulty.

"Oh, darling, you are. No one could be braver. Oh, I love you so!"

"I — I would so like a little girl, wouldn't — you?"

"I don't care if you're just all right."

Then she would grow white.

The snow kept falling. Before the doctor and Tom got back, a buggy, drawn by a horse, its feet clogged with balls of snow, drew up in their road. Jim rushed out when he heard the wheels and first rescued the poor horse's feet before he looked at the man who got out of the buggy.

"Have you no pity on your horse?" he asked. "I could hear you whipping him and the poor beast can hardly walk. Who are you?" For the snow now covered them both.

"I'm Dr. Knox," the other said with some dignity. "I

would not bother you, but I couldn't get any farther for the snow. I'm not much used to horses, but I was called to see a very sick woman."

"Oh, I'm sorry. Come in, come in. We're in heavy straits, too. My wife is in hard labor and — oh, I think this is the doctor now."

Tom took care of Dr. Knox's horse and the other two, while the doctor hurried into the house, questioning Jim as he went. "Aunt Polly not here?" He gave a low whistle. "But the girl seems good, eh? Says she's helped at births before? Well, she may know something we don't. We'll trust in the Lord, Jim, and do our best. I'm wet and dirty. We lathered the poor horses pretty well. I'll wash up."

He took off his greatcoat on the porch, shaking the snow, and then rolled up his sleeves and washed his hands carefully at the kitchen bench and went at once with his satchel up to Peggy's room. He went about his ministrations tenderly, speaking now and then to Phoebe.

"Doctor?" Jim spoke.

The doctor waved him back. "Just let her know you're near if she asks, but the fewer hanging over her, the better." Her voice was often pierced with pain and outside the snow kept falling. Duncan made soup and brought up bowls of it and buttered bread. Jim refused, but the doctor was sharp. "Drink it, Jim, you'll need it." So the watchers ate what they were told, Jim turning aside that the others could not see his painful efforts to swallow.

The anguished night went on. The doctor seemed never to rest; he eased Peggy's back, changed her position tenderly and sometimes used Phoebe's small hand to help him when he needed a desperate attempt. Peggy's screams had become weaker even as she was herself. About dawn, a small head emerged and then a tiny body. There was a faint cry. The doctor seemed to take little heed. "Take it down to the kitchen and see what you can do," he said to Phoebe gruffly.

"Oh, I'll bring it around."

As she left with the child, Jim drew a great, almost sickening breath of relief and thanksgiving.

"Doctor!" he said. "It's born and Peggy came through it. Isn't she all right?"

The doctor was sweating as he turned to Jim. "My boy, we have another enemy to fear. It's the bleeding."

And even as he looked, Jim saw with horror what the doctor meant.

And the snow still fell, so lightly, so gently, so remorselessly, as they all worked to save Peggy's life. The boys were told. They had watched in amazement as Phoebe had washed and cared for the tiny baby. She had moistened its lips with sugar water until it had feebly licked it. They had seen, some hours later, that the small nursing bottle Peggy had prepared for her child was in slow, delicate use. All the time in between they had given their strength to obey the doctor's orders. They had brought up great blocks of wood from the cellar to put under the feet of Peggy's four-poster, so that she would lie aslant, her head and breast much lower than the rest of her body. For a time, the doctor looked hopeful and raised her gently to take another dose of medicine.

The boys, hoping and praying as best they could in their hearts, went back to take turns at the shoveling, for some sort of path must be kept to the barn so that the cows could be milked and the beasts all fed. By noon, Jim knew that new remembrances were being tried, his own face as white as Peggy's which was now drained of all color.

"I won't give up," the doctor gritted once. But he knew the pulse was very low.

Dr. Knox had asked for a fire in the sitting room so he could enjoy some reading while he was "snowed in," as he put it, for he had looked longingly at the bookcase. Aside from prompt participation at mealtime, he had not entered much into conversation with the others, but had several times, taken part in shoveling the path. They could all see that he was not accustomed to physical work and changed often with him.

That night when the candles were lighted, sending a soft, golden glow through the rooms and falling as though with a special benison upon Peggy, she lay very quiet after once whispering to Jim, "What is it?" "A girl," he replied. "Just what you wanted." She smiled faintly and fell asleep so she did not hear Jim's terrible sobbing.

The candles had not burned very low when the doctor felt Peggy's pulse once more and then laid her hand softly back beside her and turned to Jim.

"It's not all — she's not —?" Jim's lips could not bring out the words.

"She fell asleep with a smile that the baby was a girl. Take comfort in that, and don't ever, ever feel remorse. It was nature's mistake, not yours, that took her life. Now, my boy, come into the other room and I'll give you a powder to help you settle. You must sleep now for there is nothing more we can do."

When the doctor entered the kitchen, Dave was the first to read his face. "Is it — ended?"

The doctor nodded. "Very gently, a few minutes ago. I've got Jim to bed. He's not quite himself until he gets some sleep."

"Good God! Not Peggy! It doesn't seem real." Tom's tears ran down his cheeks.

Dr. Knox slowly grasped the situation. He evidently had not realized how serious the birth had been. "Oh," he said. "Oh, the Lord must have sent me here to be of some comfort in such a time of trouble. I'll go up at once to the young man in his grief —"

"*No!*" the doctor said sternly. "He must not be disturbed. I've put him to sleep and I hope it will last for eight hours or so. I want no one to go near him till then."

"But surely prayer and the words of Holy Scripture will be what he needs most now. 'The Lord gave and the Lord has taken away. Blessed be the name of the Lord,'" Dr. Knox intoned.

"That depends on how you look at it," the doctor said gruffly, starting thirstily to drink what Duncan had set before him.

Dr. Knox looked startled and abashed and Dave spoke into the sharp silence. "I think we'll all of us need a prayer, Dr. Knox, when we've recovered a bit from our shock. The doctor has had a hard time and needs his food now."

A thin little cry sent their eyes upon Phoebe who sat in the rocker beside the fire, cradling the tiny baby against her breast. It had taken sips of sugared water through the day and now weakly, but surely, was mouthing the small nipple that Peggy herself had fastened to a bottle.

"It's watered milk with just a touch of sugar in it,"

Phoebe explained. "If she keeps taking a little of this, I think she's going to be well."

They all settled for prayer later, staying by common consent in the kitchen. Dr. Knox's words were lengthy, bringing in long passages of Scriptures and many supplications. When the men, especially the doctor, had begun to edge about on their chairs, Duncan suddenly, in a faint break of the flow of petition, lifted his voice in words and music they all knew. In a moment, they had all joined him.

> The Lord's my shepherd I'll not want:
> He makes me down to lie
> In pastures green, he leadeth me,
> The quiet waters by.

The voices broke but sang on:

> E'en though I walk through death's dark vale,
> Yet shall I fear no ill . . .

And on to the great climax they sang for themselves, for Jim, for Peggy, lying so quietly above with the little smile still on her lips.

> Goodness and mercy all my life
> Shall surely follow me,
> And in God's house forever more
> My dwelling place shall be.

Even Dr. Knox seemed humbled and grateful for the release of tension the old psalm had brought. He went back to his reading while the kitchen chores were being done. Little Jamie was put to bed and the baby was asleep in its cradle. Outside, the snow still fell. It was then that Phoebe went close to the doctor and spoke to him. His eyes filled up again as did hers. "You're a wonderful, brave girl," he said. "I was going to do it all myself but a woman's hands are better. I'll be with you and help all I can — anything heavy."

The boys tried not to see what they carried up with them, but in an hour they were back. It had been Phoebe's tender hands that had made clean the delicate, once tortured body with Aunt Polly's pink, scented soap; it was Phoebe who found the clothes to be used and put over them the wedding dress; it was she who spread the white linen sheets, the blanket and the feather comforter. There were no signs as they left of the struggle that had been.

"We men still have work to do, Phoebe. We can talk in the sitting room. Keep out of the way as much as possible, and eat something often to keep up your strength." And the gruff doctor did a strange thing. With his eyes wet he leaned over Phoebe and kissed her forehead. "God bless you, my child," he said adding, "we'll let the fire go out up there."

And the snow still fell, lightly now, but persistently. The cold was not bitter but over the sun still hung a dull, gray cloud. This that was happening would be known for years as the great "February Fall."

In the sitting room, the men, their faces gray and hard to hide their emotions, talked it over. It would be weeks, even after the snow stopped, before a conveyance could get through these country roads. By superhuman effort, working in relays, they had kept a good path open to the barn and therefore to the buggy shed which was also the farm workshop. As they decided what had to be done, no voices faltered; only Dave's, "Oh, my God!" broke often into the words. At last he and Tom got into their heaviest coats and went out together, Dave pausing first to look at the baby. "It's doing well," he said.

The sounds from the buggy shed were muted by the snow and its distance from the house. "We'll have to tell Jim," Tom said.

"Of course, as soon as he's awake."

"Maybe he won't stand for it."

"I'm afraid he has no choice," Dave said sadly.

They worked fast and the years about the farm had made their hands skillful. When they had finished, they lined what they had made with softest hay, and when they came down again they bore a soft, white sheet to cover the clover.

The doctor had kept a close check on Jim's pulse but always found it steady. He slept on, a relaxed, natural sleep now, from sheer physical and emotional exhaustion. He woke at noon and sat up suddenly, his eyes wild. The doctor pushed him gently back and began talking in a low voice of all that had been done and all that nature in her mysterious ways would make it necessary for them yet to do. Jim was a man of the fields, of the earth; he listened, and even though his face was like stone, he understood and accepted.

"Is it still snowing?"

"Lightly. But the sun is still covered. I've never known the like in all my years."

"I must see her."

"As soon as you feel like it. You may be a bit shaky when you get up."

He was. When dressed, he held to the doctor's arm until he reached the next door. Then he went in to say good-by to his darling.

When he came out, the doctor urged him to rest a little

longer. He himself would help him downstairs at supper time. Even then Jim staggered a little and apologized when he got to the table.

"I'm not much good just now, boys. But I do — thank you."

Loving hands rested on his shoulders and through the broken sentences they asked him what they had waited to know. "Where, Jim? Where would you want —"

"Under the Maiden-Blush tree, I guess. She liked it best."

So on the day that the first faint light came into the sun, there was a small mound under the Maiden-Blush tree. It had been Phoebe who had given the boys, on their last sad errand, a little pillow and the feather comforter. "It doesn't make any difference, I know, but we'll feel better," she had said with tears.

As suddenly as it had began, the snow stopped falling and in the center of the sun there appeared a small ball of fire with waves of pale light spreading from it. The sky slowly cleared until daytime returned as from the caves of darkness. The doctor grew restless. "I've got to get on as soon as possible. I left a good many sick people behind me."

"Not yet, Doc," Tom said. "If you try too soon, you may break your horse's leg."

So they settled then to an uneasy waiting, for the most part, in silence. Dr. Knox seemed most nervous of all. He sat in the sitting room apparently deep in thought. One day he asked Duncan if he could have supper early as he wished to speak to the family as a whole afterward. Duncan's only lightening of the spirit had consisted in seeing that Shep kept as close as possible to the minister who always tried to move away. Jim had been, for the most part, eating alone when the others had finished and had gone at once to his room. Tonight Dr. Knox asked him especially to remain. So after Jamie had been put to bed and the meal eaten and the table cleared, Dr. Knox rose from his place with a paper in his hand.

"You may all have thought, during these terrible days of grief and problems that have beset this household, that I was merely reading and keeping apart from them. That is not so. I have been praying and thinking, especially now of the days to come. In a short time, the doctor and I will go. There will be left here then this young girl, this most *worthy* young girl, and four men. I have made inquiries from her and from some of the brothers and the facts are, she is alone in the world. She has no place to go, but most importantly, she is desperately needed here. She practically saved the life of this baby. The doctor knows of *no one* who could come to take her place."

He paused and they all looked inquiringly at him. He coughed and fingered his paper nervously. "As I can see it and as I think it has been given me in my prayers, there is only one possible solution: that is for Phoebe to become the wife of one of you, and certainly the father of the children she cherishes would be the most proper one."

"That is a *monstrous* suggestion," the doctor almost yelled. "You are proposing this to him at his weakest, most grief-stricken moment. You ought to be ashamed!"

Dr. Knox did not yield. "I have thought of all this. As I say, I have prayed long and earnestly to be guided aright. I speak in this not as a man, but as God's emissary."

"Emissary be damned!" the doctor growled half under his breath. "I know better than any of you what this young man has been through."

Dave's voice was choked. "Jim, for God's sake, watch what you are doing. Don't let him urge you. Take your time."

"Careful, laddie! Careful!" Duncan said harshly.

Then Jim himself stood up.

"I am the one to speak," he said and his voice was steady, "for I'm the one to make the decision. It has always been true that the Ryall men do not love lightly nor forget easily." He thought of the crushed rose in the drawer. "I have known a great love and somehow it seems easy now to say it before you all. My heart is now cold and may always be." He stopped a moment. "This girl has done for us what we can never forget. If she stays on she will be as safe as with her own brothers, but I realize her reputation would suffer nevertheless. I could not enter into any promises where the word 'love' is involved, but I will give her the protection of my name and that is all."

"Laddie! Laddie!" from Duncan.

"Oh, Jim!" from Dave.

"It *is* monstrous," from the doctor.

Dr. Knox went on. "And you, Phoebe, would you be willing to enter into a bond of matrimony with this young man?"

"Well, you see," Phoebe said softly, "I have no one. No family, no home. This has begun to seem like home to me even though it's been so sad. But oh, most of all, I don't see how I could leave the children!"

"You are willing, then?"

"Yes." Very low.

"Please rise. I have written a few words I think you will be able to say." With no more hesitation he began.

"Do you, James Ryall, take this young girl to be your wife to give her all protection, care and kindness?"

"I do!"

"Do you, Phoebe McNair, take this man to be your husband and promise to treat him and his children with all care and kindness?"

"I do."

"According to the law vested in me by the state of Pennsylvania and as a minister of God, I now pronounce you man and wife."

It was over. Without a word, escaping Dr. Knox's outstretched hand, Jim turned on his heel and went upstairs. The doctor, still muttering imprecations, stood motionless as did the brothers who had risen for the brief ceremony, Dave leaning upon the mantel and Tom staring into the blankness of the window.

"Doctor," the minister said, "I should have two witnesses on this paper. Would you be kind enough to affix your name here, for one?"

"No!" the doctor exploded. "I will have no part in this iniquitous proceeding!" And he left the room, as did Duncan.

The minister for the first time seemed shaken. The paper trembled in his hand as he gazed helplessly about as though wondering what to do next. At last, Dave raised his head in the silence and looked at Phoebe, sitting flushed, tear-stained and a little frightened with the baby snuggled against her shoulder. He watched the movement of a tiny hand and then spoke.

"Tom," he said. "Tom! Listen to me!"

"Yes," Tom said thickly, "what is it?"

"These children have to have a mother and Phoebe has surely been good to us all. I think we should sign that paper."

Tom, followed his eyes and then laid his hand gently on Phoebe's head.

"You may be right," he said.

And the two brothers slowly advanced together to the table and set their names upon the strange document.

Chapter VIII

As the months passed, the household settled into a strange, passive routine. Dave and Tom laughed together betimes and all the men discussed the work of the farm. But Jim, who in a sense had always been the life of the house because of his seniority and his personality, too, was still quiet as though the stony depths of his heart would not soften. The others all wondered that he paid so little heed to the children, especially the baby, little Mary, named for Aunt Polly. But there came a time when the baby inevitably became "a little girl," and it was then all began to worship her. For beauty, nature's gift, lay upon her; on her rosy cheeks and tiny dimpled arm, on her bright blue eyes and the blond curls that seemed to make a bewitching cap for her head. She began to make sounds like words, imitating Jamie. It was then Jim picked her up and held her on his knee and sometimes laughed as she searched his pockets. So there was a small, general lightening of the spirits as Shep patiently allowed the children to ride on his back, when Duncan sang in a funny voice and when Dave and Tom made little toys of wood and paper for "the bairns," as Duncan called them, to play with on the big table before they were put to bed.

For they all marveled at Phoebe's way with them, so gentle and affectionate, but yet so utterly firm. Even now, Jamie at two and a half, and enchanting little Mary, not quite a year, were learning the first lessons which make good children.

"You'll say *please*, Jamie," Phoebe would say in her quiet voice.

"Please."

"That's good."

Sometimes she took Jamie for a walk along the farm road with Mary toddling beside him. One day they met Jim and he joined them, apparently enjoying the children's company. In a short space of silence, Phoebe said, "Jim?"

He looked up startled and stern.

"Yes?" he answered almost harshly.

"I've been thinking and watching you. I wonder if maybe you are just a little *too* proud of The Richlands. If maybe you are *too* set on all your big plans I've heard you talking about with the others. I hope you'll excuse me for saying so."

Jim's voice was hard. "Well, I'll excuse you, of course. But I don't particularly like being watched. Also, I'm the oldest son here, and the biggest responsibility is mine to make The Richlands greater in every way if I can. That I intend to do. I believe it's time we went inside now."

Phoebe said nothing but took the children into the house. There was a change in the atmosphere of the kitchen that night. Phoebe, who was always ready for a game of checkers after her charges were fed and put to bed and in her quiet way lent a gentle wit to the conversation, had nothing to say tonight, even as she helped the children with their little homemade toys. Jim, too, after discussing the next morning's work, was silent. Dave and Tom looked questioningly at Duncan who shook his head. It was as strange a night, the boys felt, as those terrible ones the weeks after Peggy's death. In their own room later they talked things over. They had all grown fond of Phoebe. There were no lightning flashes as there had been before. Instead, her seductiveness seemed to be of the spirit rather than the body. She was indeed to them like a younger sister. But what were the relations between her and the man who was legally, and by mutual promise before a licensed minister, her husband? They knew their brother's iron will and the terrible depth of his passion. They had only to look at him when Peggy had been near him to realize that. And now, would he ever change?

In his own room the same questionings were wrenching Jim's heart. When he thought of any woman in his arms, it was his beloved. Only her. How could it ever be otherwise? But he feared he was not being fair to Phoebe for whom, at least, he had great respect. He regretted his sharp words as she had advised him gently about his overwhelming ambition. That had not been kind. After all she had done and was daily doing for his children, he should never speak a quick word to her. Never. He was struck now with her perception. She had studied him, had read his thoughts and his determination. She was probably right, but the only comfort for his stricken heart lay in his great plans for the crops, for The Richlands. Now, again, the fall — 'How fast the seasons roll,' his father was always quoting — and never had the great fields looked so magnificently fruitful or borne such a yield. He set his face in a hard line. Let come what might. He would fix his thoughts on the farm.

So the days moved on and still there was no sign of any intimacy or even close friendship between Jim and Phoebe. One day, however, he seemed to be studying her.

"Phoebe," he said slowly, "You must need some new clothes — a pretty dress or two and — and the other things. The children will have to have some winter clothing and if Pete takes his term at school, he will need something warm. Would you like to go shopping at the General Store in New Salem and select what you like?"

Her face was radiant. "Oh, Jim! I would love to do that. It would be wonderful!"

"Then we'll call it settled. Would you drive her in when you feel you can spare a day, Tom?"

"Me?" said Tom, while Phoebe's face fell. "Why don't you go yourself?" he asked bluntly.

"I have a very busy week ahead and some papers to fill out. I think it would be better if you went."

"All right," Tom agreed slowly. "I'm a pretty good shopper and if we bankrupt you, it's your own fault, eh, Phoebe?"

"Of course you can charge what you get to my account and don't be sparing. You should have two new dresses, Phoebe."

Phoebe thanked him, but the glow had gone from her face. Jim watched them off the day they left and understood her forced smile. He felt a twinge of conscience but still knew his presence in town with her would, according to the peculiar news osmosis of New Salem, give rise to conversation that would somehow sear his heart. No, it was better for Tom to go.

That evening after the shoppers were back and supper over, all the new purchases were looked at, appraised and pronounced excellent. The clothes were all tried on to great acclaim. All but Phoebe's.

"Now your turn," Dave said to her as she folded the rest and put them in their bags. "Come on, Phoebe. We can't let you off. We've got to see yours, haven't we, boys? Tom, here, got the trip and went to the ice cream parlor, I'll warrant —"

Phoebe cried out, "I never tasted any before. It was past believing good."

"All right, then show your appreciation. Go up and put on *one* of the new dresses at least. You can't put us off."

She stood shy and blushing and looking at Jim. When he nodded, she went upstairs and came down in the new dress. As she stood before them there was quiet at first, for she was changed. She had brought with her only a flannel dress and a couple of calicos which she had been at pains to mend and keep clean. Now she stood before them completely transformed. The dress was a blue merino with a roll of white about the neck. The fit to her form was perfect. But the soft white at the neck was the thing that made her a different person, a shy and lovely lady where a little nursemaid by the fire had been before.

After a moment's silence there was a burst of applause! Tom and Dave and Duncan all shouted their compliments, and Jim smiled and said, "You made a very good choice." This last restrained compliment seemed to please Phoebe most of all and after she had turned round and round about as she was asked to do, she said quietly, "Thank you, Jim," and went back upstairs wearing a small smile as she carefully smoothed the prettiest dress she had ever owned.

As the weeks advanced toward Thanksgiving, there was quiet discussion. It would not be quite a year since the Great Fall of snow had shut them all in with tragedy. Jim urgently suggested they make nothing of the day, only a good dinner as Duncan would be sure to make. But Dave raised a considering voice. "I know that's the way we all feel, but I believe we've got to think of Aunt Polly. She's been shut in so long now and she's well again, and when I rode over last week she said she supposed it was too much to expect for them to come as usual but that she didn't know how she'd bear it on the day itself, just themselves two, when she longed to see little Mary. She's never been away from us this long, has she?"

They talked it all over again. Aunt Polly had been sick all that terrible winter of the snow, and then with warmer weather a resulting bout with rheumatism had attacked her. Now this fall her native resilience had come to her rescue and she was practically her old self again. But could she and Uncle Charley come as to the old feast?

"She says," Dave went on in a lowered voice, "that grief shared is not so sore."

Jim went out and took a long walk around the fields that early evening and came home by way of the orchard. The small mound there under the Maiden-Blush tree was hardly noticeable now and Jim had been wondering about a little marker for it. He stood there a long while and then went back to the house.

They all looked up as he entered the kitchen for they knew the final decision must be his.

"I think we should have Aunt Polly and Uncle Charley over as usual," he said. "I realize that no one should be selfish in his grief."

"Good!" the other men said as one. "We'll have to have the best dinner I can make," Duncan added, "but there will be no songs and jokes, just a quiet family time."

"I suppose we'll not have the Knoxes this year," Tom said irrepressibly.

At the glance Dave gave him, even Tom looked ashamed. "I'm sorry, Jim. I withdraw the question. It was not in very good taste."

Jim's voice was sharp. "Forget it!" he said.

So the plans went on, with Phoebe in a sense unconsulted but still in the heart of the work. She was desperately nervous. She must be sure to do everything just right for Jim's sake and for all of them. This was the first large occasion in which she herself had figured. When Duncan put the extra boards in the dining-room table and showed her where the large tablecloths and the good silver were kept, she followed all his instructions with unsteady hands. She would be glad to see Aunt Polly, but oh, she was frightened. She did her best, however, and with red berries and a few remaining bright leaves she made a little centerpiece for the table. She asked Duncan when she was not sure how to lay the silver, and did a dozen small, extra tasks.

The morning itself was bright and pleasant and the guests arrived early for Aunt Polly wanted to get home again by dark. Her coming had a soothing effect upon them all, like a mother's blessing. She kissed them once around, wiped away a quick tear and settled herself to enjoy the children, especially, of course, her little namesake.

"And wouldn't you know, she looks just like my baby pictures? I brought one along to show you. Here! Lookit!"

They passed it from one to the other exclaiming, for she had spoken the truth. The little child in the old photo had the same curly hair and sunny smile as the small Mary Aunt Polly held on her knee. Somehow, after that, all seemed easier. The prattle and play of the children filled all the conversational gaps, and when at last they sat down at the table and started the meal, there was quiet talk of the state of the crops, the yield of corn and the hopes for wheat. There was no merriment, yet no patent sadness either. Each held his memories in check for the others. Phoebe, eager, nervous, anxious that all would be well, kept passing various viands.

"Sit down, child," Aunt Polly said, "and enjoy your dinner. We can all reach. We're not strangers."

They all sat a little while later beside the fire and felt the tender words unspoken and the close tie that bound them. When Uncle Charley said they must leave, Aunt Polly did not suggest staying on, as had been usual.

"I'll get on home," she said, her voice breaking a little, "but as you see I'm able now to come if you ever need me. About Christmas —" She stopped and looked out the kitchen window. "I don't know. We got through today well and it's done us good, but Christmas is another kind of thing. I have a feeling we'd do better this year to just eat our own dinners at home and make little of it. Except for the children."

"I agree," Jim said, his face showing the strain.

"Well, we'll cross that bridge when we come to it, and it's done me a world of good to see the children. You're doing a fine job with them, Phoebe. Don't let them wear you out."

They were always loath to see Aunt Polly leave, but today everyone looked weary and glad to fall into the family silences which had become frequent. When all was cleared in the kitchen after the evening chores were done and a final snack eaten, everyone went to bed except Jim, who felt he simply couldn't sleep yet, and Duncan, who, perhaps in a mood of sympathy, stayed with him, making a business of arranging the logs in the fire. Jim suddenly realized that he now had, simply and casually, something for which he had often wished, for while fearing to make an issue of it, this was a chance to talk alone with Duncan.

They sat quiet for a time and then Jim began. "You know, Duncan, how close we all feel to you, but we can't help wondering a little about your background and what brought you here at random during a winter storm. I speak of it now in all kindness, not wanting to press you, but because the last week in New Salem I saw the Squire and he told me Watson hadn't gone north at all, as he pretended, but only somewhere near and was back here in his old haunts with plenty of money, apparently, to look round and do a little horse trading. Oh, Duncan, what did you *do* to make you run away long ago?"

Duncan crossed his legs and looked at the burning logs. Then very quietly he said, "I killed a man!"

Jim couldn't speak at once. He only stared with horror. "Tell me how it happened," he said thickly.

"Well, I've kept me own wheesh, as we say. Now it may lighten my heart to tell you my story. I was a wee laddie orphan in Scotland when a fine family, the MacClouds, took me in. They had big land holdings an' a mansion of a house with plenty of help. They was all good to me. Cook let me help her with the vegetables an' taught me many a thing about cookin'. Hannibal, the butler, had me shine the knives an' polish the silver an' later I always took Master MacCloud's early cup of tea up to him an' he sort of took a special fancy to me an' I about worshiped them all. But the mistress had come from Virginia. The master had been on a business trip an' met her an' they fell in love. But she never was really happy in Scotland. She wanted to get back among her ain folk. So at last Master MacCloud sold the big place and they came to Virginia an' brought me with them. By then I was sort of a valet to him. They soon got plenty of help. Bill Watson an' his brother Joe were stablemen, took care of the horses, drove the carriages an' such. They were jealous as the devil of me an' I couldn't abide either of them."

"Was it — was it — one of them?" Jim asked as Duncan paused again.

"There was a girl, sort of special maid to the mistress. Cindy, a pretty young thing an' we was sort of fond of each other. This Joe Watson was determined to have her an' she hated him. One day I seen her go into the herb garden an' this Joe went in after her. There was a high, box hedge around and unless you were up a bit you couldn't see into it. I thought the girl might need help so I hurried down out of the house an' went in. I found this dog trying to undress her and ready for worse. He was a dirty beast. I came up behind and hit him as hard as I could over and over until he fell flat. Cindy knew right away he was done for. His face was half hidden an' she could find no breath in him.

" 'He's dead, Duncan. You've killed him and you've

got to run for it. I think Bill was watching from the big stable window. Oh, run Duncan. Hurry! Get away!' she says. 'You saved me, but you might hang for this. Never stop going till you're far, far away.' She was cryin', mind, and me, too. I was young and scared as the devil. I never waited to think. I passed her and hurried round the house. I kep' close to field fences. I run an' kept on. I slept in barns an' ate scraps as I went an' when I was northward an' the weather cold, I made off with an old coat an' an old pair of shoes from a horse stable.''

Jim watched him in amazement, but said only, ''Go on.''

''One winter night I was caught in a blizzard. I couldn't see. I was about frozen. I thought I'd give up an' die. It would pay for what I done, anyhow. Then I saw a light. I got to the house and managed to chap at the door. When it opened there stood Aunt Polly an' when I spoke, she said, 'God save us, it's a Scotchman. Come away in, man. You'll be starved with the cold.' They fed an' warmed me an' after she had gone to bed Uncle Charley brought in the big tub and helped me get clean from all I'd been through. He found some old clothes for me and as soon as he could he brought me here. It's been home ever since. That's my story, Master Jim.''

''But — but Duncan, what about this Watson? How did he find out you were here? And what does he want when he *is* here?''

''Aye, that's what I've had a hard time figurin' meself. It *could* have been like this. Bill might have been slow to charge me with the crime for he an' Joe were always fightin'. But they're slow down there an' the years went by an' I never turned up. I guess he thought I'd come back, you see, for Cindy. Between themselves an' with the Mac-Clouds doin' everything to save me, he might even get the thing put on *him*. The Watsons both had enemies an' he could have named one of them. I just don't know how he worked it. As to how he got here, I finally found out about that. You mind the chap that was here a while back sellin' patent corn shellers?"

"I certainly do. You wanted so badly for me to buy one and it was no good. He was a fraud."

"Aye, an' he was a bletherin' one at that. I bet he covered three states an' everywhere he would brag about The Richlands. When he was at the MacCloud place you can be sure he had it all down pat an' spoke of the Ryalls and a *Scotchman* livin' with them and I guess Watson could have been loafin' around the back door and Cindy had come into the kitchen. They both, I guess, remembered what this blatherskite said. He likely come on up. Cindy wrote me a note later which he tried to grab. Always snoopin', he was. The postmaster kep' the note an' Tom brought it. I kep' it. You can be readin' it. There's nothin' much in it."

He handed it over. It read:

Dear Duncan, I heard from a traveling man where you were and glad to know you are well and have a good place. I am all right too. I'm married to the butler and he's a good man and so am still at the MacClouds'. The old man is pretty poorly now. He'll be eighty come Michaelmas.

> Best regards,
> Cindy

"I still don't see why Watson keeps eyeing you all the time. What does he think he can do?"

"Well, he may just like to keep me on pins an' needles. Just make me feel any time he wants to he could turn me in. He's such an ornery cuss, he's just mean enough for that. Meanwhile, he'll get off out of sight for a while an' pretend he's lookin' at a farm or a horse or somethin'. But in a way he keeps track of *me*, an' more than that, he makes sure I know where *he* is. It's sort of like he's blackmailin' me. I think he'd sure like to get me. Come on, Master Jim. It's time we went to bed."

"I don't like this," Jim kept muttering. "I don't like this at all."

No one, strangely enough, except Dave, noticed that Phoebe had not been the same since Thanksgiving. She moved more slowly, smiled less and gently refused the checker games in which she had before been delighted to join. She often went to bed herself after she had put the children to sleep. Jim's mind was so full of Duncan's strange story and the fears and problems it engendered that he paid little attention to anything besides it and the ambitions he held for the farm. Then one night, suddenly, after the children were in bed, they heard a fall. Duncan was the first to reach her as she lay on the floor, her hands very cold, her head very hot. Phoebe roused and demurred, but Duncan carried her to her bed in the small spare room which had been allotted to her. "I'll send Jim up," he said. "You may need a bit of help to get ready for the night."

Her voice was suddenly strong. "No, please, Duncan, you just stay on a little longer with me. I'll be all right. Don't, don't bother Jim."

Duncan went down to the kitchen and expounded it to the others. "It's just a plain *overdone,* poor child, that's what it is, an' we was too dumb to see it. She was scared about the Thanksgiving an' nervous as a witch, I mind it now, for she near let a glass fall an' then cried at the thought. She was so afraid she wouldn't do everythin' just right an' I doubt if any of us praised her when the day was over."

"But is she sick now, Duncan? What do you think?"

"Oh, I think she's been a bit doncie for a while an' now she seems to have a touch of fever but I'm sure a good rest will settle her."

Jim went out and slowly climbed the stairs to Phoebe's room. Behind him, the other men looked at each other and wondered. They all had grown fond of Phoebe, but with all their quiet watching no one of them had ever detected the slightest intimacies between her and her strangely wed husband. Jim tapped now on the door and went slowly in. Phoebe looked up listlessly.

"I'm so ashamed," she said weakly, "to stay in bed like this but the room keeps going around when I try to get up. I feel," she added with a faint smile, "like a clock that's run down."

"You're just overtired. You did so much at Thanksgiving time and did everything so *very* well."

"You — you think so?"

"Of course. We all thought you were wonderful and should have told you then more than we did. Do you still feel feverish?"

He came close and hesitantly laid a hand on her forehead. It was very hot.

"I'll be — all right soon," she murmured. "The children?"

"They're fine. We're seeing to them. You just rest." And he went out for she was drowsing again into sleep.

Jim wrestled with his conscience. He was concerned about this strange illness. He felt they should have the doctor come out or at least go in and report to him and get medicine. But the very thought of the doctor brought a wave of anguished memories over him. And he knew the doctor felt he himself had played a weak part. "We'll give her another day or two," he thought, "and then I'll take some action. We can't let this fever go on indefinitely."

On the second day of his delay when the other men were in the fields, Jim went up again to Phoebe's room. He walked softly over to the bed and then stood transfixed, paralyzed by what he saw. For Phoebe lay heavily asleep but in her fever had evidently thrown aside her night shift and the sheet that had covered her. Before Jim's eyes she lay completely bare. He looked, moved back and came close again, his eyes devouring a beauty of which he had never dreamed. He had never seen an unclothed woman before. He had once or twice asked Peggy if he might see her when she took off her clothes for the night, but she had always modestly demurred, "Oh, Jim, I think I'd feel so queer." And so he had never pressed the matter.

But now here was a loveliness more than the face. His eyes followed her brown hair spread upon the pillow down to the tender, young, molded breasts, the soft hair above the genitals and the perfect sculpture of the limbs. In her long skirts he had never thought of their enticing curves. She lay upon her back, her arms at her sides, the only marring feature to the loveliness of her body being the small, work-worn palms. As Jim watched them, thinking of the way they had worked for him and his children, the hot tears rose in his eyes. But more than that. He felt a tremendous upsurge of feeling, of tenderness and of overwhelming desire, until his legs shook under him. The words he spoke came from no volition of his own. He hardly knew he spoke them but they sounded on the quiet air.

"Oh, my love! Oh, my little love!"

She stirred, opened her eyes and seeing Jim, smiled faintly. "It's you," she said. "I — I always hope it will be — you."

"It will always be me when I possibly can come," he said, and heaving a long breath, looked again at the form before him and drew up the sheet. When he heard a sound at the door, he went quickly to find Duncan there with a small basin and a cloth.

"I was passin' by the spring an' I brought up some water. It's good an' cold. I was goin' to wipe her face a bit."

Duncan's tone had an edge to it as he handed it over. "Weel, I'll no be denyin' you're the proper one for it."

When he came back to the bed, Jim drew up a chair and began gently to cool the hot face, then pushing down the sheet, wiped the arms and breasts. She seemed scarcely conscience except to say occasionally, "It feels so good." And once she held on to his hand. He knew then she was not quite herself. "Jim!" she had murmured as she held his fingers with her own. "My Jim."

When he went down to the kitchen at last, he thought or imagined that her head was cooler. He had looked in a drawer and found, neatly folded, a thinner night shift and managed to put it on her. Then he drew up the sheet halfway and hoped no other eyes than his would look upon the beauty now hidden. He found Duncan preparing hot broth for her and stopped him in time. "Not *hot*, Duncan, when she's so hot herself. Let it get very cold and maybe she'll drink it."

"Lawks me! If the man hasna' a bit of sense in him! I wisht I'd thought of it mesel'."

She did sip most of the cool broth and assured Duncan faintly that she was better. Jim, meanwhile, had stated his intention of keeping up the cool applications during the night and then of riding into New Salem the next day to see the doctor, either to get medicine or bring him out. "I've been guilty of neglect before this — just letting her suffer, there. I'm ashamed and I mean to right it now."

"Listen, Jim," Dave said, "if you are planning to keep up the cool cloths on her head all night, I'll spell you."

"So will I," said Tom. "If you're on your way to the doctor's tomorrow, you'll need your sleep."

"Thanks, boys. I think I can manage, but if I get drowsy I'll call one of you."

Before he left Phoebe for the night she asked hesitantly, "Did I sort of talk in my sleep, Jim?"

"Well, a little."

"Oh dear, what did I say?"

"You kept saying, 'It feels so good' when you had a cool cloth on your head."

"That was all?"

"That was all." Jim, of course, would keep his own little secret.

The next day, even though the fever was down a bit, found him with mixed feelings entering the doctor's office. That redoubtable gentleman covered his surprise, offered Jim a chair and sat down watching him keenly.

"Now what can I do for you, Jim? Tell me straight off what's the matter and I'll try to help you. How's the girl, Phoebe?"

"Well, that's the problem. She's sick." He told about how hard she had worked for Thanksgiving and all the time, for that matter, and described her symptoms. The doctor asked a few straight questions and finally gave his diagnosis. "That girl is tired out and she's been under a heavy physical and mental strain. I'll give you something for her."

They talked of the farm, of the children and of Aunt Polly and when Jim rose to go the doctor gave him a little package.

"Now," he said, "here are some powders to bring down the fever and a bottle of tonic to build up her strength. What she needs to relax her and relieve the tension is not put up in bottles. You're a bright boy, Jim. I think you understand. I'll tell you how it is with me. When I think a thing is wrong, I fight like the devil against it, but later when I think it over and decide maybe after all it was right, then I back it with all I've got. Anyway, good luck, Jim, and remember me to Phoebe. She's a remarkable girl."

Jim flushed, thanked him and then, on impulse, went across to the ice cream store. There wasn't much chance, but oh, if he could transport it, wouldn't ice cream taste good to Phoebe now! Billy Wester was as jolly as usual. When he heard the problem he insisted that he had an answer. "Just got new measures, metal ones. Always just used scoops before. I can let you have one till next time you're in town. If the little Missus has a fever, nothing tastes as good as ice cream. Or that's what they tell me. Could you use one this big?" He held up a large metal container. "Used mostly for festibles an' picnics an' such when you want to measure out big lots at a time. Too large for you?"

"Couldn't be," said Jim. "We're a big family. I'll take the biggest you have. But will it keep till I get home?"

"Well, we're takin' a chance, but man to man, I believe it will. I'll get my biggest an' fill er up. Then, you see, there's a little lid clamps down — the salesman made a great fuss over that — then we'll wrap it in a big feed-bag or two, an' then you skite home as fast as you can. It's a gamble. Take me up?"

"I'll take you," Jim answered.

He rode as fast as Beauty could go through the brisk, late autumn air and before he thought possible was back at the farm, with the medicines in his pocket and the precious package of ice cream in one of the saddlebags. He took it out. It still felt solid. He hurried into the kitchen, removed the bags and lifted the lid. Wonder of wonders, it had not melted. Pete was dispatched in haste to call the men or ring for them and Jim took a little saucerful up to Phoebe.

"You've been gone so long," she said languidly.

"I went to get you some medicine to make you well, but I've also brought you a treat."

He raised her a little on the pillow and gave her a spoonful. She took it slowly and then looked up in amazement. "Oh, Jim," she said, "it's past believing. It's so good and so cool. Even my head feels better now."

"I thought you'd like it."

"You got it — *for me?*"

"Especially for you though there is more in the kitchen for the boys."

"You're so good," she whispered.

He choked a little. "No, I haven't been really, but I'll try to make up."

He gave her the first powder and the doctor had been right. In a few days, the fever gradually disappeared. Then came an afternoon when Phoebe dressed and Jim, even though she expostulated, carried her down to dinner with the family. She wore one of her new dresses, and the long sleeps had brought additional youth and freshness to her face. There was a joyful reunion with the children until Jim saw the color fading a little from her cheeks and then carried her up again to her little spare room.

As Dave and Tom strolled around the farm road as they often did of an evening, Tom spoke after a silence.

"Well, it looks as though Jim and Phoebe have broken the silence at last. You can tell by the way they look at each other. For my part —"

"What is your part?"

"It isn't quite a year yet. Phoebe is a sweet thing and I'm fond of her, but when I think of how we felt ourselves —" His eyes wandered to the Maiden-Blush tree "— I don't see how Jim can —"

Dave's voice was harsh. "Let's talk of something else," he said. "We've got to get at that fence round the little pasture."

But a change had come in the household, very subtly, very quietly, but still there. It was evidenced by a difference in tone as Jim and Phoebe spoke to each other; it was shown by the look in their eyes when their glances clung and sometimes, when their hands met, there was a blush upon both faces. This was all, but it was enough to show the other men that something deep and hidden was happening. Phoebe was strong now and busy about her usual duties. Only once had Jim mentioned their strange relations to her. When they were alone with none but the children near, he had said hesitantly, "I'm sure you know how great my sorrow was and it is now not quite a year since it happened. But I've learned much in between and I've thought a great deal about life and about — you and me. I want to ask you if you'll give me a little longer time —"

Phoebe had raised her gentle face. Her eyes were adoring. "But of course, Jim. Of course."

Jim's heart was lighter, somehow, after that. Sometimes he could be heard whistling again and once in while he would join the others in a song. The burden now that weighed upon him steadily was not that of marital duties nor even the times when depths of grief overwhelmed him. The thing that followed him through the fields and woke him by night was Duncan's strange confession. That he, their trusted servant and friend, had been guilty of *murder*, even long ago, was something so unbelievable, so shocking and thoroughly frightening, that he couldn't clear his mind of it. There were questions which baffled him. If Duncan had actually killed the man — and after his own fight with Dave that time he could imagine such a circumstance — and had run away while the brother, Bill Watson, saw it, then why had not Watson gone to the police? Of course, the girl Cindy would not have testified and the rich, dominant MacCloud family would have pulled all strings to save Duncan, and yet —

Also, if because of the traveling corn sheller, a hint of
Duncan's whereabouts had reached Watson and he had
made the long distance between them, had actually found
him, then why had he kept all knowledge of this, apparently, from Virginia authorities? Jim often tossed and turned
in his bed and finally gave up the mystery. The years
between the crime and the present must have somehow
dimmed the scene and the attendant anger with Watson,
and his malicious joy now was in locating Duncan and,
as the latter had said, playing cat and mouse with him as
a witness who might at any moment emerge to destroy him.
December was quiet and Christmas, as Aunt Polly suggested, had been a day for the children only, with a few
toys from the General Store which Tom and Dave insisted
upon buying. There was a good dinner and this was all
that marked the day. January was easier, for the men sat
over the table with paper and lists and decided what seeds
they should order and how much. Also Jim said there
should be extra fertilizer.

"You know," he told them, "I have an idea we should
plough up the lower pasture and plant it in timothy and
clover. And we might even plough the west wheat field
and rotate the crops. You know Father always said that
was good for the land, but he never did it partly because
the fields still seemed rich. But it would be pretty important to keep them so. What do you think?"

There was plenty of discussion pro and con although
Jim's word was always final.

February was hard. There was no snow to remind them
of the Great Fall a year ago, but the calendar spelled out
the weeks and as day followed day the countenances of all

of them showed what their hearts were remembering. It was a relief when March came blowing in with flying clouds and wind songs in the chimney. It was ploughing time for grain and as the men bent their strong shoulders to the task there seemed room for only physical reactions. The lower pasture was planted and seeded for hay and April brought more ploughing and the planting of corn. The oats were already in and would be well up in May.

One spring night, Dave and Duncan went early to bed and Tom dozed in his chair.

Jim looked up from his game of checkers with Phoebe. "You'd better get on to bed, Tom. You're half-asleep already," he said casually.

"I think I'll do that. Thanks for the advice. Well, good night!"

When they were alone, Jim quietly swept the checkers into the box. "You've won, anyway," and then, hesitantly, he added, "Could I — may I — come into your room tonight, Phoebe?"

A soft color diffused her face. "Yes," she said, very low, adding, "you will always be welcome there, Jim."

He rose, came over and kissed her. "Thank you," he said. "You go on up and I'll take care of things down here. I won't be long."

No one saw Jim go into Phoebe's room. No one knew that love had been made there with tenderness and tears. No one knew that in Jim's heart there had been rising a strange desire such as he had not known before to possess the beautiful body he had once seen. Even Jim himself could not explain the contradictions of his heart. With Peggy there had been a glorious passion that wrought upon his senses like a flame; with Phoebe there was a different beguilement, a seductiveness born, in a way, of gentleness. He often pondered upon these contrasts as the furrows turned beneath his plough. One thing he had decided upon after a few weeks of their real union had passed. He wanted a real marriage ceremony, and to this end he wrote all the story to Pater Donaldson. He received a prompt and affectionate letter in reply. If Jim would bring Phoebe over on a Saturday he would perform the regular ceremony with great pleasure and his blessing. He added that considering all the sad circumstances Jim was doing the right thing.

The boys were more than agreed. They all wanted to wipe out the stress of that awful night which Dr. Knox and his slip of paper had forced upon them. Now, by all signs, Jim's heart had found a new home, even as their own, with February passed and spring in all its beauty upon them, had found life and hope covering over the memories once unendurable.

So, on a Saturday in May when they all said he could be spared from work, Jim took Phoebe in the best buggy and left early for the Academy, empty now for the summer. The farm was in excellent shape, fences mended, ploughing done, oats already nearly eight inches tall, corn planting to begin on Monday. All the mastering ambition of his heart rose at the thought of being, indeed, the Master of The Richlands. As they drove along they talked together more than they ever had done before. Jim found Phoebe had gone regularly to their country school where there had been a good teacher. She had tried to get the most from it and had read all the books the teacher had lent her. There were just the three of their family on a very small rental farm. When the "black sore throat" struck the countryside, her parents had died and left her alone with no relatives. She had worked unhappily here and there until Uncle Charley had found her. Then Jim knew the rest. He knew, too, as they talked, that she had a clear, active brain which met his own at many points. There would now, then, be not only the desire for her body but an interest in her mind as well. To her surprise, he suddenly leaned over and kissed her.

Dr. Donaldson received them warmly. It was plain he was fond of Jim and also quickly approved of Phoebe. He inquired about the farm and gave advice as to the form Jim's advertisements should take and then, after hearing about the other boys, he led Jim and Phoebe at once to the church opposite the main Academy building, signing to his wife and one of her friends waiting beside her who, he explained as he introduced them, would act as witnesses. Then within the church, the minister took his Academy robe and his Geneva Bands from a front pew and indicated that he was ready for the young couple to stand before the pulpit. They came and the ceremony proceeded with all due reverence. The vows were taken, the tender prayer and benediction offered. Then when all was over, Dr. Donaldson bent down and kissed Phoebe's forehead. "It's a minister's privilege, my dear; you have a good man. Make him happy. And Jim, you have a gentle wife. See that she lacks nothing."

After refusing food as they had some with them by grace of Duncan — they made their good-bys and thanks and started back toward Aunt Polly's. Jim longed to see her and it was necessary to break the long trip home, but one feature of the visit twisted his heart like a knife. Once there, Aunt Polly received them with cries of delight and "mothered" them to her heart's content. She rejoiced over the day's news and said she always knew it would turn out that way. Then she said quickly with a quaver in her voice. "You'd never think it but Charley and I have takin' a liking for the spare room an' we'll be sleepin' there tonight if you two can use ours. How about it, Jim?"

"Fine," he said, "and thanks, Aunt Polly." Then he turned to look out the door. "She knew," he thought to himself. "She understood and she's made it easier for me."

It was, as always, a happy visit with Jim inspecting the small farm and Aunt Polly showing Phoebe the quilt she was making for her. They left next morning refreshed and eased in heart by all they had experienced. They got home by early supper time and were just giving their news when they heard a rattle of loose wheels and a buggy stopped before the kitchen porch. It was Mrs. Bumper who got out and rushed through the door. She was overwrought.

"Duncan!" she almost screamed. "Come on with me. There's not a moment to lose. The law's caught up with you. Bumper was gettin' the horse shod at the Four Corners an' he seen these two policemen askin' for the Ryall farm. Hurry, Duncan. Get in the buggy an' come home with me. I'll hide you under my bed where the Lord himself couldn't find you. *Hurry!*"

Duncan stood, stone white. "Go on, Duncan," Jim said. "There's no use just walking into trouble. We'll keep in touch somehow, but *hurry!* God bless you!"

Duncan got into the buggy and the sound of wheels retreated while the family looked at each other in a kind of horror.

"I'm afraid this is it!" Jim said at last. "We've always felt he ran away from something."

"But *what*, Jim? Do you know?"

"He told me he had killed a man but not to tell the rest of you. I've kept my word."

"Murder!" The word seemed to sear their lips as they said it. "Oh, my God," said Dave, "and after all these years they've caught up with him! Watson knew of this?"

"Duncan thinks so."

"Then that's it, but why has he waited and how —"

"It's a tangled web," Jim said, "but we must stand by Duncan whatever comes."

They could not eat. They all sat stunned, and waiting as though for a blow. At nine o'clock they heard the sound of hooves and then of two riders stopping at the hitching post. In a few minutes they were on the back porch, knocking at the side of the door, which was open. They were in officers' uniforms. Jim, terrified at what he was about to hear, went to greet them.

"Good evening, gentlemen," he said politely. "What may I do for you?"

"Are you Mr. Ryall of The Richlands place?" the one asked with a heavy Southern accent.

"I am James Ryall and these are my brothers," he said, indicating them.

"We came round the upper road through the Four Corners, they call it, and they told us there where we could find you. The point is, we've trailed a man clear from Virginia an' we think now we're on the scent. Any help you can give us will sure be appreciated.''

Jim moistened his dry lips.

"Who is the man?" he asked.

"Watson," the two said at once. "William Watson."

At the words, Tom and Dave sprang as one man from their chairs. "Watson?" they both all but shouted.

The officers looked surprised. "I guess you know something about him then. Could any of you tell us where we might find him?"

Jim's voice shook. "Let me get this straight. You are looking for Watson in order to arrest him for a crime. Is that right?"

"Right as rain, an' we want to find another man just to talk to him. That's a Scotchman, Duncan McPhee, who used to live at the MacClouds' back in our part of the country."

"Did — did he also commit a crime?"

"Good Lord, no," said the one officer. "He knocked a dirty dog down years ago, Bill Watson's brother, an' then took to his heels and no one has seen him since. I guess he was afraid Mr. MacCloud wouldn't like it. But the old man was terribly fond of Duncan and we'll have a bit of nice news for him when we see him, that we'll tell him if we catch Watson in time."

"What is the charge against Watson?"

"Armed robbery and we've got to get along if you'll just give us a hint or two."

"You don't mind strange roads in the dark?"

"We've been over a good few."

"Good." Jim smiled. "Then follow our farm road out

to the Pike, we call it, and it runs straight west to a little town called New Salem. There's the old Stone Hotel there. Go in quietly, for I think you might find Watson in the taproom. And the best of luck to you."

When they were gone, Phoebe quietly reheated the uneaten dinner and they sat down to it, ravenous from hunger and all but sick from the relief of fear and an intolerable burden. They were still eating and talking and planning it all when the tall clock struck eleven. Suddenly, they heard a step on the stones and then on the porch. Duncan himself came in, his face white and strained and his clothing disheveled. He didn't even give them time to speak.

"I left in such a hurry I had no time to think. But after I was at the Bumpers', I thought plenty. Who was I, I sez to meself, a grown man to be hidin' under a woman's bed! I'll hae nae mair a' that, I sez, an' I got' out. If I was guilty of a crime, I'll stand up to it like a man an' take me punishment. I only hope if won't be hard to the rest of ye."

"Duncan!" Jim cried as Phoebe brought a cup of tea and some food to him. "Duncan! The officers have been here already."

"Aye, I thought as much. You needn't try to be shieldin' me!"

And then one after another they poured out the amazing news. Duncan sipped his tea with unsteady hands. He said, "*Watson! Watson!*" in a queer, squeaky voice. "It was Watson they wanted! An' all the time he knew I never killed Joe an' yet he held it over me like a gun at me head." There followed then a torrent of swearing not before heard in the farm kitchen, both Scotch and English and the most eloquent of each.

"Steady, Duncan," Jim laughed. "There's a lady present."

Phoebe laughed, too, a frequent sound of late. "This lady would excuse anything tonight."

"I'll tell you," Dave said, "if I were you, Duncan, I'd ride in now to the squire's. You may get there faster even than the officers for you know the roads. I'll warrant you they'll catch Watson in the taproom. They say he sneaks in and always faces the door."

"It may be the officers will be there with Watson with them. Anyway, they want to talk to you, too. Let's go," said Jim. "I'll ride with you."

"Belike I will," Duncan agreed. He spread his arms wide. "Lookit!" he said, "I'm a free mon the now, an' I'll tell you, it's a *gra-a-and* feelin'. Why, I can tell the Squire the whole damned business."

There was an arrest in the taproom of the old Stone Hotel that night, a very quiet one, for the officers had come in soft-footed while Watson had been in the midst of one of his tales about horse trading in the South. When he looked up suddenly and recognized uniforms, he made a flying leap toward the open window, but the officers were too quick. They handcuffed him while Watson cursed and moaned like a schoolboy.

"But listen here! What's the charge? You can't arrest me without charges! Let me loose here till you state your business."

"Shut up! We know just what we're doing, but a pretty chase you've led us. Come along. Have you a lawyer or a good squire here?" one of the officers asked, turning to Hartman.

"That we have. Best Squire in the state."

240

"Then, Watson, we'll be going to see him."

They almost hauled the prisoner to his feet and dragged him to the Squire's iron gate not far away. Jim had pressed his horse to take the miles swiftly, as had Duncan, so they were there to meet them, with Duncan, still abashed and unbelieving but with angry shoulders squared as though his life had just begun for him.

The Squire opened the door, saw the crowd, glimpsed the handcuffs and knew his favorite work was about to begin.

"Come in, come in! You're gentlemen of the law, I take it."

"From the sovereign state of Virginia," the one answered promptly.

"Well, come away in. I believe I am acquainted with the others. There's a wee nip in the air so I have a bit of fire. Duncan, me lad, would you tie your horse and make up the fire a bit? Oh, a fine man is that. I've known him since he was quite young. Well, well, come away in."

The men entered, all but Duncan who went for more logs. Jim, familiar with the book-lined room, sat down to await developments.

"I see," the Squire said calmly, "that you have Mr. Watson here under arrest."

"That we have an' if you'd care to hear the story —"

"Please tell it," said the Squire, licking his lips, as it were.

"It's a queer one an' it's pretty long."

"We've got all night for it," the Squire assured him, "an' I'm used to queer stories."

"Well, it was like this. One of the richest men in our parts was Mr. MacCloud. He had a lot of servants an' Duncan, here, was a sort of valet to him an' he was mighty fond of Duncan. Bill Watson here an' his brother, Joe, worked in the stables. There was a girl, too, that liked Duncan. This Joe was after her, but she couldn't abide him. One day he followed her into the herb garden that was all set round with box, so you had to be up higher to see into it. Duncan saw Joe grab her an' heard her scream an' he tore downstairs and give this Joe a couple of mighty good blows from behind with his fists an' the girl an' Duncan both thought he was dead 'cause he fell pretty hard, so Duncan took to his heels an' has never been back since. You see, he thought he'd really killed Joe." The officer stopped for a long breath and they all waited. "Well," he continued, "things went on this way with Mr. MacCloud always missing Duncan, an' Bill here always trying to worm himself into bein' a house servant. At last, Mr. MacCloud tried him out an' let him bring up the early cup of tea. But he didn't like Bill. He told some that the man was always asking questions about his business an' snoopin' around an' he didn't like a snooper, so he put Bill back to drivin' the carriage an' Bill was mad as hell, you might say."

"An' then what? We're waiting for the climax," said the squire.

"Well, about six months ago, old Mr. MacCloud died under strange circumstances. He was awful sick and one of the maids in the house heard a sort of weak scream an' went to him. She swore there was marks of an end of a pistol hard on his forehead. Of course, they soon faded, but she swore they were there as if he'd been scared to death by somebody. The packet of bank notes an' some stocks marked plainly for Duncan McPhee and left him in his will was gone. And Bill Watson was gone. What think you of that for a climax?''

It was a strange night. It had not taken New Salem long to spread the news. They had commented, of course, upon the sporadic appearance of the strangers during the last days, but to have a real arrest in their midst was shocking and almost incredible. Much usual work was laid aside until every new bit of evidence had been discussed. The doctor had found Watson's leg in definite need of attention, so the small "lock-up," as the little room of the hotel was familiarly called, was fitted with a few more comforts and, although there were locks, the officers stood guard. At the end of their three days' residence, a short, nondescript-looking man who could pass unnoticed in a crowd came into the hotel carrying a small battered suitcase. He engaged a room and asked if by chance Mr. Hartman had seen any officers about. When told where such might be found, the shabby man took a smart-looking card from his pocket and presented it. It bore the wording: S. J. Sanders, Investigative Detective.

All this Jim learned later when Duncan, after a visit with Billy Wester during which, it was reported, they had done the Highland fling with variations, had managed to get off his horse and reach the kitchen door singing "Green Grow the Rushes, Ho!" at the top of his voice, bringing several convivial spirits with him. Why should it not be a night of rejoicing? For the shabby detective had unobtrusively searched the deserted farmer's shack to which Duncan had led Watson when he was afraid of discovery in the Stone Hotel, and had found beneath some tumbled comforters the precious packet which would one day probably give Duncan a little fortune, a modest nest egg, or at the least "a wee bit siller."

Oh, it was a great night in The Richlands kitchen with Duncan the center of it as they all asked him to tell his story again and slapped his broad shoulders with affectionate delight in his good fortune. The Bumpers came over, too, for they had done their best for their friend.

"You're all talkin' about the money," Duncan called out once when he could be heard through the loud conversation and laughter, "but you're forgettin' the main thing. There's no denyin' I'll like unco well to hae a nice bit of siller put by, but that's naethin' to the fact I've had a burden lifted from me heart an' conscience. I'm an honest, free man with no murder hangin' over me. Now give three cheers for the biggest thing of it all!"

It was past the hour when good farmers were up and in their fields that Phoebe, having set Pete at the milking, looked in shock at the apparent shambles of the kitchen: chairs overturned, many mugs and glasses scattered over the table and a strong smell which was not that of Temperance. She had started on to bed when she had heard all the stories, but on the last step she stopped and looked back and listened. Duncan, whose speech was somewhat impaired, could still be heard distinctly as he spoke. "Genlemen, an' Master Jim, an' Mrs. Bumper there, it's once in a lifetime ye get the chance to see a man freed from hangin'. You've got it now an' I'll take it a verra great kindness if you'll all drink a toast whether ye ever taste another swig in your lives."

Phoebe was astonished at how many bottles and jugs

appeared on the table. She waited until glasses and mugs were filled and the men on their feet. Then the heavy throated voices rose to the rafters:

Here's to Duncan! May he live forever!

And even Phoebe, slipping quietly away, knew that the real celebration had begun.

Chapter IX

When Phoebe came down first into the kitchen, the morning after the great carousal, and had sent Pete to do the
milking, she looked about her in despair. Thank good-
ness the children were still asleep after being kept awake
most of the night with the noise.

As she stood tearful and aghast, she heard soft, padding
feet and Duncan appeared from the stairs, shoes in hand.
He saw her tears, whisked her round the waist and danced
her about the floor where he could find a vacant space.

"Ah, dinna' greet, lassie, after the fine evening we had.
I'll have this all cleaned up in a minute."

"But, Duncan," she said, "where did all these bottles
come from?"

Duncan scratched his head as though in deep thought.
"Now, that's just fair mysteerious, that is. Seems to me
there's a verse in the holy Book that the Lord opened the
bottles of heaven. I doubt that was for rain, but who are
we to look miracles in the face. Help me get them all out
under the back porch, lassie, an' we'll ask no question of
the mysteerious ways of Providence."

"Duncan, that's sacrilegious!"

"It was a *gra-a-a-a-and* night," was Duncan's only reply.

Once the debris was cleared, the chairs on their legs as usual, a cloth and dishes on the table, Phoebe went up to wake the children, and Jim and Tom, roused by the pungent smell of hot bread and flitch, came sheepishly down. Duncan took the first word of them.

"An' what's a bit headache in the mornin' compared to the glorious hubbleshoo we had last night? Did ye ever in all your life feel so *lifted*?"

"Well," Tom said with a grin, "as to being 'lifted,' as you call it, I thought my head would hit the rafters when you danced around with Mrs. Bumper."

Duncan's face was scarlet, as he rattled the pans on the stove. "Havers!" he said, "canna' an' auld friend trip it a bit with another auld friend? Eat your breakfast an' don't be bletherin'."

When Phoebe brought the children down Jim did an unusual thing. He crossed over to them and kissed them each one. "I'm afraid you didn't get much sleep last night," he said apologetically.

Phoebe smiled at the men and her voice had a tinge of mirth in it. "I did hear something once," she admitted. "It sounded as though Sheppie might be knocking something off the table." She gave a sly glance at Jim and then, with a general laugh, the great carousal was over.

The marriage of Jim and Phoebe seemed as though it had always been, with a growing tenderness and congeniality in evidence between them. The other boys still studied them. They saw that while gentle and loving,

Phoebe had a quiet will of her own which was perhaps good for her husband. She was wise in practical matters, too, and brought evidence to bear, for example, that wheat ripened in the moonlight. And with her quick, contented laughter, there came to her face a growing beauty, a serenity, a glow of peace.

As to Duncan, the whole episode of Watson had left him a trifle more sober, but the strains of "Hunting Tower" and "The Crookit Bawbee" still rang gaily out as they used to do at intervals. One day Jim asked, "When matters are settled, will you be wanting to go back to Virginia, Duncan?"

"Me? Go back when me heart's here with the family? Not if you'll keep me. Many's the time through the years when you boys had grown up, I kep' thinkin', 'if worst, ever come to worst, they'd stand by me!' "

"Could you ever doubt it?"

Duncan turned his back and lapsed into his childhood speech. "It gars me greet," he said.

"Me, too," answered Jim, wiping his own eyes.

Official papers came to Duncan after the officers and detective *and* the precious packet had returned to Virginia. The lawyer wrote him that after the settlement of old Mr. MacCloud's estate and the trial itself, which would all take some time, he would receive the money willed to him which, he added, was a very considerable sum. Duncan read the letter aloud. "Look at me," he said as he went on to set down the supper. 'I'm goin' to be an independent gentleman the noo! Who'd a thought it. If you ever want to borrow a shillin' or twa, any of you, just ask an' I'll never be refusin' you!"

T.R.

R

Everyone laughed happily knowing that no money could ever spoil Duncan. They did see him sometimes, when no one seemed to be looking, fling out his arms and shout: "I can look any man in the face! There's no cloud hangin' over me."

They all knew this was his real riches.

A year after Dr. Donaldson had performed the true ceremony, there was a new baby in the cradle. Jim marveled at the comparative ease with which it had come into the world. Aunt Polly, able to come over now, explained it to him.

"She's born for motherhood, that girl. The Lord took care of that."

Jim, never forgetting, still looked with pleasure at the new little girl. "I hope she'll be as lovely as her mother," he said, looking down at Phoebe.

"Oh, Jim," she cried, "do you really think I'm pretty?"

He smiled, remembering the day he had seen her sleeping body.

"I think you're beautiful," he said.

She held his hand to her cheek, which was wet. In a moment, very softly, she said, "We should choose a name at once. I had wondered about — Margaret. Of course she would then be — be Peggy. Would you mind?"

He stood silent. It was as though she were pleading with him. "When she didn't get her own little girl, you know."

"I wouldn't mind," he said slowly. "Indeed, I believe I'd like it very much. Let's call it settled and then we can tell the others. It's wonderful of you to think of it."

So the little Peggy took her place in the family and the name sounded sweet upon the tongue.

As the next late winter moved toward the spring Jim, while learning deep happiness with his wife and children, was much of the time tense and preoccupied. In a big new book, he was keeping records of farm activities: plough and harrow in *March* for grain; early *April*, plant seed for hay, plough for corn; *May*, roll ground for planting corn. Oats should be eight inches tall then. *June*, plant corn, mow hay. Oats then should be two and one-half feet tall, corn four inches tall. *July*, corn should be knee high by fourth of July —

And so on. The notes were definite, covering all phases of farm work, and as Jim wrote he also set down his expectations for the coming year. It was here his eyes shone and his face grew tense. The great dream of his for The Richlands was going to have substance. There had indeed been a magnificient yield of crops this year, but nothing to what was yet to come.

In the notebook, too, Jim wrote out examples of the advertisements he was about to send to the farm journals:

> Wheat, corn and oats for sale
> At The Richlands, halfway
> between the Four Corners and New Salem.
> Inquiries and orders taken.

J. Ryall, Prop.

A great pride rose in his breast. As great as the spreading acres around him. The lines in his face grew stronger and more tense and his voice, as he gave orders, had a tinge of mastership in the tones.

When the first farmer's catalogue reached them, they all pored over it with eagerness — until The Richlands' advertisement was found. Tom read it aloud, then repeated the last: "J. Ryall, Prop."

"Now, ain't that elegant," he said.

Jim's face flushed. "I thought it sounded more businesslike to have one name instead of several," he defended.

"Sure, sure," said Dave, flipping the catalogue back across the table to Jim. "It looks fine. As long as it's businesslike, let everything else go hang. Now me, I'm going to hang myself right up in bed now. It's been a heavy day."

Jim stood up, his face scarlet. "Boys," he said, "I'm sorry if I hurt you. We're all in this together; you surely know that. I still think the one name is better in the advertisements but I can easily change that. You know the oldest is supposed to take the main responsibility. I can change the notices and say "Ryall Brothers.'"

Tom gave a short laugh. "Let the notice stand. 'Ryall Brothers' sounds like a hardware store or something. Well, I think I'll go up now, too. My legs feel stiff. Good night, Phoebe."

Duncan had already left at the first hint of dissension. Jim and Phoebe now sat alone. "I don't see why they took it like that," Jim said at last. "They were downright sarcastic. After all, as the oldest son I *am* the Master of The Richlands, and on top of that, I love every inch of it, more I'm sure than they ever did. Those fields are mine by right of what they call primogeniture in England, but they *belong* to me because of my affection for them, my plans and hopes for them. I would sacrifice for them. I tell you, in the heart of me, they are *mine*!"

"And what about Dave and Tom?" she asked quietly.

"But they'll always have what they now have: a farm to

work and make a living from. I'm sure that's all they think about."

Phoebe laid her hand on his arm. "Don't be angry with me, Jim. I think you were, once before, but now this trouble with the boys has made me want to speak to you again: I think you are *too* ambitious for The Richlands or maybe dear, it is for yourself without your knowing it. You look so — so strained sometimes, as though you were just pouring all your energy into your plans for bigger and better crops. Your eyes look so sharp and far away and you don't always hear what we say the first time. I worry about you."

Jim closed his notebook with a snap and put it in the drawer.

"No, I'm not angry," he said. "But I do feel tonight I've taken all I can stand for I believe I got too tired in the fields today, too. Don't let's talk about it anymore."

The next day was normal with no echoes of the previous night's biting remarks. And so was the next. But on the third day, Dave spoke to Jim as they were coming in from the field.

"Jim," he said, "for some time Tom and I have had something on our minds which we'd like to talk over with you in private. Could we go into the sitting room this evening after the children are in bed and sort of thrash the thing out?"

Jim looked at him astonished. "Is anything wrong, Dave? You know I'll change the name in the advertisements."

Dave gave a careless fling of his hand. "Let's just wait till we can discuss things in full," he said.

"I'll get Phoebe to take the children up and Duncan always goes to bed early. I'll be at your service then," Jim said, feeling that the words sounded strange and ominous between brothers.

All day Jim was anxious. He thought he knew the nature of the conversation he would hear. Dave and Tom were hard workers but never looked far ahead. Why, they would ask, must the fields be urged and men's backs broken to make larger crops when they were big enough already? There were always enough buyers to put ready cash in their pockets while the old farm still quietly held its rich beauty. He had been wrong to use his name alone on the advertisements and the boys were hurt. He would have to make that right some way. He mulled over the idea all day. "It was through my damnable pride," he muttered once.

In the evening Phoebe, at a word, had gone up early with the children; Pete always was drowsy when he finished his kitchen chores; and Duncan, with his usual perception, had seen that something was not right and had pleaded a headache. "Och," Aunt Polly often said, "he could see through a stone wall, that one!"

At last the three brothers were alone and Dave led the way into the sitting room where there was a chill dignity in contrast to the coziness of the kitchen table.

Jim spoke first. "This seems like some sort of serious meeting, boys. Do get on with it as fast as you can. Can you lead off, Dave?"

They all looked uncomfortable and as though they were controlling themselves with difficulty.

"Well, first of all," Dave began, "Tom and I would like to see that deed or paper or whatever it was the Squire and the lawyer fixed up for you. You may remember you just told us about it and didn't show us."

Jim's face was crimson. "I'm sorry for that," he said. "I was so glad to get anything that would legally hold for The Richlands if we were challenged, I just put it away. But here it is, now."

He drew from one of the drawers of his father's desk a folded piece of foolscap and handed it to Tom who immediately read aloud: "Know all men by these present—"

"Where does that funny word come in?" he interrupted himself.

"Down further," Jim said, "where it tells that the tract of land called The Richlands has been held for four generations by the family of Ryall without formal deed and has been under cultivation and yield. Therefore, it is now pronounced title by adverse possession and will remain under the legal ownership of James Ryall and his heirs and assigns forever —"

There was a dead hush. Even Jim, in his buoyancy on the day when the precious paper was given to him, had not stopped to read the words aloud. His only thought was that now The Richlands was safer and that he, the Master, had brought this about.

Now he stood silent, while the others read again and again the paper he had seen as a future necessity, had labored to bring about and then cherished in pride. The deed to The Richlands was in his name. How else should it be?

But Dave was speaking. "This old law term sounds crazy but I guess it must hold water all right."

"It does."

"I see you have signed the paper as the owner of The Richlands."

"Yes, I did."

"Well, now this brings us right up to the thing we want to say. No one's life is sure, Jim. We've had some sad lessons on that. If anything should happen to you, you have a wife now who might inherit more than any of us think. Have you made a will?"

"Never thought of it."

"Well, you'd better. But here's an even better way Tom and I have thought of. You tell him, Tom."

"You see," Tom began. "We've been born here, grew up here and worked here as hard as you have. Now the point is, neither of us is thinking of getting married right away, but you can't tell about these things. If we married and had families we certainly would need homes of our own and a farm to work. So —"

Dave eagerly took up the thread. "The Richlands is the biggest tract of farm land not only in the county but in the whole end of the state. Big enough to make three big farms. We'll have to get two more men to work here at harvest and husking times, because our crops have got so big. But as I was saying —" Dave swallowed hard and went on, "Tom and I thought if you'd get a first-rate surveyor out you could have him measure off three sections, yours the biggest since you're the oldest and then two equal ones for Tom and me. Afterward we could all discuss which fields should be included and all that. What do you think, Jim?"

Jim was not scarlet now. His face was stone white and his hands gripped the table. He seemed unable to speak.

"*The Richlands*," he brought out at last with difficulty, "you would cut up, you would destroy The Richlands —"

"No, no," Dave shouted. "We'd do it no harm. We

will all be here together as before, only each working on his own ground which would be a good feeling and the division would not be hard."

"Wouldn't it?" said Jim. "How would you divide the maple grove and the walnut clump, the spring and — how would you divide — the *orchard*?"

He felt their hands on his shoulders then. "We don't want to hurt you, Jim. Just forget it for now. You may think of a better way for us. Talk it over with Phoebe. She's so calm and sensible. One thing remember, Jim, as you think it over. You've always been generous. Just giving us money wouldn't be the same as owning a bit of our own land especially if we know every inch of it. Well, good night and God bless us all."

The boys went upstairs. Jim sat by the kitchen fire which was always kept alight especially in the evenings. He put his head in his hands as he leaned on the table. Of the blows he might have imagined this was the most utterly unexpected and incredible. That The Richlands which had always seemed to him like a sentient thing, worthy of affection, the center of his life and plans, his hopes, his intense ambitions, should have its spreading beauty cut up into three farms, no longer able to bear the great name which had signified the magnificence of its acres? This he could not accept. He was *Master* of the Richlands, he was the legal owner. The boys could not destroy it without his consent. This he would never give. He would make it up to them some other way.

He was restless that night. His dreams were troubled. Tom and Dave stood pleading once before him. "Just a little land we can call our *own*," they said.

For a long two weeks nothing more was said in connection with the deed or the request. There was a visible effort in making conversation at meals. Phoebe, the most sensitive of all, felt for Duncan whose great uplift of heart and general condition had been allowed to sink into a minor place, since the great celebration of that first night. She tried often to tease him by bringing up the subject again, but Duncan, with a quieter manner than usual, only smiled and cooked more and more of their favorite dishes. The three brothers did not walk out together in the evenings. Dave and Tom strolled along the country road, or played with the children while Jim, gaunt and heavy-eyed, walked the farm itself, pausing at this familiar spot or that as though to check on the growing grain. And he thought constantly and without release of the problem his brothers had presented. He could not shake it, neither could he solve it for, first of all, what he felt most was anger.

How *could* his brothers think of dismembering The Richlands? How *could* they ask this of him, almost casually when they knew by every mark and sign that his love for the land was greater than their own. From these hours of anger, Jim entered the house stony-eyed, avoiding the gaze of the others, even that of Phoebe and Duncan, who he knew were somehow on the side of the boys. There was always the next day's work to discuss and then, bedtime.

One early evening as he walked alone as usual, he felt a mist in his eyes. It came not from anger, but rather from *hurt*. His heart suddenly felt sore and bruised and longing for sympathy. If Dave and Tom had only once said,

"Think no more of it and we won't either!" If they had said something to comfort him after the shock of it! But they had kept their silence after that hard night. "Forget it for *now*," they had said, so the request still stood unanswered.

He began to think deeply about his brothers. They were strong men now, tall, broad shouldered like the rest of their breed. He realized sharply that in time they *would* want to marry. The happy arrangement of the present could not go on forever. And there could not be a second mistress or a third in the big stone house over which Phoebe presided. He should have realized all this before the boys had spoken.

His eyes wandered over the spreading fields. It was the size of the tract, taken up years before by his forefathers, that had perhaps influenced him in wanting to make the farm his career, along with his great love of it. A small farm would not have attracted him after his Academy days were over. But slowly now as he allowed himself to face the fact, he knew there was land enough here for *three* large farms — enough and to spare, and though divided, The Richlands would still lie together, soil touching soil, fruitful under the touch of skilled and familiar hands. What if Dave and Tom had been right? What if it had been his inordinate ambition and pride that had blinded him to his simple duty? Suppose his father could know, would he not want his sons to share together in their great heritage?

The anger had left him and also, slowly, the hurt. There had come instead, painfully but clearly — understanding. He drew a long breath. It was strange when he made his decision how inevitable it seemed; how almost easy the acceptance was. The evening was still young and he had seen Tom and Dave already going into the kitchen. He crossed to the house and joined them all. The muscles of his face were relaxed and the tension was gone from his eyes.

"There's a full moon tonight," he said in a casual tone.

They all looked up at him in surprise, their own faces lighting.

"I was just thinking," Jim went on," that maybe it's time, boys, for us to have another conference in the sitting room when the house is quiet. How about tonight? Are you agreed?"

"Oh, Jim!" Tom said, his voice breaking.

"We're ready," Dave replied strongly.

Jim looked at Phoebe and his eyes were tender. "We have quite a lot of things to discuss but we shouldn't be too late. While you're getting the children to bed, I may go out and take another look at the moon."

As he passed Duncan, he laid a hand on his shoulder. "How's old Money-Bags?" he forced himself to ask.

Duncan raised his face, "Oh, laddie, laddie, I thought I couldna' thole things much longer. Laddie —" He turned abruptly back to the stove. "God a'mighty, I'll be makin' you buckwheat cakes the way you like thm, in the mornin.'"

There was general laughter and in the midst of it Jim slipped out and made his way back to the edge of the farm. He was not truly happy, but he was at peace.

It was spring, the loveliest of all seasons in the country, and now the moon was sending soft, misty rays down upon the young green, growing things. As he watched, the moon, the shimmering half light, the solvent air, all seemed to speak to his heart with new knowledge. This land was not really his own nor would it be his brothers'. It belonged to the Maker of it. The snow, the rain, the sunshine, the fruitfulness and the great blessedness of work came from his hand and left no room for pride. Suddenly, Jim remembered standing beside his father years ago, enjoying an early evening and looking at the land as he was doing now. Then the older man had half smiled as he gazed from acre to acre, and had quoted a line from a poem. The young boy had been deeply impressed and asked to have it repeated. He had thought of the line many times in the following months and occasionally over the years when a half-formed feeling craved expression. Then it had drifted away. But now, in his time of need, it rose from the depths of his memory and he, as his father must have done, felt the relation between himself, the farmer, and the Power that brooded over The Richlands. There was no one to hear, but he spoke the words aloud:

God advances across the fields.